Praise for Monique Gilmore's work:

Monique Gilmore's first title, *No Ordinary Love,* won best multicultural romance by *Affaire de Couer.*

Praise for *Hearts Afire:*

"Ms. Gilmore has written a mesmorizing novel that plunges the reader into a vortex of romance and suspense."
—*Romantic Times*

Advanced praise for *The Grass Ain't Greener:*

"The Grass Ain't Greener is a . . . story that is solid in content and inspiring to read. . . . I look forward to more outstanding work."

—Shelby Lewis,
author of *Delicious*

"Monique Gilmore is a wonderful storyteller who has a knack for telling it like it is. No additives, no preservatives, just 100% real."

—Chrisena Coleman,
New York Daily News

"Monique Gilmore is a rising talent, who provides the audience with a . . . romance that is well worth reading . . . brilliant."

—*Affaire de Couer*

TIMELESS LOVE

Look for these historical romances in the Arabesque line:

BLACK PEARL by Francine Craft (0236-0, $4.99)

CLARA'S PROMISE by Shirley Hailstock (0147-X, $4.99)

MIDNIGHT MOON by Mildred Riley (0200-X; $4.99)

SUNSHINE AND SHADOWS by Roberta Gayle (0136-4, $4.99)

Available wherever paperbacks are sold, or order direct from the Publisher. Send cover price plus 50¢ per copy for mailing and handling to Penguin USA, P.O. Box 999, c/o Dept. 17109, Bergenfield, NJ 07621. Residents of New York and Tennessee must include sales tax. DO NOT SEND CASH.

THE GRASS AIN'T GREENER

Monique Gilmore

Pinnacle Books
Kensington Publishing Corp.

PINNACLE BOOKS are published by

Kensington Publishing Corp.
850 Third Avenue
New York, NY 10022

RPB

3 6626 10120 250 5

Pinnacle, the P logo, and Arabesque are Reg. U.S. Pat.
& TM Off.

First Printing: October, 1996

Printed in the United States of America
10 9 8 7 6 5 4 3 2 1

This book is dedicated to my grandparents,
Robert Braye, Sr. and Doris Braye

Thank you for instilling the foundation—
moral fiber, unconditional love
and endless words of encouragement.
May God continue to bless you both.
I love you.
"Poogie"

Special Thanks To:

My heavenly Father for making this all possible in the first place.

My brother, Herman Joseph Gilmore, for being my gauge and giving me the necessary feedback and feeling about my manuscript even while basking in the sun somewhere far on vacation.

My sister, Dr. Renee D. Gilmore, for squeezing in my manuscript between exams and boards. Yeah, I know.

My parents, Herman and Janeth Gilmore, for staying down on bent knees and calling on the name of our Lord and Savior Jesus Christ. I'll be on meat one day soon.

My trustworthy best friend, Melonie Wilson, for always being in my corner no matter what. Remember all that fasting and praying? He heard us. Thank you, Mel!

My sister-writer friend, Shelby Lewis, author of Delicious, for making time in your busy schedule to share your thoughts about this book.

My sister-writer friend, Aliona Gibson, author of Nappy: Growing Up Black And Female In America, for thinking enough of me to find time to give me some input on this book and to share whatever resources you have available. It's a tough arena. Let's hang!

My long-time Detroit friends, Dr. Angie Robinson and her husband, Aaron Robinson, for making this story easier to write by providing me with accurate details about the Motor City. Love you.

My girl Kym Wells from Detroit for lending a supporting ear and hand.

Prologue

Truthfully speaking, Ramona Shaw was not usually an unhappy woman. Unless, of course, if she was tired. And right now, she was tired. Don't get it wrong, she loved her husband and her children. It's just that she was beginning to despise her daily routine. Unappreciated, overlooked, misunderstood, and overworked have all been feelings she'd been forced to cope with of late. Yes, she would say, she was feeling a little disenchanted about the mommy-wife, family stuff. So, what woman hadn't at one time or another?

If society had their say, she might have been classified as an unfit, undeserving mother. But this was her life, her emotions and her story, and what was wrong with a wife, a woman, a mother, wanting to take a break—a vacation, a mini-sabbatical from whatever it was that had her stressed? It did the soul some good, you know, to search and wonder if indeed a decision was sound, if your feet were planted, if the foundation was solid or, in Ramona Shaw's case, if the grass was greener.

Ramona sat stiffly behind the leather steering wheel, with her eyes closed. She expelled a deep breath, allowing her thoughts to run rampant. *I just need to escape for a moment,* she thought, inhaling again. *Every now and again, a mother, a wife, a human, must snuff the sound of voices and listen to the music, the rhythm, the beat, the voice of her car. Meka, my ride, a 1991 Volvo station wagon loaded with gadgets and city miles, is telling me I need a break—a vacation from the clutter of little voices, the strain of the city streets, and the constant of my daily routine. Eighty thousand miles reads the little white numbers protected in the glass circle. So why am I about to slap another few clicks on the odometer? Because it is necessary, mandatory that I dodge away for a minute to escape the bores of my everyday routine. Click-tock-click-tock has been the beat of my days. But today will be different, and so will tomorrow for that matter.*

Now, with Meka loaded up with a few bags, some yogurt, oranges, and turkey sandwiches, I can head west. Not too far west, but just far enough to be considered west of my current living quarters. My destination? My older sister, Lalah's house in Detroit. The drive is only ten hours from my humble abode in Montclair, New Jersey. I probably should have given Lalah more notice but then again, she's my sister. More than likely Lalah's high-priced attorney husband, Gordon, will not be home. Makes no difference either way, because at this particular point in my life any home besides my own would be a welcome change. One thing's for sure, things won't be the same when I return. If I do. Well, no matter, it's something that has to be done. So, hold on Meka, here we go . . .

Back in the beginning . . .

They had been considered newlyweds, even then, two years later. Ramona diced the tomatoes and green onions. Her nostrils fluttered softly in and out—the strong flavorful smell overtaking her senses. The onion aroma made her eyes tear. Madrid was basting the chicken on the charcoal hibachi with his secret barbecue sauce. He hated gas grills and the chemical taste that soaked into the food. Besides, it was a "girlie" way of preparing a man's feast, he would often say. He brushed the extra sauce left on his hands onto his baggy jeans.

June was coming into its own. Mature maple trees, habitat for various birds returned from their winter hiatus, edged the backyard. The humidity for this time of year in New Jersey was—comfortably tolerable. The flames blazed up suddenly through the blackened rows on the grill, singeing two thighs. Quickly, Madrid reached for the plastic cup he always kept close by and doused the coals with water. Startled, the flames jumped back. But not before a speck of the grease, mixed with water, pricked Madrid's hairy forearm.

"Damn," he shouted, gingerly examining and wiping the area that had begun to turn red. Ramona walked out the back door from the kitchen with a large wooden bowl filled with tossed salad in one hand and two smaller wooden bowls in the other hand.

"What happened?" she asked.

"Nothing," he shrugged, taking the bowl from her and placing it on the tiny glass table meant only for two. He couldn't really remember when he'd become so macho. "Part of the job," he said, still favoring the spot, which would soon be classified as a battle story. "Did you bring the dressing?"

Ramona rolled her eyes upward as she let out a disappointed breath. "I knew I forgot something." She turned toward the kitchen door to fetch the Russian dressing. They both preferred the thick, creamy, calorie-infested salad topping over all others.

"I'll get it, sweetheart. You sit down and relax," Madrid said softly.

"If you're still cooking the chicken, I can go in and straighten up for a while until it's done." There was still a load of clothes to wash and fold, and dusting and vacuuming that needed to be done. But she was tired. Her feet ached and so did her lower back. Probably overworked it calling on too many hospitals today, she thought, running her slender hand across her back. But she had to do what was necessary to uncover the secret committee members in order to get the new cardiovascular product on formulary at the hospital. She let out a dramatic breath. Life as a pharmaceutical sales representative. Thank God it was Friday.

"Don't worry about the house, Ramona. I'll do my share and help you before we turn in. Just relax, darling. Really. I've got this," Madrid smiled. Using the long metal fork, part of a rotisserie set they got as a wedding gift, he snatched the four drumsticks and four thighs off the grill and placed them on a fruit-design platter. Tiny pieces of skin sprinkled with barbecue sauce, where the chicken had stuck to the grill, remained sizzling on the hot iron.

While Madrid went to retrieve the salad dressing, Ramona plopped down in the colorfully-cushioned wrought iron chair. It was a cute set and fairly inexpensive, due to Fortunoff's summer clearance sale. To tell the truth, she wasn't hungry in the tiniest proportion. She easily would have settled for a fruit drink instead. Regardless forgetting things had never been her habit. Perhaps Madrid's occasionally, but certainly not hers. Not until lately.

During the past few weeks though, she'd felt like if she hadn't had her brains firmly tucked away in her skull, she would have left them somewhere, too. The midnight oil she used to burn for energy had become like one of those enormous tanks off the New Jersey Turnpike near Newark Airport—empty. But now she knew the reason why her tank was dry. Dr. Murphy had told her so earlier this afternoon. She would share the information with Madrid in a few minutes, maybe before dinner. No, probably during dinner—no, after dinner. No matter, she didn't know much except that she was tired. Madrid closed the screen door behind him.

"Keep the mosquitoes out," he smiled, taking his seat beside her. He piled three pieces of chicken and a severe heaping of salad in his bowl. Ramona stared blankly as he let the excess dressing run down the side of the bottle. Nothing annoyed her more than constantly wiping crusty excess from the mouths of mayonnaise or jelly jars—or the salad dressing bottle.

Her mind shifted. A yawn followed. "How did things go today at the office?"

Madrid's chewing accelerated. He swallowed deep, then said, "Better than ever anticipated." There was a certain secrecy, elusiveness about his answer. He tore another bite out of the chicken, concentrating on its delightful taste. "This is good, babe. Aren't you going to eat?"

Ramona clasped her hands together under the table and slouched against the back of the chair, the one habit she was very familiar with whenever she got nervous. Should she tell him now? Or wait till he stopped shoveling all that damn food in his mouth? She wondered if her news would choke his last breath out of him.

"I'm not hungry just yet. The day is still long, though."

"You don't know what you're missing," he boasted, jaws still champing.

Good Lord, she thought. Just like a squirrel packing away food in his cheeks for the winter, that's what Madrid reminded her of now. Her laugh was unexpected and fairly hysterical.

"What's so funny?"

She laughed harder now, focusing in on his blowfish-like cheeks. "Your face . . . your cheeks." She cracked up again. "It's funny, is all."

"Ugh-hmm," he grinned, causing his cheeks to swell up even more. "You keep laughing and I'll keep grubbing. All right?"

No response followed. A few seconds, a few more bites, and several more chuckles elapsed before Madrid finally came up for air. He grabbed the sweating beer can, leaned back in his chair and studied his wife's sleek, model-perfect face. He found the dimples in her cheeks quite sexy, not to mention all that smooth, even, chestnut-colored skin, which had sucked him in the first time he'd laid eyes on her three years ago in the Miami heat.

"Why are you staring at me?" she questioned.

" 'Cause I can. And because you're so damn fine!"

She blushed. Her hair was tucked neatly off her face in a granny bun although Madrid despised the conservative appearance. He always felt her face was further enhanced by letting her hair hang free.

Ramona cast her eyes down, but not before they'd tangoed with Madrid's sparkling eyes. She grinned slightly. They were the very reason for her being where she was right now, she thought. The way Madrid had looked at her with those intense, dark eyes that first evening at the hotel in Miami left her speechless—just as it seemed she was now. How could such a barely-bronzed brother have such deep, mesmerizing eyes?

"I've got something to tell you," she finally confessed after searching the mediocre-sized backyard of their new home. She would plant a tiny vegetable garden right in that corner next to the ivy-coated garage sometime before the summer was over. A new home and now a new addition. How would they be able to do it?

"What is it, Mrs. Shaw? You know you can tell me anything. We're a team, remember?"

"I'm pregnant," she blurted with a half smile, unsure of her statement.

There was a brief moment of silence. Quiet enough to hear the birds chirping past the tree that towered above them, obviously in search of another place to build a nest.

Madrid smiled. Build a nest. That was a good thing. Yes, a good thing to do. He would have to build a nest for his wife and his unborn child.

"Do you think it's a boy?" he quickly asked while scraping his chair across the cement toward her. He could feel his insides beginning to flutter like a loose feather roaming around unhindered. Ramona shrugged her shoulders, letting her grin ease into a bright, full smile.

"If it is a boy, you know that Madrid is the best name a brother can ask for," he half-teased.

She chuckled lightly. He sucked the side of her face a little before unfastening one of her hands so that he could hold it. He kissed the palm of her hand and thanked her. His other hand gently stroked her belly.

"I've been so tired. I went to see Dr. Murphy today. I figured I might be pregnant. I just couldn't shake this sleepy feeling." She yawned hard. "Can we afford the baby, Madrid?" She didn't mean for it to come out like that, but it had. Between the two incomes they should be able to manage. But she had to ask, had to be reassured, for whatever it was worth.

Madrid's cheeks got fuller. She wasn't sure if he had left some of his dinner stuffed in the corner of his mouth, preserving a snack for later. Perhaps it was a smile. Yeah, that's what it was—a smile.

"I've got some news of my own. Actually, I believe this is all working out the way God intended it," he said, stroking her hand again. "They offered me the district manager position for this territory. That means a little more money. So, don't stress, okay? This is our child. I'll make a way for us, baby. Don't you ever worry about that."

"But what . . ." He silenced her with his index finger pressed softly against her smoothly curved lips.

"Shh," he whispered, the sound coming out like velvet. "I'm so happy, Mona. Let's just enjoy this moment. It may never be like this again. Like it is now. Please don't worry, sweetheart. I love you and I'll be here for you, my baby, and all the other children we may have in the future. I'll support you," he vowed, softly pulling Ramona's head toward his chest until she rested it on his shoulder. "I'm here for you, sweetheart." He stroked the top of her forehead with a sweeping kiss. "Thank you, baby. Thank you."

One

This is a nightmare for sure, she thought as she opened her eyes. Ramona was curled up in her warm, fluffy, king-sized bed. On the one side of the bed, Madrid stood towering over her with an iron in one hand and a wrinkled white shirt on a metal hanger in the other. On the opposite side of the bed, a great deal shorter than Madrid, was his eleven-year-old daughter, Leslie, from a previous relationship. She too stood peering at Ramona, holding a comb in one hand and a brush in the other. Sitting at the head of the bed and leaning over the right side of his mother, was Nathan, Ramona and Madrid's son. He was clasping a bowl in one hand and a spoon in the other. Contemporaneously, like a West African band, they begin creating rhythmic sounds by loudly clashing their objects together while chanting, "Mona, mommy, wake up, we need you. Mona, mommy, wake up, we need you! Wake up, we need you! Wake up, we need you!"

Instantly, Ramona popped up from the covers drenched with perspiration, her heart pounding like a jackhammer. "Jeez," she mumbled, squinting so she could focus on her whereabouts. She was dreaming again. *Thank God.* But then again, maybe not. Before she had a chance to turn down the volume on the clock radio, Anita Baker's sultry voice oozed out of the tiny speaker. The sun's rays, which cut through the gray mini-blinds, bounced off Ramona's wet face as she wiped the tiny speckles of sweat from her forehead.

6:30 A.M.

Ramona Shaw, struggling to shake the sleepy feeling from her right arm, realized that the culprit of her lack of circulation was Nathan. He had crept into their bed early this morning, using her arm as his pillow. Looking to the far side of the bed, and hearing the shower running, she knew that Madrid had already begun his day.

The daily rituals that had been so much a part of Ramona's life for the last few years were about to begin again. She lay in bed for a minute longer ingesting Anita's lyrics. God, how her *body* or *soul* didn't feel much like being a part of today, yesterday or tomorrow for that matter. Laying Nathan's head down on a pillow, she eased out of bed and walked down the brightly lit hallway to the second bedroom. Leslie lay curled under the blanket with her head covered.

"Leslie," Ramona called groggily while leaning against the doorframe. "Time to get up. Come on, you don't want to be late for school this morning."

Ramona stood in the doorframe until she saw the covers stir, then made her way downstairs to the large, sunny, L-shaped kitchen. Like clockwork, she turned on the coffee maker, placed some strips of turkey bacon in the oven, flipped on the TV perched high in the corner of the kitchen, and began searching for ingredients to make lunch for Leslie and Madrid.

"Tsk!" Ramona exhaled, sucking her teeth. There was no bread for sandwiches. *If only Madrid had taken his butt to the grocery store last night while I attended class, perhaps he and Leslie would have some lunch today.* She frowned, slamming the refrigerator door shut. No bread, no sandwiches. *I guess they'll just have to settle for cafeteria food for the day.* What would she have to do to get more cooperation around here?

6:50 a.m.

She could hear Madrid calling for Leslie to get into the shower. Then, in another part of the morning ritual, Madrid yelled downstairs for her. "Mona, have you seen my blue socks? I don't have any in my drawer. Could you check the dryer for me while you're down there?"

Methodically, Ramona walked over to the clothes basket that had been sitting there since yesterday, ruffled through some clothes and found a pair of blue socks. Walking past the large, oval mirror hanging on the wall along the staircase, she stopped and gazed into the glass.

"God girl, you look whipped," she said, pulling wild strands of hair behind her ears.

"Honey, where are you? You know I have that meeting with John today," Madrid said, grabbing the socks out of her hand once she reached the top of the stairs.

"And a good morning to you too, my love," she said sarcastically. Madrid didn't respond directly. He mumbled something under his breath and went on about his business. *Not even a good morning, kiss my toe or nothing from anyone around this house in the morning,* she thought. Except for Nathan, of course, who was now standing in the doorway rubbing his eyes.

"Mommy, I'm hungry," Nathan whined, holding his blanket and rubbing his large, brown eyes.

"Just a minute, precious. Mommy has some strips of bacon in the oven right now. Can you wait until I take my shower?" she asked, scooping him up and cradling him against her chest for a few seconds before releasing him.

He shook his head "yes," then lay down on the carpet right in the middle of the doorframe.

Ramona had fifteen minutes to jump into the shower and pull herself together enough to be seen in public. Standing under the hot, running water, she could hear Madrid as he poked his head in the bathroom, mumbling something about not forgetting to pick up his shirts from the cleaners and stopping by the bank. More than likely, he would be gone by the time she went back downstairs. Madrid would have his cup of coffee, some toast and maybe some strips of bacon, and be out the door in a hurry, with no hugs or kisses to linger over; a newly developing habit that was beginning to annoy her.

Ramona dried off as quickly as she had showered and slipped on a pair of jeans and an oversize University of Michigan sweatshirt. Dashing down the hallway, she called out to Nathan, "Come on Nathan, let mommy brush your teeth and wash your face."

Nathan wobbled down the hall, dragging his blanket behind him. Hastily, Ramona drenched the washrag with warm water and wiped Nathan's round face. She grabbed the tiny toothbrush, placed a dab of toothpaste on the tip and brushed Nathan's teeth.

"Here, rinse your mouth," she said, handing him a Dixie cup filled with warm water. She placed the little stair-step up to the counter, allowing Nathan to step up and spit the water out into the sink. Stripping him bare, she ran the washcloth under his arms and between his legs. Wrapping a towel around him, she whisked him back down the hall to his room where she dressed him in a navy turtleneck and a pair of denim overalls and sneakers.

7:25 A.M.

"Leslie are you ready yet?" Ramona yelled while descending the stairs with Nathan in her arms. "Let's go, girl. We go through this every day. Come downstairs so you can have your breakfast, and don't forget to bring your comb and brush."

"I'll be down in just a minute," Leslie's voice promised.

Ramona knew that Leslie's definition of a minute meant more like ten. It wouldn't be so bad if she didn't have to tangle with Leslie's thick, long, and tender head of hair everyday. Ramona had tried, on several occasions, plaiting Leslie's hair on the eve before a school day and wrapping it with a scarf. But that proved a waste of time because Leslie was what old folks would call a wild sleeper, which meant her hair looked wilder than ever in the morning.

Both Ramona and Leslie dreaded the morning duel between the comb and thirteen inches of thick, woolly hair. But it had to be done. Especially since Madrid wouldn't allow Ramona to have Leslie's hair cut into a short style or braided. He just refused to understand how much easier it would be for everyone involved if Ramona didn't have to tackle Leslie's hair on a daily basis.

But no! Madrid wouldn't concede. Something about a haircut being too old for Leslie and braids being too grown, too hoochie-like. As if he really knew the meaning of hoochie. Madrid only repeated what he heard his brother, DeMar, say because he was too busy as a regional sales director for a Fortune 100 telecommunications company to really spend time researching information for himself. Or doing things for himself, for that matter.

"Come on, Leslie," Ramona yelled up the stairs once again before returning to the stove to pre-heat the skillet for the eggs. Normally the kids would eat cereal and fruit for breakfast, but Ramona enjoyed adding some variety. So, she often opted for turkey bacon, eggs and grits whenever time would permit, which was rarely.

Strangely enough, Nathan knew the routine of the house better than anyone else did. He would try and help out by dressing himself, usually something Ramona had to redo. The truth of the matter was that she appreciated his efforts, as small as they were. Nathan attended daycare three times a week and today, praise God, was one of the days he attended. While Nathan crunched on the pieces of bacon and played in the scrambled eggs, Ramona tackled Leslie's hair.

Ramona sat down in the dining area chair with Leslie seated on the floor between her legs. She used her left hand to hold and steady the back of Leslie's neck and used the other hand to brush her hair. Leslie was so godawful tender-headed that Ramona dreaded brushing and combing her hair as much as Leslie abhorred having it done.

"Ouch! Mona," Leslie wailed. Mona was the name Leslie used with Ramona.

"Oh Leslie, I'm barely touching your head."

"It hurts, Mona. Ouch," she cried again.

Ramona didn't bother to respond to Leslie's whining. She was used to the ceremony and figured that Leslie should be too, by now.

"I'm going to have your hair braided so we won't have to go through this everyday," Ramona said, running the brush through Leslie's hair.

"But my daddy said he didn't want my hair braided," Leslie said, bending her head forward so that Mona could brush her hair.

"Yeah, well, your daddy doesn't have to deal with this every day, now does he?" Ramona charged back.

Leslie didn't notice the sarcasm in Ramona's voice. She was too preoccupied with her stinging head.

"What are we having for dinner tonight, Mona?" Leslie managed to ask through crocodile tears.

"I really don't know yet, sweetie. Why? You plan on cooking tonight while I'm in class?" Ramona teased, placing a rubber band at the end of Leslie's braided ponytails.

"No way! Not me. I don't want to be a housewife when I grow up," Leslie said, her smile exposing the silver braces that girdled her teeth.

God, Ramona thought, *kids can say the damnedest things.* Actually, it wasn't her idea to stay home and fall into the category of housewife. But after Nathan was born, Madrid had insisted and she'd agreed that it would be better for their child if she stayed home and nurtured Nathan instead of having some stranger do it.

Initially, it really wasn't that hard for her to give up her pharmaceutical job as a hospital sales representative to stay home with her son. But after two and a half years of Betty Crockering-it, her pots had runneth over, which was when she decided to go back to school and get her master's degree in family counseling. It was the least she could do to keep her mind sharp. She had always been fascinated by the cause and effect of family rearing and how it directly related to a person's current life.

7:55 A.M.

Having fed the children, Ramona cleared the table and placed the dishes in the dishwasher. She decided to wait until the load was full before running the cycle, which would probably be the case after dinner tonight.

"All right guys, grab your coats and let's go," she said hurrying them out the door and locking it behind them. Quickly, she strapped Nathan in his car seat while Leslie fought to buckle her seat belt. Looking around the backseat Ramona realized that her car was filthy. Meka, the silver Volvo station wagon, was filled with papers, pencils, crayons, empty McDonald's bags, books, and several used and unused tissues. Meka was also in need of a thorough wash and wax job, which Madrid had promised to do this past weekend while he was out beautifying his Jeep. But of course, he hadn't gotten around to it.

She had several errands to complete before her own day got started. But first, she would drop Leslie off at school, which was eight miles or so from the house.

8:15 A.M.

Ramona pulled in front of Leslie's school, careful not to run over the other children who were beginning to pour into the streets.

"Here's some money for lunch," Ramona said, handing Leslie three dollars.

Leslie looked at the money, then let her gaze set upon Ramona again before saying, "Three dollars? Is that all, Mona?"

At first Ramona was slightly taken aback. But she collected her thoughts before replying, "I believe three dollars should be enough to cover your lunch Leslie. Don't you?"

"No, because the turkey sandwiches are $1.75 and the lemonade is 75 cents and the yogurt is 65 cents and the Jell-O—"

"Okay, I get the picture," Ramona cut in. "Here's another dollar. That should do it. If not, you'll have to decide whether you prefer yogurt to Jell-O."

"My daddy would have given me at least five dollars," Leslie mumbled under her breath while stepping out of the car.

"What did you say?" Ramona said, lurching forward toward Leslie's side of the car.

"Nothing," Leslie replied, pouting.

"I didn't think so. Because you know better than to talk back like that. Don't lose your mind, girl. You hear me?"

"Yes," Leslie exhaled, while rolling her eyes up into the back of her head.

"All right then," Ramona said, still eyeing Leslie intensely. "Be good. I'll see you at 2:50."

She was going to be tall like her daddy, Ramona thought while watching Leslie mingle with the other students as they all made their way into the building. *The nerve of that child. What she needs is some more chores around the house so she can earn her allowance. Then she can buy whatever the hell she wants for lunch.* Ramona shook her head in an attempt to snap the string of thoughts. She didn't have any more time to waste on the situation, especially since she had to drive back across town to drop Nathan off at daycare.

"Fire truck, Mommy!" Nathan beamed, pointing to the large, red ladder truck.

"Aww, and what a pretty red truck it is. We'll have to get your daddy to take you to see one."

"Yeah! When, Mommy?" he screamed.

"Soon, Nathan. Soon." Ramona smiled. She'd never imagined how much joy Nathan would bring to her life. Even when her days were bombarded with chaos, she could always count on Nathan's unconditional love to bring her through the day. At least for now. To hear a few of her girlfriends tell it, the days of unconditional love, respect and loyalty would come to a screeching halt from about age thirteen to twenty-something.

8:40 A.M.

Turning into the Wee-Wacs Daycare parking lot, Ramona pulled alongside of another car, flipped on the hazards and unbuckled Nathan. The lot was cramped with cars belonging to other parents who were dropping off their children. This was Nathan's first year at daycare and he was enjoying his newfound friends tremendously. As soon as they entered the lobby, Nathan broke free from her hand and began running down the hallway.

"Nathan," Ramona called after him. "Stop running. Hey, aren't you going to give Mommy a hug?" Too late. He was already engrossed in the activities taking place in the room and didn't hear her. She stared at him briefly, feeling a twinge of

disappointment. She smiled before waving good-
bye, then turned and left the building.

Someone had boxed in her car, so she sat patiently, waiting for them to move. After a few minutes, a young man ran down the stairs and jumped
into the car in question. He waved to her as he
drove by, smiling broadly. She returned the wave
and the smile, only not so extensively. After all,
she had to conserve as much energy as possible
to make it through the rest of the day. Oh yeah,
the rest of her day. What a line-up it was:

9:00 a.m.: Stop by the bank to withdraw cash
from savings and transfer it into the checking account.

9:25 a.m.: Drive across town and pick up Madrid's dry cleaning from the cleaners.

9:40 a.m.: Drop by the gas station to fill Meka
up with gas and check the oil.

9:50 a.m.: Stop by the local car wash and run
Meka through the full-service wash.

10:17 a.m.: Bee-line into Pathmark to shop for
food.

11:33 a.m.: Drive back across town to her home
at 1437 Sanford Place and unload eight bags of
groceries, along with Madrid's clothes from the
cleaners.

12:13 P.M.

The cordless phone mounted to the wall near
the counter rang. *Break time.* "Hello?"

"Mona, my baby sister," sang the female voice
on the other end.

"Hey Lalah. It's good to hear your voice. What
are you doing?"

"Obviously not as much as you. Child, you

sound winded. What the heck are you doing, jumping jacks?" Lalah laughed.

"I wish. No, I just got back from grocery shopping and now I'm putting away the food." Ramona paused to pour herself a glass of cranberry juice. "The house looks a mess. Figured I'd straighten up a little before class." Mona took a deep gulp of the juice then continued, "It's neverending around here, I swear."

"I thought you had exams this week?" Lalah asked.

"I'm almost done. I have an exam tonight and a take-home due by mail on Friday."

Lalah sighed heavily. "Then why the heck are you worried about some damn housework? Shouldn't you be studying now?"

"Nope. I've done all the studying I'm going to do for my exam tonight. If I don't know it after five hours of reviewing last night, then I guess I won't know it." Ramona chuckled. "Besides, I couldn't concentrate with this house looking like it is. Honest, Lalah, I don't know who's worse—the kids or Madrid."

"See, that's why I don't have any kids. The little monsters can make you old before your time," Lalah teased. "You should have listened to your older sister and kept yourself single and childless. That's what you should have done. Then maybe there would be a time I would call and hear you say you just got back from the salon or the masseuse, instead of completing some household chore or another."

"Yeah, yeah, yeah, Broomhilde," Ramona cut in. "We've been down that avenue before. Perhaps you can tell me why you're relaxing in the middle of the day? No major high-profile client to service today?" Ramona was referring to her sister's part-time interior design business that had started off with a bang.

"Nope. I just finished one of the Pistons' houses yesterday. I'm taking a break for a few weeks."

"Must be nice to have your own business and do what you will when you want to."

"I keep trying to tell you, Mona, but you won't listen to me. Am I such a bad example that you feel you can't take any of my advice?" Lalah teased.

There was a brief moment of silence while Ramona toiled over Lalah's question. Come to think of it, she couldn't really say why she refused to listen to her older sister.

"Naw, you're an all right older sister," Ramona finally replied. "I suppose I'm just hard-headed," she laughed. "Lalah, sometimes I feel like I'm not cut out for this housewife stuff. Lately, it's really starting to work my last nerve."

"I would imagine so. You've been doing it for four years now. A lot of women go through this, from what I hear. Don't worry about it. This too shall soon pass," Lalah replied yawning loudly.

"Am I boring you?" Ramona asked, placing the boxes of cereal in the cabinet.

"No, not at all, Mona. I just had a late evening, that's all. Anyway, sounds to me like you need a little vacation. Why don't you come home for a few days? It's been too long anyway. Besides, it definitely will do you some good to get away for a while. Poppy was just asking about you and so was Sophia. Now that mom and dad have moved to Saudi Arabia for an undisclosed number of months, Poppy and Sophia are feeling mighty lonely." Their Aunt Sophia was only a year older than Ramona.

"How is Sophia? I haven't spoken with her in about two months." She put away the last bit of food before flopping down on the sofa in the family room. She opened a box of Cheez-Its and laid the box between her thighs.

"Why don't you bring your buns out here and see for yourself? This way, we can all grab a peek of you, too. How you looking these days, sis?"

"Tired, exhausted and chunky," Ramona replied, throwing her head against the back of the sofa and stuffing several crackers in her mouth.

"What do you mean, chunky? Sounds like you're feeding your face right now," Lalah told her. "How much do you weigh, Mona?"

"Oh, Lalah, let's not talk about that now, okay?" Ramona said—with her mouth full.

"No, it's not okay, Mona. I warned you after you had Nathan you probably were going to have to watch it with the scale. Just because you're thirty-four years old and have a child doesn't mean you have to lose that cute figure you've always had. Please, at least tell me you haven't shrunk in height," Lalah joked, trying to lighten up the conversation.

"No," Ramona snickered along. "I'm still standing at five-eight and blank number of pounds."

"How many pounds?" Lalah pushed.

The phone line fell dead for a couple of seconds before Ramona shyly responded, "One hundred-and-sixty pounds."

"One hundred-and-sixty pounds! What? Ramona, what are you doing falling to pot around there?"

"See, that's why I didn't want to tell you. I knew you'd make a big deal about this," Ramona exhaled, glancing up at the clock on the kitchen wall. Break time was almost over. She would have to cut the conversation short soon, because she still had more things to do around the house.

"Being twenty pounds overweight is a big deal. Bigger than the actual pounds themselves. Is it school, or is Madrid stressing you out?"

"All of it. This entire household is beginning to stress me out. They're killing me softly. I feel so unappreciated," Ramona admitted. "Everyone thinks they have a damn live-in maid around here. It's driving me crazy. If it's not cooking, cleaning, running errands or tending to the kids' needs, it's Madrid and his need for constant attention and sexual satisfaction. Sometimes, I feel like he could care less about me and the business of the household other than where his blue or black socks are—or when he can get some loving. I need more help from him. I want more cooperation around here. And it wouldn't hurt to hear a compliment or something warm and nice from him from time to time. It would make me feel better."

"Mona, please. All of the household problems you mentioned can be remedied by calling a maid service to come in once a week and lend you a hand. You and Madrid have enough money to fork out $65 or $70 dollars a week to get someone to assist you. Tell him that's what you want. And if he gives you some static, cut his supply off until the blue balls syndrome talks some sense into him."

Ramona and Lalah fell out laughing for several seconds. Lalah was right again. Maybe what she

needed was a maid to come in periodically to
help her with the chores around the house. And
Lalah was right about one other thing—they certainly could afford it on Madrid's salary. She
would have to discuss it with him later on this
evening.

"And another thing, Ramona—I know you.
Don't start worrying about the so-called stigma
that is attached to sisters who seek housekeeping
services. European women have been doing it for
years and when a sister does it, our society at-
tempts to cremate her. Child, just get you some
help. To hell with what everyone may think."

"I won't have a problem with it, Lalah. Not with
the way things have gotten out of control around
here over the past few weeks. Don't worry. I will
have a housekeeper in here next week."

"Good for you, sis. It's high time you do what
you have to do to make it easier on yourself.
Guess who I saw today?"

"Who?" Ramona replied absentmindedly. She
had stuffed more Cheez-Its in her mouth.

"Ronnie Ware."

The chewing ceased suddenly. Ramona's heart
skipped slightly. *Ronnie Ware? My college sweetheart?
Mr. Popular Kappa Alpha Psi fraternity brother? The
captain of the football team for the University of Michigan? Mr. Pro Bowl for eight years straight for the Kansas City Chiefs? The man who broke my heart?*
Ramona realized that she had skipped off to a
private world reminiscing about Charles "Ronnie" Ware. She had to fight to return to the conversation with Lalah. "Really?" She swallowed
hard. "How's he doing?" she asked matter-of-
factly.

"Still fine as ever, with a body to die for. He

said he just moved back to the Motor City to open a fine Italian clothing store."

"Good for him. No doubt he'll be a success at that, too." Ramona couldn't help but feel cynical about the news. After all, when it was all said and done, Ronnie could probably care less about her and her life.

"He asked about you. Said something about it being a mistake letting you go."

"Is that right? Well, he's married to who he chose to be with." Ramona was getting annoyed now. Couldn't Lalah sense that she really didn't want to hear much more about Ronnie Ware?

"Not anymore. Supposedly, he just went through a painful divorce," Lalah pushed some more. "Anyway, he just told me to tell you hi. And asked me to ask you if Coodles was still intact? What's he talking about, Mona?"

"A raggedy old, decrepit stuffed animal." *Hmmph. Some nerve of him asking about a damn stuffed animal that was well over ten years old.* Ramona shook her head then let out a deep breath. It had been eight years since she had last seen Ronnie Ware and his ice princess wife, Nina. *Nina Richardson, that . . .* Once again Ramona caught herself delving off into deep thought. She cleared her throat and said, "Listen Lalah, I have to go. I've got a few more things to do before I pick the kids up from school." She rose from the sofa, brushing the crumbs onto the carpet. "I'll call you this weekend. Hey, how's Gordon doing?"

"Who?"

"Your husband, woman," Ramona said knitting her brow. "Was it anything serious?"

"Oh yeah. He's fine. Too much fried foods and

spices. A simple case of angina, turning forty-two
years old and not exercising properly. You'd have
thought someone was trying to kill him, the way
he performed." Lalah snickered. "I'll tell him
you asked about him. But if you come visit, you
can ask him yourself."

"I'll work on it," Ramona told her.

"You promise?"

"I promise, Lalah. I love you, now good-bye."

"I love you too, Betty Crocker," Lalah laughed.
"Talk to you later."

Ramona hung up the cordless phone smiling.
She needed Lalah's humor to help her escape
from the bores of her life. All work and no laughter was not good, Ramona thought while plugging in the vacuum cleaner. But then that's what
it had been like lately around here.

The house looked like a tornado had whizzed
through it. Toys, clothes, papers and junk were
strewn everywhere. Ramona looked over at the
overflowing basket of clothes, then sighed.
Leslie was supposed to fold the clothes last
night. She'd see to it that Leslie did it tonight
for sure. Pushing the vacuum cleaner across the
carpet Ramona realized she had forgotten to
sprinkle the carpet with deodorizer. Ah so what,
she shrugged. It wasn't the smell of the carpet
that counted as much as the neatness of the
house overall.

Ramona attempted on a daily basis to keep
the house clean and presentable for two reasons: one, because she liked her house to be
spotless to begin with, and two, because she
never knew when her annoying brother-in-law,
DeMar, would drop in unexpectedly. It wouldn't
be so bad if he knew how to stop by alone, but

he always had some woman or one of his partners attached with him. And as if that wasn't
bad enough, he always managed to time the
dreadful visits around dinner.

My God—nothing flared Ramona's nostrils
more than her brother-in-law stopping by unan-
nounced and then proceeding to make himself
and his company comfortable at the dinner table,
devouring everything in sight. It was sometimes a
thrice weekly habit, with DeMar. She didn't know
how many times she had talked to Madrid about
DeMar coming by the house swinging nothing but
his arms, and never any bags of groceries unless
it was a six-pack of beer.

1:25 P.M.

Ramona switched on the half-full dishwasher
just to get the dirty dishes out of the way then
continued with the household tasks.

1:30 P.M.

She cleaned the master bathroom as well as the
kids' bathroom before continuing with light dusting, sweeping, and more vacuuming, finally placing a load of clothes in the wash. She stumbled
on the nebulizer, Nathan's asthma machine, in
the laundry room. She had meant to put it back
in the upstairs closet, where it belonged, but
there was no room. She'd leave it here in the
laundry room for now—making sure to let everyone know of its whereabouts. Thank God there
wasn't much to do in the living room. It was the
only part of the house that was forbidden territory.

2:15 P.M.

Ramona drove back across town to pick Nathan up from daycare.

"Mommy," Nathan screamed with excitement, falling into his mother's arms in the lobby of the center.

"Hey pooh," Ramona said, kissing him on both cheeks. "What you do today?" she asked while snapping his jacket shut.

"We did ABC's. Want to hear, Mommy?"

"Sure sweetheart," Ramona said, walking outside. She could hear him singing the ABC song when she closed his car door. She was starting to feel signs of a major migraine coming as she pulled out of the daycare parking lot to drive back across town to pick Leslie up from school.

2:45 P.M.

Ramona laboriously guided Meka through the side streets to avoid the late-afternoon traffic before reaching Leslie's school. Leslie was leaning against the school yard fence talking to a tall, lanky boy, clearly older than she. Ramona shook her head and sighed. *Not already*, she thought, honking the horn. Leslie smiled at the boy widely, waved good-bye then ran over toward the car.

"Hi Mona!" Leslie sang at her highest octave, causing Ramona to stretch her ears back a good bit as Leslie stepped into the car.

"Hello, Leslie," Ramona smiled. "Where's your jacket?"

Leslie lowered her head and hesitated for a moment before replying, "I lost it."

"What? How did you lose your coat? Where did you see it last?"

"I had it hanging on the back of my chair at lunchtime, but when I went to take my tray to the garbage can, it wasn't there when I got back."

"Who was that young man you were talking to?" Ramona questioned her.

"Oh, him?" Leslie said, pointing toward the school yard. "That's Truth. Misha's cousin."

"Um hum," Ramona replied. She flashed back to a familiar time in her life, when she was about Leslie's age and her mother had questioned her about her first so-called boyfriend. Smiling, she realized that as Leslie got older and naturally more curious about boys, she would have to brace herself to deal with the dating scene and Madrid, the ruthless, over-protective father. Ramona lowered her head toward the steering wheel and let out a deep breath. Thoughts of that stress was the kind of thing that could make her migraine manifest faster than she wanted.

After a few seconds of silence she finally lifted her head, looked at Leslie and asked, "Did you inform your teacher about your jacket?"

"Yes. Ms. Roland said she would try to find it for me. I'm sorry, Mona. All I did was go to the garbage can."

"Don't worry about it, Leslie. I'll call Ms. Roland when we get home. How was school for you today?"

"Okay," Leslie mumbled. "I got an A on my spelling test."

"You did?" Ramona smiled. "That's very good, Leslie. I'm proud of you. I knew you could do it if you concentrated hard enough. I guess all that studying paid off then, huh?"

"I guess. Thanks for helping me, Mona" Leslie smiled sheepishly, braces glittering.

"You're welcome, sweetheart," Ramona said, grabbing her hand.

"I'm starving. What are we having for dinner?"

"Girl," Ramona chuckled. "Is that all you think about is food? Tell you what, maybe you can help me with dinner when we get home. How about that?"

Leslie didn't reply. Ramona could see from the corner of her eye that Leslie's body language had slouched at the thought of having to do any work around the house. *This girl is lazy,* Ramona thought quietly. There was no doubt about it.

3:14 P.M.

Meka came to a slow halt in the narrow driveway. Leslie was the first person to bounce out of the station wagon and toward the back door of the house. Ramona unbuckled Nathan and helped him out of the car. "Where are your keys, Leslie?"

"I don't know," she shrugged, looking down at the ground.

"What do you mean, you don't know? When's the last time you had them?" Ramona asked, unlocking the door with her key. "You need to find your keys, Leslie. What if there's an emergency and you have to get in and we're not here?" Ramona shook her head in the typical disgusted-mother gesture upon entering the house. She could feel the small pain in her head returning again and went straight upstairs to her medicine cabinet and the bottle of Advil.

Two pills and a glass of water later, she was on her way back downstairs when she heard Nathan scream, "Leave me 'lone, Leslie!"

"Leslie," Ramona said with a raised voice. "What are you doing to your brother?"

"Nothing, Mona. He keeps trying to take the remote control away from me and turn the channel."

"Turn that TV off and go upstairs. Straighten up your room then come back down to this table—" Ramona paused to point at the table in the dining area "—and do your homework."

Leslie stood gazing defiantly at Ramona but not moving. Then, after seeing Ramona's face turn from that of a friendly buddy to that of an unsettled foe, she turned and stomped up the stairs two at a time.

3:34 P.M.

Ramona began preparing dinner while Nathan watched *Sesame Street* and Leslie plunged into her homework.

"When you're done with your dinner, Leslie, I want you to fold the clothes in the basket like you were supposed to do yesterday. Please don't let me come home from school and find these clothes still sitting in the basket. You hear me? I also want you to sweep the kitchen floor after dinner."

"Okay," Leslie said, careful not to let Ramona see her rolling eyes.

4:43 P.M.

Ramona served the children spaghetti for dinner, then went upstairs to freshen up before class. She wasn't thrilled about attending class tonight, solely due to the exam that awaited her. Hopefully, she had gotten in enough study time to pass the test. Either way, she would just have to ask God to hook her up one more time.

5:20 P.M.

Madrid walked in the door with his suit jacket in one hand and his briefcase in the other. His tie hung loosely around his thick neck and his large, otherwise sparkling, black eyes were drowned with exhaustion.

The children sang in unison, "Daddy," as they ran over to embrace him. "Hi, Daddy," Leslie said, trying to kiss him on the cheek. Madrid lowered his six-three stature down to accommodate the children as they fell into his chest.

"How's Daddy's beautiful children?" he asked, whisking them up for a quick spin before releasing them.

"Fine!" Nathan yelled. "Any treats, Daddy?"

"Maybe," he said, pinching Nathan on the nose lightly. "Have you been a good boy?"

"Yes," Nathan giggled.

"What about you, Leslie? Have you been good, too?"

Barely, Ramona said to herself as she reached the bottom of the stairs and noticed that the children's plates had hardly been touched.

"Yes," Leslie smiled, trying to pry open Madrid's palm to see what he had hidden inside.

"Well, I guess you can have what's in my hand then," Madrid teased.

"Not so fast, Madrid. They haven't finished their dinner. Look at these plates," Ramona said circling the table. "You guys haven't even touched your food."

Madrid looked up at Ramona then back at the kids before saying, "Well, I guess you guys need to finish your dinner before you can see what's in my hand." He had a disappointed look on his face.

"Hi, Mona," Madrid grinned before placing a kiss on her lips.

"Hey," Ramona responded, kissing him back lightly. "Gotta run. I have finals tonight. See you later." She kissed Madrid again, then kissed Nathan and Leslie before they took their seats at the table.

"Mona, we don't feel like spaghetti tonight. That's why we haven't eaten it," Leslie whined.

Ramona shot a quick glance at Madrid, then back at Leslie. "Handle this for me, dear," she said, letting out a deep breath. Then she grabbed her bag before racing out the door.

5:28 P.M.

Ramona drove Meka down Bloomfield Avenue through Montclair, Glen Ridge, and Bloomfield, before reaching the Rutgers campus parking lot in Newark. She rushed into the classroom, where her fellow classmates had already begun the exam. She picked up her test from the instructor and took a seat in the front row. For the next three hours, Ramona struggled with the grueling exam in Family Systems before she returned to

the parking lot where Meka sat covered with the
evening dew.

9:25 P.M.

Ramona pulled into her driveway, weary from
her day and starving for something to eat. Perhaps
she should have eaten something before she left
for class—maybe then she would have been able
to concentrate better, she thought as she walked
into the house. At first glance of the lanky body
sprawled out on the love seat, she wanted to
scream.

"Hey, Mona," DeMar sang in his resonant
voice.

"Hi," Ramona replied in a disgruntled tone
while surveying the house.

"This here is my partner, Elmwood. He and I
bowl together on Friday nights," DeMar grinned.

"Pleased to meet you," Elmwood said, rising to
his feet to shake Ramona's hand.

Ramona passed off a smile while looking Elmwood in the eyes. After a few seconds she turned
her back and asked, "Where's Madrid?"

"Upstairs, I believe. Hey sis, you missed a good
fight, you know that? George Foreman still got
it!" DeMar laughed while keeping his eyes glued
to the TV.

A good fight? Hell, if stuff didn't start shaping up
around here, he was about to witness the fight of
the century. The first round would center around
how the house got trashed so quickly after the energy and time she'd spent cleaning it up earlier
today. The second round would be with Leslie, because the clothes were still balled up in the basket
in the corner by the sofa. The third round would

be with Madrid, because there were beer cans and plates scattered about the family room coffee and end tables. The fourth round would be because the damn TV was blaring and the pillows from the sofa had been tossed all over the family room floor.

Making her way into the kitchen, Ramona noticed that the crusty dishes were still piled in the sink from dinner and to top it off, no one had bothered to save her anything to eat. Now for sure all hell was going to break loose. The pots were still sitting on the burners with spaghetti sauce splattered all over the stove and the adjoining counter. The floor hadn't been swept and the garbage can was overflowing with trash. The table hadn't been wiped down, nor had the glasses from dinner been removed from the table.

Walking up the stairs, Ramona stopped abruptly, as she had done on so many occasions, and gazed into the mirror hanging on the wall.

"Mirror, mirror on the wall, what the heck is going on?" Ramona whispered. Everything about her life, her looks and her enthusiasm reeked "tired." Her oval-shaped eyes were starting to show signs of dark circles, her smooth cinnamon face was starting to look fuller and her dimples were starting to fade into the fullness of her cheeks. Her brown shoulder-length hair needed to be trimmed, and her thick eyebrows needed to be arched. Ramona Shaw stood at the mirror staring, searching, scanning in disbelief at her current image.

With a flash as quick as a lightning bolt, she reflected back to her college days and the days just a few years back when it was just her, with no husband, no children, no housework. What had happened? She fell in love, that's what happened.

One thing was certain, her heart was burdened and her mind exhausted. And it didn't help her self-esteem knowing that her body was a tad out of shape. She desperately needed a change, a break, a savior, a plan of recourse before it would be too late. She was drowning in housework, in motherhood. It was already 9:45 P.M. and she still had to complete a take-home exam that had to be postmarked by tomorrow.

Just as she was about to escape into a fantasy of crystal blue waters and white sands, she heard the familiar patter of little feet racing above.

"What the sam hill is going on around here?" Ramona spewed while racing up the stairs, only to find Leslie and Nathan running up and down the hallway.

"What are you still doing up? Get your butts in the bed right now!" At that, Leslie raced into her room and hurled the door shut, while Nathan attempted to plead his case.

"I'm not sleepy, Mommy," he whined in a low tone.

"I don't care if you're not sleepy, Nathan," Ramona said with a raised voice. "You are going to bed. Now go to your room and get under them covers. Now!"

Nathan dropped his bottom lip then stared at Ramona for a few seconds before dashing down the hallway toward his room. He slammed his door shut behind him.

"And you all better stop slamming these doors around here, too," Ramona threatened. "Madrid? Madrid, where are you?" After a few seconds without a reply, she walked down the hall toward their bedroom and flung open the door.

Madrid's burly body was propped up against the

back of the bed with the phone wedged between
his ear and his shoulder. He was obviously on a
business call because he was jotting some numbers
on a pad. Madrid acknowledged Ramona by winking his left eye, but continued his conversation
with the person on the other end of the phone.

Ramona could feel her blood pressure escalat-
ing. Her heart was racing wildly and her breath
was seasoned with fury. She was going to get to
the bottom of this once and for all when he hung
up the phone. She was going to finally tell Mr.
Madrid Shaw about his shiftless, scrounging
brother, DeMar, and his foraging partners; his recent nonchalant attitude about the going-ons of
this house; the wise mouth of his daughter; the
increasing stubbornness of his son; the broken
promises to help out around the house; the grass
that needed to be cut—and a number of other
things. Yes sir, buddy, as soon as his 230-pound,
smooth-talking, Hugo Boss-wearing butt got off
the phone, Ramona Shaw was going to express
herself.

Two

"Hey Mona, ba*by*," Madrid beamed, hanging up the phone and easing off the bed. "How about we sneak in a quick one?" he whispered, moving closer to her with extended hands. "I got something to make all your troubles disappear," he crooned while running his tongue over his top lip. When he got within an arm's reach of Ramona, he could sense that something was wrong. Ramona stood with her arms crossed and tucked firmly under her breasts. Her eyes were seething with rage and her cheeks were puffed out like a clown.

"What's wrong with you, Mona?" Madrid said, backing out of her personal space and taking a seat on the foot of the bed.

A few more seconds that would never be recaptured slipped past as Ramona began pacing. She was burning with anger that heated her body more than any type of fever she had ever experienced. *This brother actually expects me to put in nine hours of household maintenance, three hours of educational stimulation, and no hours of personal edification, and then come up here and fine-tune his Scooter while his rowdy, self-centered brother is downstairs slurping it up in a nice neat, but now littered house? He*

*must be smoking crack, inhaling glue, shooting heroin
and popping pills simultaneously.*

After several short breaths, Ramona finally
opened her mouth and let the hot words sear
into the air, like a dragon releasing fire. *"Madrid."*
She paused to search for some way to articulate
her frustration and disappointment without cussing and yelling like a wild woman. Her voice was
shaking and she tried to calm her heart rate by
reciting a quiet prayer, but she was too worked
up to even ask God to help her.

Instead, she cleared her throat and spilled, "I
need some help around this house. I'm not the
only one living here, in case you hadn't noticed.
You and the kids and your fat-head brother think
this is some type of Motel Six. I am tired of feeling like I have four helpless children in this house
all the time."

"Hold it," Madrid said, throwing up both
hands firmly. "Maybe we should discuss this later,
when you're not so worked up. This way, you
won't be tempted to say something you might, or
we might, regret. Okay?"

"Actually Madrid, it's not okay. I need to vent
right now because I'm about to burst with anger."
She moved her hands with each word as if she
were giving instructions.

"Yeah, well, maybe you should, 'cause you're
looking pretty swollen to me," he replied, leaning
back against the bed on his elbows.

"What's that supposed to mean?" she fired
back. The thought had flashed across her mind
that quick. Was he trying to say something about
her weight on the sly?

"Nothing, Mona," he said, shifting his body

some. "I just mean it's obvious you're angry about whatever it is, so let's get on with it."

"I'll tell you exactly what this is about," she said, tucking her arms back under her bosom. "It's about me not getting any cooperation around here. It's about feeling unappreciated for all I do."

"Like what, Ramona?" Madrid cut in, sitting straight up now.

"Like all this housework I do by myself for the sake of our family. That's what."

Madrid perused his wife's body trying to figure out where this stuff was coming from all of a sudden. She had been content being home for the last four years and now she was griping about housework? "Tell me what you want from me, Ramona, 'cause I don't have a clue what you're trying to say, or trying not to say, for that matter."

Shaking her head with frustration she finally verbalized, "Let me just start by saying that I'm going to get us a housekeeper to come in once a week to help me. Then, maybe I can—"

"Wait. Hold it," Madrid said, abruptly slicing off her sentence while chuckling at the same time. "A housekeeper? This has to be a joke. You actually think I'm going to waste money paying some stranger to come sift through our house?" He paused. "It's a waste of money."

"Oh, come on, Madrid. Spare me with the money talk. We can afford it. Unless you plan on helping me around here?" she said, eyeing him coldly.

"I do help you. I pay the mortgage so we can have a roof over our heads. I don't see why all of a sudden it's so difficult for you to keep the place together. It looks fine to me," he said, rubbing his knees with his hands. He was getting annoyed with her gibberish now.

"Oh, it does, does it?" she said placing her hands on her hips. "Then let us take a stroll downstairs and see just how together it is after I spent most of today shaping it up. Matter of fact, I'd like to know who is going to clean up that mess in the kitchen and family room? You? I doubt it." She kicked off her shoes before walking around the room to search for her slippers. "You probably didn't even notice how filthy downstairs is, because you're always too busy with outside stuff to know what's going on inside this house."

At that Madrid stood up and began walking toward the bedroom door. The conversation was hovering and he was content to leave it there like a pilot circling around a city until it was considered safe to land. Bottom line, he didn't feel like discussing it anymore or being the target of her sudden rage. Reaching the door, he turned back and said, "The housekeeper idea, theory or whatever you want to call it, is out, Ramona. There's no need to waste the money. I don't want to talk about it anymore."

Ramona spun around so quickly she saw stars. "What did you say, Madrid?"

"You heard me," he said, brushing her off, then opening the bedroom door.

Ramona was at the door in less than a tenth of a second. She pushed the door shut with force before Madrid could step foot into the hall. Standing in front of the door, she spouted, "Don't dismiss me like I'm some child. Who do you think you're talking to? One of the kids? I

don't ever remember it being stated that something isn't open for discussion."

"Yeah, okay Ramona," he said, trying to keep
his voice lowered. "We'll discuss it later. Okay?
Satisfied? Now can you please move out the way
so I can go downstairs and see my brother out?"

"Don't try and patronize me, Madrid, all right?
Furthermore, later for your brother and his pea-
cock-sucking friends. We need to handle our business and get this settled." She was steaming with
anger, a side of her Madrid rarely had to encoun-
ter. But damn it, he was going to see it tonight
because she was tired and this discussion was long
overdue. Ramona took a few more deep breaths
trying to calm her voice, because she knew Madrid wouldn't talk to her if she became too excited. Nor would she oblige him if the shoe was
on the other foot and he was raving out of control.

Madrid's eyes locked with hers momentarily before he assumed the akimbo stance, then he softly
said, "What is it Ramona? Because the housekeeper conversation is not one I want to revisit."

"It's deeper than some housekeeper thing, Madrid," Ramona said, mimicking his soft tone. She
knew that two sides to this story existed. *If he
wasn't so darn busy trying to solve the problem, he'd
be able to listen to me.* "I'm trying to tell you I am
feeling overwhelmed and unappreciated for my
contributions around the house. I get the feeling
that everyone, including you, thinks that I'm
some kind of nanny or maid or something. Very
rarely do I get a thank you, or a please, or an
excuse me, or a good morning, for that matter.
It's the same old thing, day in and day out. I'm

truly unhappy feeling like I'm surrounded by people I love who don't appreciate me."

"Really, Ramona? Well, I guess I'm feeling pretty damn unappreciated myself right about now. I don't recall having any thank you banners hanging from the ceiling when I arrive home from a hard day of smiling with people I sometimes can't stand, while I'm at my office ten, twelve, fourteen hours a day. No one says 'Thank you, Daddy,' or 'Thank you, Madrid' for going out to work everyday rain, shine, sleet, hail or snow, and bringing home a paycheck every week so that we can have a house to live in or complain about cleaning. Or so that we can have a car to get around in, or so that we can have electricity to juice the cable lines when we choose to watch TV, or have a dial tone when we pick up our telephone. So, what do you think I should do? Blast you out about it?" He sat back down at the foot of the bed. He was tired and ready to go to sleep. He had a long day ahead of him and an early wake-up call to go with it.

"You're twisting this around, Madrid," she said through clutched lips. *Remember, Ramona, try not to overreact.* She sucked in a deep breath and continued, "The reason why you don't have a thank you banner swaying from these nine-foot ceilings is because your thank you leaves with you in the morning when you have on a clean, white shirt, and when your stomach is full with a warm meal, and when your brown bag lunch serves as your commuter companion. Thank you greets your nostrils when you return to a kept house in the evening, and when your children have put in their hours at school and greet you with completed schoolwork, full bellies and open hugs.

Gracias, señor is whispered in your ear faithfully while we lie in each other's arms in the wee hours of the night even after I've had a full day of roughing it as a house mommy and toughing it as a student in a grueling master's degree program. So don't ever think for one minute that *thank you* isn't oozing out at you, Madrid."

"Well then, Mona, what's the problem? Seems like we both can read between the lines. What's your gripe? I don't seem to verbally acknowledge you with thank you and you don't verbally acknowledge me with it either."

"To hell with it," Ramona sighed. "You're not hearing me because you're too busy trying to negate the issues."

"No, I'm not trying to negate anything. Like I said, we seem to have an unspoken understanding. Everybody has a job to do around here, Ramona. Me, you and the kids."

"The kids? Have you even noticed that Leslie has to be told a trillion times to do something before she finally decides to listen? And that Nathan is really not at the age to contribute, and your brother—well, I won't touch that one."

"Good, 'cause I'm exhausted and I'm ready to turn in for the night," he said, rising from the bed.

"Perhaps you and your brother and his friend, what's-his-name, can help me clean up the kitchen and the family room. I would appreciate it."

Madrid didn't respond. He waltzed out the door with his head high. Ramona was sure that the position of his head had more to do with his height and not so much with arrogance. She pulled herself together and followed Madrid downstairs.

Once she reached the bottom step, DeMar and

his friend had disappeared out onto the front porch. Madrid stood with the front door partly cracked, bidding them both a good evening. Ramona stood in the kitchen looking dumbfounded. She didn't even know where to begin or if she cared if the mess was cleaned up tonight, a real unusual attitude for her.

Ramona heard Madrid flipping the pillows onto the sofa, then stacking the empty cans of beer before tossing them into the garbage can. A few minutes later, she heard him switching off the lights in the family room and going upstairs.

"Good night, Ramona," Madrid's voice faintly trailed as he reached the top of the landing.

Ramona stood leaning forward at the kitchen sink. Streams of tears began to run down her cheeks. *This can't be happening. I'm too young to be this fed up, this burned out with family life. Mother handled it with me and Lalah. Grandmother handled it with my mother and her two sisters, and the family tree goes on. So why do I feel so inadequate? So helpless? So resentful? Oh, Lord.* She sighed, letting her tears douse her face. She stood at the sink for a long while trying to grasp some type of solution for her feelings. Madrid was being so confrontational lately that she felt like she was in a neverending battle with the man she had married six years ago.

It hadn't always been this way. Things were a lot easier when it was just the two of them. Two years after their marriage, Leslie came to live with them when her mother died unexpectedly of cancer, and Nathan followed shortly thereafter. Yup, things were much more sedate when it was just her and Madrid. But now it was the four of them and things had gravely changed. After wiping down the dining room table, she tossed her bag onto the table and plopped down into the chair. She had to get started on her take-home final for the quarter if she was going to have it completed by tomorrow. And with all the distractions that normally accompanied her daily routine, it would be best if she completed as much of it, if not all of it, tonight.

Ramona's mind began to drift back to the conversation she had had with Madrid. She laid her head down on the table and closed her eyes. What she needed was a hot bath to soothe away the tension that had been mounting like an active volcano. Perhaps Lalah was right, she rationalized. No, she knew Lalah was right. What she needed to do was jump into Meka and make the drive to Detroit for a few days. But what would she do about the kids? She needed a vacation away from the house, kids included, even if it was only for three or four days. Madrid could handle it. She always managed to hold things together whenever he left town for a business meeting.

Yes, that's exactly what I will do. I will drop my take-home exam in the mail, pack a bag, and make my journey west as soon as Madrid gets home from work tomorrow. Maybe spending a few days in my shoes will be a good experience for him. Then maybe the next damn time I try to come to the plate to discuss my feelings, he'll be a bit more understanding.

She thought about making the climb up the stairs to the bed that she shared with her husband, but she opted for the family room sofa instead. Grabbing the comforter out of the hall closet, she let a winning smile crease her cheeks. "Ramona Shaw," she whispered aloud while

drawing the comforter over her. "Tomorrow evening it is then. It'll be my turn to take a little
much-needed break from the business of this
house."

Ramona awoke at 2:30 A.M. with an agonizing
crook in her neck. Tossing the comforter onto
the floor, she clumsily made her way upstairs to
her bedroom and slid into the king-sized bed. Madrid, still asleep, wrapped his arm around her
waist and pulled her toward him, cuddling her
close, something he often did during the night.
She lay with her back to him, trying desperately
to doze off again.

Madrid's hand began to fondle her breast. She
could feel his hard manhood pressing against her
bottom, but fought to stay asleep. After a few
more seconds, he started rubbing his hands between her thighs.

"Come on, Madrid," she whined in a cracked
voice. "I'm tired."

"Umm, baby," he purred back. He had rolled
her over on her back and was on top of her in no
time, balancing his weight with his large, firm
arms.

"Madrid," she said again, trying to discourage
him, but it was too late. He hadn't heard a thing
she'd said to him. She lay there with her eyes
shut while he smothered her face and neck in
kisses, intent on making her moan.

Ramona looked at the clock. 3:00 A.M.

"Aw, Mona baby," Madrid passionately
strained, kissing her face all over. He was butter
now, all soft and mushy. Ramona stared up at the
ceiling and caressed his back. Madrid was still
purring for a few seconds before she heard the
familiar snoring sounds.

Madrid sound asleep. Ramona? Wide awake. She lay with her eyes still fixed on the ceiling, trying to get a handle on her emotions. She loved Madrid and the children, there was no question in her heart about that. It was who she had become when facing the mirror that she didn't like. She was gradually slipping downhill. Her battle with the twenty pounds she had gained over the course of six months was at the bottom of her feelings, she was sure of it. Or was she?

A double chin was sneaking up on her and the circles under her eyes were more pronounced. She was beginning to hate her hair and the way it did nothing to contribute to her self-esteem. Perhaps she should change the color from her natural sandy brown to a deep black or dark brown color. Or maybe she should cut it. Perhaps her vision of herself wouldn't be so bad if she heard a compliment from Madrid or the kids once in awhile.

She let out a deep breath then rolled over onto her stomach. What she could use at this point in her life was a trip to one of those retreat spas in Phoenix for a week. But she guessed that Detroit would just have to do for now. Before dropping back into slumber, she winced up at the clock—3:33 A.M., definitely time to go to sleep.

Wednesday . . .

The alarm sounded. 6:30 A.M.

"Already?" Ramona groggily whimpered. She had gotten a mere three hours of sleep. How was she supposed to get through the day with just that? Hearing the familiar sound of water gushing out of the shower, she knew for sure that she was awake. Laying on her side, she contemplated telling Madrid about her plan to drive to Detroit soon, perhaps even as soon as tonight. She imagined that he would not be the least bit thrilled about her news. In fact, she was fairly certain that a disagreement would ensue as a result of her decision. Oh well, she resolved. It was the only remedy she could think of for now.

Ramona's morning kicked off in its normal routine. The kitchen was in shambles when she left to drive the children to school. She had decided early this morning that she would spend the day at the library and complete her take-home final. Besides, what was the rush to get back home? she thought, walking through the library doors. The house could wait for a change. She spent the next two-and-a-half hours plugging away at her psychology exam undisturbed until it was completed. Peeking up at the clock she noticed that it was 11:40 A.M. That left her about fifteen minutes to drive to the center of town and make her annual visit to her gynecologist, Dr. Robinson. Hurriedly, she gathered her belongings together and left the library.

Peeping into the rearview mirror at her appearance, Ramona let a smile creep across her face. She was exhilarated and feeling very productive for completing her final and mailing it on time. Thinking about her life as a student as well as a mom and wife, Ramona realized she could use a break, even if it was only for a week. The one thing she liked most about quarters as opposed to semesters was the mini-breaks that fell in between during the school year.

Shifting the car into park, Ramona turned off the ignition and leaned her head back against the car rest. Every year, she experienced the same thing when she pulled into the office complex parking lot. Ramona dreaded the yearly visit with Dr. Robinson. She found it distasteful having some doctor prodding, sticking, roaming and searching through her private area. Ramona let loose the air she had sucked in and stepped out of the car. She was dressed casually in a pair of jeans and a poet's blouse with ruffles. Although the jeans were labeled baggy, they snugly fit around her size 39 hips. She vowed to herself that she'd have to do something about the extra twenty pounds as she walked into the doctor's office.

"Good morning, Mrs. Shaw," the tiny receptionist greeted her. It was Adeline, the office manager who had been a part of Dr. Robinson's staff since its inception. This was Ramona's fourth year with Dr. Robinson and everyone in the front office knew her.

"Good morning, Adeline. How are you doing?" Ramona smiled then jotted her name down on the paper attached to the clipboard.

"Fine, thank you. How's that handsome young son of yours doing?"

"Busy and inquisitive as ever. His favorite word now seems to be *why*. Why this mommy, why that mommy, why, why, why? Sound familiar?" Ramona had taken a seat and began flipping through the latest edition of *Essence* magazine.

"Sure does. But I'm past all that stuff thank God. It's the defiant actions of a fearless adolescent I'm forced to deal with now. Honey, wait till you get in that stage." Adeline grinned while perusing Ramona's chart. "You're here for your yearly, correct?"

"Yes," Ramona replied, never lifting her eyes

off the page. She was engrossed in Susan Taylor's uplifting monthly article. A few more minutes passed before Adeline called for her.

"Come on back, Ramona," Adeline advised, holding the door open.

Still clutching the magazine, Ramona walked toward the back of the office. Adeline guided her to examining room two, where she instructed Ramona to undress entirely and put on the blue gown with the opening in the back. "I'll be back in a minute to take your blood pressure," Adeline said, closing the door behind her. "Oh yeah, do me a favor and step into the hall and weigh yourself before you undress."

Weigh myself? Why on earth would I want to do that? Don't they have my weight in my chart from last year? Ramona taunted herself, knowing full well that last year she was twenty pounds lighter and fifty clicks happier with her life. She made the short walk down the hall to the scale.

"Here it is," she sighed. "This godawful piece of man-made machinery." She took a deep breath, then stepped onto the black rubber base of the scale. She slid the large silver piece of metal over to the 100-pound groove until it clicked. Then she grasped the smaller silver piece of metal. Purposely, she slung the tiny piece of metal as hard as she could to the far right. *Clink*, she heard, as the tip of the scale fell down onto the metal base. She smiled and whispered to herself, "Well, at least I know I'm not *that* heavy."

Slowly, she inched the small piece of metal back toward the left side of the scale, stopping suddenly at the number 59. She eyed the scale as it swayed lightly up and down before stopping in the center. *Hallelujah, 159!* her inner voice screamed as she stepped down off the base and walked back down to the examining room. *How wonderful! I'm less than 160 pounds after all.*

Hearing the rapid knock on the door, Ramona sat up straight and answered, "Come in."

Dr. Robinson, a tall, dark woman with a short salt and pepper natural haircut, entered the room.

"Hello, Ramona," Dr. Robinson sang in her vibrant voice, walking over to the counter where she grabbed the chart and began fingering through it.

"Hi, Dr. Robinson, how are you?"

"Near perfect. And how have you been?"

"Honestly?" Ramona grinned, looking directly at her. "I've been feeling very tired and cranky."

"Really? Well, let's try and figure out what's going on with you, shall we? Let me see." Dr. Robinson paused, flipping through the papers in the chart. "I don't see your blood pressure reading. Did Adeline take it?"

"Not yet. She was supposed to come back and do it."

"She must have gotten busy. Let me get it." Dr. Robinson strapped the blood pressure gadget around her arm before squeezing it until she couldn't squeeze any more. Once the pump was fully expanded around Ramona's arm, she took her stethoscope and listened to Ramona's pulse. "Seems well enough, Ramona. Your blood pressure is 120 over 80. I would say that's excellent. Why don't you lay back and rest your arms behind your head?"

Dr. Robinson examined her left and right breasts. "Don't feel any lumps, which is always a good sign." She walked to the end of the examining table, turned on the light attached to it, and put on a pair of latex gloves.

"Slide down some and place your feet in the stirrups for me. That's good. What seems to be the problem, Ramona?" Dr. Robinson asked, taking a seat on the stool at the foot of the table.

"I don't really know," Ramona replied, staring up at a picture of a killer whale gliding through what looked like arctic blue waters. "I suppose I could use a break from motherhood and wifehood, if there is such a thing." She could hear the metal tongs clashing together when Dr. Robinson opened the drawer.

"Sounds to me like you're experiencing what some at-home, full-time mothers go through. It's called boredom, Ramona."

"I don't know Dr. Robinson. Sometimes— ouch!"

"Sorry, Ramona. Your cervix is hiding from me again. Go on. What were you about to say?"

"I can't say it's boredom, because I'm busy working on my master's degree. There are times I really feel like I made an error getting married, having a child, staying home—the whole bit. Don't get me wrong, Dr. Robinson, I love my family. I just feel trapped. Everybody leans on me so much. They totally depend on me."

Dr. Robinson was standing now, peeling off the latex gloves. "Everything looks normal, Ramona. Maybe you should go over to the lab to have some blood drawn so we can check your thyroid to be safe."

"Thank you Dr. Robinson," she said, sitting up on the table. "I hope I didn't bore you with my problems."

"No, you didn't. I'm used to it. A lot of women who had careers prior to starting families go

through similar bouts. What you need to do is
some soul-searching to find out what's really eating at you. Get away for a couple of days and do
something special for yourself. Okay?"

"That's exactly what I plan on doing. I just
hope I don't go on a guilt trip for leaving my
family for a couple of days."

"There's no need to feel guilty because you
want to do something for yourself. But if you decide to take the guilt trip with you, make sure
you dump it off as soon as you can so you can
enjoy yourself. Love yourself a little more, Ramona. That's all you need, honey. I'll have Adeline set up an appointment at the lab for you.
See you next time."

Ramona left Dr. Robinson's office feeling sure
of her decision to take the trip to Detroit and
sure about spending more time loving herself. It
was 12:29 P.M., just early enough for her to stop
by the fish store to get some whiting for dinner.
But when she saw the many cars clogged on
Bloomfield Avenue, she chose to go home and
prepare a spinach and turkey sausage roll instead.

Pulling into the driveway, Ramona noticed Madrid's Jeep parked in front of the garage. What
was he doing home this time of the day, she wondered, closing the car door behind her. She could
hear the music blaring from inside before she
walked into the house. John Coltrane's "A Love
Supreme" was tweeting out of the JBL speakers.

Immediately, her eyes perused the living area.
Still no change. Everything was left in the same
mess as it had been last night. The garbage bag
was still swollen and leaning against the wall next
to the kitchen counter, the cereal bowls from this
morning were still stacked in the sink along with

the plates from last night, and the family room carpet was still sprinkled with popcorn kernels.

Apparently, Madrid hadn't heard her come in because when he turned the corner and saw her standing in the family room, he jumped. "Mona," he said nervously. "You scared me." He walked over to the stereo and turned the volume down. "I wouldn't have heard you over this music anyway, huh?"

"I guess," Ramona dismissed. Already she was in a bad mood. Who wouldn't be miffed if they came home to an untidy house knowing that they'd be the only one to clean it up? How long had Madrid been home, she wondered, looking around the house. Good God, he could have at least taken the trash out.

"What are you doing home?" she asked, placing her purse and leather school bag on the stool.

"My meeting with the staff ended early, so I decided to sneak out. I even dropped by the gym to pump some iron before coming home. And somehow I lucked out and got tickets for tonight's Knicks-Chicago game. Larry, the marketing manager, couldn't attend the game, so he gave his tickets to me. Another reason why I needed to get home early." He plopped down on the sofa and stretched out. His feet dangled over the end of the sofa as he attempted to get situated.

Ramona's attitude dissipated as hastily as it had developed. She was tickled silly at the thought of visiting the Garden. In the five years they had lived in the New York metropolitan area, they had attended only two Knicks games and one Nets game. Perhaps it was because she was a staunch Pistons fan and Madrid an unrelenting Cavaliers fan. How sweet, she thought, ready to shower him with a juicy kiss. "What time is the game?"

"Seven-thirty. I'm supposed to meet DeMar at the Steak and Ale across the street from the Garden at six. We'll grab a little something to eat and a few beers before the game so we can be fully energized."

Ramona knew her face had cracked. "DeMar?" She frowned. "What, have you forgotten how much I love the game as well?" Her eyebrows were knitted now.

Madrid looked up at her with the stupidest expression on his face before replying, "Oh, Mona, I'm sorry, baby. I just assumed that you had some schoolwork to do. I wasn't thinking. With the kids and all." He was stuttering now. "I'm sorry, baby," he said, sitting up on the edge of the sofa.

"Just for your information, Madrid, I'm on break from classes for the next week. All you have to do is call DeMar at work and tell him that there's been a change of plan. I'm sure he'll understand that if you don't take your wife to the game of the century you'll be homeless." She grinned diabolically. "I'll ask Karen to babysit for us." Ramona was already reaching for the phone to place the call.

Madrid rubbed his hand across his forehead and took a moment to consider her proposal—or her threat, whichever it was. Truthfully, he didn't want to go to the game with his wife. He wanted to have a boys' night out with his brother and do some bonding. He carefully mulled over his words before responding, "I can't, Mona. I told DeMar we'd have a boys' night out. Sorry," he said, shrugging his shoulders timidly.

Ramona stared at him, feeling her temples tightening. She tried to marinate her words before letting them bake. But it was too late, they were already oozing out and ready to burn him. "A boys' night out? What the hell, Madrid, are you regressing back to your college days? Tell me if I'm wrong, but it seems to me we just had a boys' night here recently. Take a look around you," she said, illustrating with her hands. "Have you forgotten about last night?" With that she turned her back and sauntered into the kitchen. "I mean, look at this mess." She was referring to the sticky kitchen floor that she had mopped on Monday, the sauce stuck on the stove from last night, the dishes overflowing in the sink, and the trash that was beginning to stink up the house.

He stood up and followed her into the kitchen. "Do you need some help?" he asked in a guilt-ridden voice.

What the hell you think? she answered inwardly. She was so wound up that when he touched her shoulder she unconsciously jerked away from him.

"Okay, fine then," he murmured, walking out of the kitchen.

It was obvious he wasn't going to try any harder. How pitiful, Ramona resolved. But she refused to let him off the hook so easy. Without giving it much thought she blurted, "You could pick the kids up from school."

"What time do they get out?"

Damn. He doesn't even know what time his own kids get out of school. It was probably safe to assume he didn't remember where the schools were either, she fretted internally. She pulled her thoughts together long enough to respond, "You can pick

Nathan up around two-thirty. Leslie gets out at two-fifty."

Madrid glanced up at the clock—1:10 P.M. He still had over an hour before he needed to pick up the kids. "I'm going to stop by the gas station to fill up the Jeep. You need anything while I'm out?" he asked, swiping his keys off the kitchen counter. He couldn't understand why she was being so bitchy lately. It was starting to make the hairs on his chest rise. When she didn't answer him, he picked up the trash and said, "Okay then, I'll see you when I get back."

"Yeah, well, if I'm here," she mumbled over the running water and rattling dishes.

"What's that supposed to mean, Ramona?" Madrid asked. He was annoyed with her snide remarks. "You plan on going somewhere?"

"You mean besides to the store, the bank, the schools, the grocery store, the cleaners, the gas station and the office supply store? Yes, Madrid, I just might. I'm thinking about driving to Detroit for a few days."

"And when did you decide all this?"

"Last night," she replied matter-of-factly, soaping the pots.

"Really? And when is this supposed to happen?" He dropped the bag of garbage and crossed his arms in front of his chest.

"I'm not sure yet. Maybe in the morning, maybe tonight, maybe this weekend. I don't know."

"Ramona, you must be delirious to think you can up and drive to Detroit on such short notice," he huffed. "You must be planning to take the kids with you."

"Maybe I am delirious, but I'm going. I could really use the break, Madrid." She frowned, wiping the bottom of the pots with the dishrag. "And as far as the kids are concerned, as much as I'd like to take them with me, they're not included in this little retreat."

Madrid's stout body had moved back into the kitchen. He had to read Ramona's body language to be sure that she was serious. "I know you're not seriously thinking about doing this. Especially since we haven't discussed it or made plans to see to it that the kids can go."

"I told you Madrid, the kids aren't going. Not this time anyway. Besides, they're in school. I need a little break. Since I can't fly to Cancun and soak up some sun like some housewives can, I guess Detroit will have to do. It's been awhile since I've seen Lalah and the rest of my family anyway."

Shaking his head back and forth a few times, Madrid turned up his top lip, then stated, "I knew your man-hating sister was behind this. She just doesn't have enough business in Detroit to tend to, does she?"

"Lalah doesn't have anything to do with this, Madrid, okay? So just leave her name out of it," Ramona said, pushing her lengthy bangs out of her eyes.

"Fine. But I tell you what, you can leave this house if you want." He paused, then walked over to the back door once again. "If you go, you can stay gone because there is no rational reason for what you're going to do. I think you're being very selfish about this."

"Selfish?" she responded in shock. "I know you aren't trying to let that word even part your lips. Matter of fact, if we look up the word 'selfish' in the dictionary, your mug should be flashed right next to it. Listen to what you're saying. It's okay

for you to disappear for a business meeting, or a
fishing expedition, or a skiing trip with the boys
for a few days, but I can't go see my sister? Now
that's pretty selfish if you ask me. Sounds like
you're the one hallucinating, Madrid."

"Call it what the hell you want to, Ramona, but
like I said, if you leave without taking the kids
with you, you can stay gone. That's final!" he
barked, turning his back to her.

"Final? Who the hell do you think you're *final-
izing*? I'm not one of your damn employees. I'm
your wife, in case you forgot. More importantly,
I'm a grown adult, okay? I'm not going on a scuba
diving expedition, I'm going to visit my family
and I don't feel like I need your permission to
do that. You don't have to worry about visiting
your family, because your only immediate family
member is always here in this damn house."

Madrid was furious now. His deep, rich face
burned with redness. He was sure his blood pressure had jumped a few notches. He turned
around and eyed Ramona like a boxer would do
his opponent before a bout, hoping that the cold
stare would rattle her. But after a moment of silence, he could see that his piercing gaze hadn't
rocked her in the least. She was obviously serious
about this. Well, so was he. If she thought that
she could leave anytime she damn well pleased,
she was the one dreaming.

"What kind of mother are you to leave your
kids stranded?" he questioned. He was reaching
now, trying desperately to grab control of the situation. But seeing Ramona's face flush, he knew
he had struck a nerve.

"You know what, Madrid? I'm not even going
to go there with you, okay? You and I both know

that you're hitting below the belt. A better question would be what kind of father are *you* that you don't want to spend more quality time with your children? What, are you afraid of a little work around here?"

"Work? *Work?*" he repeated with a chuckle. "If you think this little housework bull you do around here is so much work, try going to a job every day and bringing home a paycheck so that me and the kids can be provided for."

"Don't hand me that nonsense, Madrid. In case you've forgotten, I used to be out there every day working professionally just like you, and still coming home and keeping the house in order. Sure, it was just you and me at the time, but I was the one putting in eight hours a day in the field and another two to three hours at home on a daily basis. So please spare me that tired line. I contribute just as much around here, if not more, than you do." She slung the few pieces of hair away from her eyes again.

"Yeah right," he laughed. "I'm sure it's real hard work lounging at home all day watching Sally, Oprah, and God knows who else while I'm out there busting my butt. I would gladly trade places with you and stay home and rest on my laurels all day if you want to go out and do some real work every day."

"This *is* real work, Mr. Man. I bet you couldn't handle half of what is required to keep this house and the children in order," she smirked. "You can't even take the trash out without me reminding you constantly."

"That's just it. You don't remind me—you nag me constantly. That's what you do. I go to work every day, sometimes twelve, thirteen hours a day.

So if I don't feel like I want to take the trash out or tell you how the sam hill my day went when I get home, so be it. Hell, I shouldn't have to do too much of anything around here but go to work and pay the damn bills!"

His voice was strident and strong. "I'm not going to discuss this anymore, Ramona," he vowed, picking up the trash bag and walking toward the back door for a third time. "All I've got to say is, if you choose to take a so-called break and leave, your unappreciative behind can stay gone for good. And you'll be sure to find some papers waiting for you when you get back!"

The door shut so hard that one of the tiny windowpanes cracked. Ramona heard the tires squeal as the Jeep sped down their driveway. Immediately, she stopped what she was doing and picked up the telephone, angrily punching in the eleven digits. Her hands were trembling so much and her heart racing so fast that it felt like someone had just injected her with speed.

After the third ring, the answering machine picked up. She waited for the outgoing message to finish and when she heard the beep, she blurted, "Lalah, this is your sister. I'm packing up Meka and heading your way. Expect me late this evening. Don't bother to call back, because by the time you get this message, I'll be on the road. See you soon. Oh, and do me a favor. Schedule me a hair appointment with Jonathan." Slam! The phone crashed into the cradle.

Who the hell does Madrid think he is ordering me around like I'm his child? Ramona jogged up the stairs two at a time. Her adrenaline was flowing like crazy. It was evident her hormones were out of control when she reached into her bedroom closet and snatched her overnight bag from the top, causing everything else to come crashing down. She didn't care. She was pumped as she raced around the room tossing clothes into the canvas Polo bag. She wasn't even thinking clearly when she went into the bathroom and stuffed her cosmetic bag with her toothbrush, facial cleanser, lipstick, mascara, face powder and deodorant.

Ramona was moving at a tremendous rate. Ten minutes later, she was toting the overnight bag downstairs. Swiftly, she rummaged through the kitchen cabinets and refrigerator looking for some food to accompany her on the trip. She yanked one of the plastic supermarket bags out of the pantry and began swelling it with yogurt, two apples, a banana, two oranges, a couple of Pepsi's, a liter of spring water, and a bag of potato chips. She slapped some mustard and mayonnaise on four pieces of bread, then laid a good portion of turkey breast and Swiss cheese between the slices before wrapping the sandwiches in foil. She stood in the kitchen for a few more minutes to make sure she wasn't forgetting anything. "Oh yeah," she mumbled. "A spoon for the yogurt."

Making her way around to the opposite side of the kitchen bar, Ramona slammed her pocketbook on the counter to check her wallet for the ATM card, the gas card and the Visa. "Check," she whispered, finding the plastic cards in her wallet. Pulling the money out of her wallet, she counted five twenty-dollar bills and three ten-dollar bills. "Cool," she mumbled. Thinking about the possible emergencies that might arise, she checked her wallet once more to make sure she had the AAA card as well. That too was tucked in her brown leather wallet. Meka had three-quarters of a tank of gas and had successfully passed the motor vehicle inspection last month, so she knew the trip would not be difficult.

Ramona perused the coat closet in the foyer before selecting her trench coat and her burnt orange leather jacket. May was such an unpredictable month for the weather that she opted for the two coats to be safe. Standing in the family room for a few minutes, she looked around to see what other items she needed to bring with her in order to make her trip more enjoyable. By the time her eyes reached the stereo, she realized that she should probably grab a few CD's as well.

Flipping through the three hundred or so CD's they had collected over the years, she chose a slew of jazz, gospel and R&B artists. Placing the CD's in her duffel bag, she seized the overnight bag and slung it over her left shoulder before picking up her keys. If only she could have told the kids she was leaving for a few days. She let out a defeated breath. Hopefully, they'd understand.

She wondered if she should leave Madrid a note letting him know that she was indeed serious. Quickly, she picked up the pen and pad by the phone and jotted down, "Went to Detroit. Call when I get there." It killed her to be even that thoughtful, considering. *Whatever,* she thought, while looking around the kitchen, then the family room, which was still partly a mess. She tossed the duffel bag on her other shoulder with her pocketbook, grabbed the plastic bag of food and walked out the back door locking it behind her. Now she was ready for her journey.

After loading up Meka, Ramona sat in the driver's seat and fastened her seat belt. She tilted the rearview mirror toward her face so that she could take a good look at herself. Never before had she put her marriage on the line like she was about to do now. But never before had she felt so strangled, so empty, so worthless, so unidentifiable. Ramona took a deep breath before putting the key in the ignition. Madrid thought that maintaining the house and looking after the children was bull.

"Well, Mr. Shaw, it's all yours for a few days," she said, turning the key until she heard the chant of Meka's engine. Meka was ready for a change and so was she, for that matter. Ramona put the car in reverse and softly pressed down on the accelerator. Gliding to the end of the driveway, Ramona carefully backed out onto her street. Placing the gear into drive she looked down at the numbers on the clock: 1:45 P.M. Smoothing her hand over the black leather steering wheel, Ramona let out a deep breath and whispered, "Let's journey, Meka. Motown, we're on our way."

Three

Madrid pulled into the driveway, heart thumping loudly the closer he got to the back of the house. He quickly perused the area, searching for a sign, an indication, that the Volvo station wagon would be parked in the front of the garage, which sat behind and to the left of their seven-room brick home. Arriving at the end of the driveway and noticing that Meka was nowhere to be parked, Madrid let out a grieved breath. Sure enough, someone had severed his heart in half. *I don't believe it,* he frowned. *How could she do this to me? To us? To the kids?*

Madrid quickly gathered his racing thoughts, shut down the engine to his cherry red Grand Jeep Cherokee and unbuckled his seat belt. He couldn't help but wonder if the kids would detect anything strange about Ramona's sudden disappearance. *How could she do this?* he asked himself a second time. Nathan and Leslie's bickering snapped him back to the immediate situation at hand.

"Leslie, leave Nathan alone," Madrid ordered, stepping out of the Jeep.

"He hit me first, Daddy," Leslie whined.

"I don't care who hit who first. I want you to

stop picking with him. Now come on," Madrid
said, helping Leslie and Nathan out of the Jeep.

Once Madrid unlocked the door, Nathan
darted through the doorway in search of his
mother. "Mommy, Mommy," Nathan shouted,
racing through the bottom portion of the house
before making the climb up the stairs.

Leslie, who had plopped down on the family
room sofa and switched on the TV, was more concerned about what was for dinner than with Ramona's whereabouts.

"What are we eating tonight, Daddy?"

"I don't know yet, Leslie. Why? You want to
cook?" Madrid teased as he walked into the
kitchen. Glancing around the modern kitchen,
he spotted a piece of notepaper sitting on the
corner of the counter, next to the telephone. His
heart fluttered as he lifted up the note in anticipation of its content. Maybe it wasn't what he
thought or, then again, maybe it was.

Slowly he lifted the piece of lavender paper, hoping, praying that it was Ramona's grocery list or
the sometimes, dreadful, "honey do" list. The
hand-written words, which seemed to have been
written in a hurry, cut him to the core. His head
was about to explode as he read the large, swag-
gering print: *Went to Detroit. Call when I get there.*

"I'll be damned," Madrid whispered, shaking
his head in disbelief. "I don't believe it." He
crumpled the paper, tossing it into the blue plastic garbage can. He was furious that his wife had
chosen to ignore his warning. He stood in the
kitchen for a few minutes trying to collect his
thoughts and grab hold of his sparking emotions.

Sudden, piercing noises from the other room
shook him free from his deliberations. Glancing

toward the family room, he realized that the disturbing shrills were coming from the 30-inch TV screen.

"Don't you have some homework to do, Leslie?" Madrid said, walking toward her. But when Leslie chose to move her head around her father's stout body in order to see the TV instead of answering him, Madrid continued, "Give me that remote, girl," taking the black remote control out of her hand. "I know this is not what you do when get home from school every day."

"Yes it is!" she screamed fiercely, then poked out her lower lip.

Madrid stood quietly peering down at his daughter. Fury was starting to swell up inside him. *Was this his daughter yelling at him like she had lost her mind?* he marveled. His first reaction was to yank her narrow little butt off the sofa and spank her. Instead, he eyed her down with the deadliest look he could possibly give. It worked; Leslie scurried over to the kitchen table with her book bag trailing behind her.

Madrid followed her over to the table, still giving her the serious eye. He would have to address her behavior now to ensure that she would never raise her voice at him again. At least as long as she was still living in this lifetime as Leslie Shaw.

"Look at me, Leslie," Madrid said as calmly as he could. Once his daughter's big eyes were locked with his, he continued. "Did I yell at you when I asked you about your homework? No, I didn't. So, in the future when someone in this house asks you a question, you better make sure you think about your answer before responding. Because you don't want to know what will happen the next time you yell at me. Do we understand each other?"

"Yes. I'm sorry, Daddy," she whimpered.

"It's okay this time, Leslie. Just remember what I said. Now, if you need some help with your homework, let me know. I'm going to figure out what we're having for dinner," he said, walking back into the kitchen.

"You're going to make dinner, Daddy?" she giggled. "How come?"

Just as Madrid was about to answer her, his attention was diverted toward Nathan, who had slid down the shellacked wooden banister before crashing onto the floor, laughing wildly.

"Nathan!" Madrid drilled as he ran over toward him. "How many times have I told you not to slide down that banister, boy? You could bust your head open! Is that what you want?" he questioned, leaning down to whisk his son up with one hand. "Do you?"

"No," Nathan giggled. "It's fun, Daddy."

"And it's also dangerous. So don't do it again or else—"

"You're going to spank my behind," Nathan chimed in.

Madrid felt the laughter brewing in his belly and tried, unsuccessfully, to hem it up. After a few seconds of laughter with the kids, Madrid felt better, less irritated. *Maybe spending some time playing Mr. Mom with the kids won't be all bad. But this is not how it was supposed to go down. Ramona and I were supposed to talk about this, plan for this.*

Madrid reflected on how desperately he had tried to exert his authority by telling Ramona she could stay gone for good if she chose to leave. Perhaps that wasn't the best way to handle it, he thought. The telephone's ringing snapped him out of his reverie. Reaching for the cordless phone, he secretly hoped that it was Ramona calling to tell him that she had just gone for a drive to sort things out and that she was on her way home to discuss things with him. But when he heard the familiar, thick voice on the other line acknowledge him, he was quickly reminded of what a bind Ramona had left him in.

"Madrid," DeMar said in a hurried tone. "I'm glad I caught you. I need you to swing by my crib and pick up my overnight bag before you head over this way. It's next to my nightstand."

Madrid hesitated for a moment trying, once again, to sift through his emotions. *Why would she do this? Why now? Why at all?* Hearing DeMar deliberately clearing his throat, he responded, "Hey, D. I was just about to call you. Something's come up. I'm not going to be able to make it to the game tonight."

"What do you mean something's come up? Is Ramona giving you some flack?"

"You could say that," Madrid groaned, snatching a beer out of the refrigerator.

"Well, did you tell her you've got tickets to the game of the damn decade? Certainly she has to appreciate the importance of two brothers getting together to see the Bulls stampede the Knicks," DeMar chuckled.

"Yeah, I mentioned it to her earlier today. But she's not here and I can't leave the kids by themselves."

"She's not there? Well, if you told her about the game she's sure to come back in time so you can go. Right?"

"I don't think so, D. I came home and found a note saying she took off for Detroit."

"Detroit? Was there a family emergency or something?"

"Nope. She just decided to break camp," Madrid said, shrugging his shoulders.

"You've got to be kidding me. So, she just left you with the kids?"

"Something like that," Madrid replied before taking another gulp of his beer.

"Ain't this nothing! I can't believe she just took off and left you stranded. See," DeMar paused briefly before continuing. "That's probably why I'm not married yet. How the hell can your wife just leave on the spur of the moment, without taking into consideration how that effects the rest of the household?"

Madrid's mind went numb. He wanted to forget, for a moment, that Ramona had deserted him and their children. Basically, he didn't want to spend any more time on the phone with his older brother discussing or crucifying his wife. He had to figure things out, get a game plan together so that his emotions, the household, and, more importantly, the children wouldn't fall apart. The thing he had to do now was cut DeMar's rambling comments off and handle his business.

"Listen man, I'm sorry about the game tonight. But right now I need to find some dinner for the kids. You can always come by and pick up the tickets if you have the time."

"Naw, that's all right. Besides, by the time I get over to your house to pick up the tickets, then swing by my house to pick up my overnight bag, it'll be too late. Next time, bro. What about you? Are you all right?"

"I'm fine. I'll handle it. Anyway, what's all the fuss about your overnight bag? Is there some special reason why you're not coming home tonight?" Madrid teased.

"Special is what special does," DeMar answered. "Her name is Connie. She's got a little studio over here and, you know, I offered to keep her warm if she got chilly tonight."

"What happened to Lisa?"

"Lisa who?" DeMar joked.

"The Lisa you brought over here last month," Madrid said, shaking his head.

"Oh, that Lisa," DeMar paused. "Her husband came home."

"She was married?" Madrid asked, shocked but not surprised by his brother's behavior.

"That's what she says. You never know about these women today. They can't be trusted. Maybe it's a blessing you don't have to deal with the dating game. I try to be good, Madrid. I really do. But Mr. Mac just won't let me behave," DeMar laughed.

"Boy, you're something else. I just hope you're wrapping Mr. Mac up properly," Madrid said, joining in with the laughter.

"Oh, you know that! I ain't crazy now. I better go. But on a serious tip, Connie just might be the one to reel me in."

"What?" Madrid replied, almost choking on his beer. "Reel you in how? As in the big M word? *Please,*" he laughed.

"Yeah, you laughing now, but don't be surprised if this little lady has the makings of another Mrs. Shaw. Hey, I gotta run. I'll call you tomorrow to see how your first night as Mr. Mom went."

"Yeah, you do that. I may need you to pick the

kids up from school for me tomorrow, so be sure to call me in the morning."

Madrid hung up the phone and let out a long yawn. Fatigue was already beginning to set in and it was still relatively early. The first thing on his agenda was making sure that the children were aware of Ramona's departure. He sat down at the table in the breakfast nook, next to Leslie. After a few moments of watching his daughter tackle her last math problem, he reached out and lightly touched her hand.

"Leslie, I want to talk to you and Nathan about something. Nathan," Madrid called out in his deep voice. "Come here, son." A few more seconds passed by before everyone was situated at the cast iron and glass breakfast table.

"What is it, Daddy?" Leslie said eagerly.

"I just want to let you guys know that Ramona has gone to Detroit. So it's just going to be the three of us for awhile. Okay?"

"Did she go to Grammy's house, Daddy?" Nathan asked.

"Yes, Nathan, she did."

"How come?" Leslie cut in.

"Because she needed to get some rest, I suppose," Madrid softly said.

"When is she coming back?"

"I don't know when she'll be back, Leslie. But she did tell me to tell you guys that she loves you very much and she would be back fairly soon."

"I want to go to Grammy's house," Nathan whined.

"Next time, big man," Madrid promised. "In the meantime, I need for all of us to help keep the place together while Ramona's gone, all right?"

82   *Monique Gilmore*

"Okay," Nathan replied sadly. "But I want to see Mommy, Daddy."

"I know, son, and you will. Just as soon as she gets back. So," he smiled while bouncing Nathan on his lap. "What you guys want for dinner?"

"McDonald's," both Leslie and Nathan sang out.

"McDonald's?" Madrid blinked with surprise. "How about I order a pizza instead?"

"Yeah!" the kids agreed in unison.

"Pizza it is then. Leslie, go ahead and finish your homework. Nathan, you go upstairs and put your toys away in your room and by the time you all do that, the pizza should be here," Madrid said.

Madrid ordered the pizza then went upstairs to the bedroom. Right away, he could tell that Ramona had left in a hurry because her things were scattered all over the room and all over the bathroom counter. Removing his crew neck sweatshirt to expose a white, sleeveless undershirt, Madrid somberly stood at the gray marble bathroom counter and gazed into the mirror. His chest, which was bejeweled with loose curls of hair, still had the rock hardness that had made him so desirable during his college days. Though the six-pack stomach had dropped to a four-pack, his biceps were still mounted high and thick as he leaned with both hands onto the counter.

He scanned the figure standing before the mirror, hoping that the man with the five o'clock shadow facing him would have some answers, some input as to what the hell was happening to his marriage. Instead, he found himself studying the face of a thirty-five-year-old, well-manicured, African-American, corporate-climbing brother.

Hopelessly, he attempted to efface the negative

picture Ramona harshly painted, trying to sift through and locate the father of two, faithful husband and loving family man. Madrid's gleaming eyes bounced off the mirror once more as he let out a tiny breath. A small circle, the size of a quarter, fogged the middle of the glass. Regardless of what image was reflected before his eyes, or Ramona's eyes for that matter, he was certain that in spite of it all, a few things remained constant: he loved his wife, he was a damn good provider, and a faithful husband. Ramona better go ask somebody, he determined, shaking his head before heading downstairs to answer the doorbell. *Yeah, she better know what time it is.*

Ramona had jumped on Pompton Avenue driving toward Route 46 West, trying to beat the evening traffic before she began her journey on Route 80. The afternoon sun, which was shining brightly for this time of the year, penetrated the windshield and flushed her smooth face. She was ecstatic that Daylight Savings had taken effect, because it meant another five to six hours of daylight driving before reaching 75 North, the route that would land her in downtown Motown. Scanning through WBLS, KISS and CD101.9, Ramona turned off the radio and settled for the Fatburger CD already in the CD player.

In no time, Ramona and Meka were coasting along Route 80 and the cars from the early rush hour traffic had begun to surface. She let out a held breath. This pilgrimage was going to help her sort some things out regarding her life, her goals and her recent onslaught of mixed emotions about her marriage and identity. Whoever said thinking and driving didn't go hand in hand, she smiled, as she thought about Madrid's earlier statement that had sent her spinning over the edge.

How could Madrid say all those things? At one point during their argument, she was sure she didn't recognize the man who was talking at her with such a barbaric attitude. Could that have been her husband of six years telling her that if she left, she could keep her unappreciative butt gone for good? *Surely not,* she thought, switching on the cruise control then leaning her head back against the head rest.

Perhaps it was the unappreciative part of Madrid's sentence that caused Ramona's nostrils to flare, and then her lips to part with a few negative proclamations of her own. Regardless of the reason, the disagreement was senseless and unnecessary. How could Madrid tell her that her duties as a loving mother and a devoted wife, as well as a bonafide domestic engineer, was nothing in comparison to what he contributed?

"I don't know," she confessed out loud.

It would be nine more hours or so before Ramona would arrive at Lalah's house in the Motor City. She was happy that Lalah had suggested she get away for a while. At least she knew that there was someone in the world who cared about her well-being enough to try and offer a solution and listen unconditionally. Madrid certainly didn't seem to care too much about her emotional state of late. But he hadn't always been so self-absorbed, she recalled.

There was a time when Madrid appreciated the little things she did around the house and for him. But of course, that was before she had

Nathan, and before Leslie came to live with them. Now, the two years they'd spent together alone before the rest of the clan arrived seemed like a blur. In fact, trying to remember the first time she'd ever laid eyes on Madrid was beginning to cloud with cobwebs as well.

It was during one of the national launch meetings with Pont Pharmaceuticals in Miami, Florida, seven-and-a-half years ago. What a glorious time in her life. Pont Pharmaceuticals had launched a new drug that had been approved by the FDA, and she had just been promoted from an account representative in Detroit to a hospital representative for an expansion territory in Cleveland. There were more than five hundred representatives nationwide attending the week-long meeting at the Hyatt Hotel in Miami. And every night, Pont had provided some type of entertainment for its employees.

One particular night, Ramona and her roommate, Tina, decided to leave the corporate festivities early in order to meet some of Tina's friends at the local club in Miami. As Ramona and Tina stepped off the elevator into the lobby of their hotel, Ramona's eye had wandered magnetically over to the tall, well-tailored, handsome, copper-colored brother resting up against one of the columns in the lobby. Madrid had returned the intense gaze as their eyes locked for some time before Ramona smiled and turned away.

Ramona, having flashed her radiant smile, sashayed through the hotel's revolving door, leaving Madrid with just the back of her hourglass figure to view. Madrid darted over to her before she was able to get into the cab and quickly introduced himself. He had spoken just a few pleasant words to both her and Tina before he had been asked to accompany them to the club. It turned out that Madrid was staying at the same hotel and was in town for a national meeting with his tele-communications company.

At that time, he held the position of sales manager for the Toledo and Cleveland territories. Naturally, when Madrid found out that Ramona had accepted a job in the Cleveland area, he offered to serve as her tour guide when she relocated. For the remainder of that long, hot week in Miami, Ramona and Madrid spent as much time together as possible. When it was time for them to return to their respective homes, they had vowed to keep in touch.

Two months later, Ramona had relocated to Cleveland and had taken Madrid up on his offer to play tour guide. Their attraction was strong and their relationship evolved. They spent countless nights sampling various restaurants, visiting several art galleries and historical museums. They saw every movie that was worth seeing, every play worth applauding for, and every concert worth standing in line to get tickets for.

Once Madrid, a Cleveland native, discovered that Ramona was a dedicated sports enthusiast, as well as a Detroit native, he'd bought tickets for the Cleveland Cavaliers vs. Detroit Pistons game. The trash talking that ensued between them during the week before the game was fierce. With Ramona swearing that the Cleveland fans would never have to worry about attending a championship game and with Madrid promising that Lenny Wilkins was a better coach than Chuck Daley with his eyes closed, they had made an interesting transition in their developing relationship.

The game had come and gone in a flash. And so had Isiah Thomas and the rest of the Pistons, who had successfully annihilated the Cavaliers, forcing Madrid to wear a Pistons sweatshirt the next time they went to visit one of his friends. That wager wasn't nearly as hard to fulfill as the one that followed, after they had attended the University of Michigan vs. Ohio State football game. The bet had been set prior to the beginning of the football season and the stakes were fairly high. The losing team's fan had to wear the winning school's paraphernalia on the weekends for a whole month.

It must have been lady luck watching over Ramona every time she placed a bet with Madrid, because sure enough, Madrid was stuck purchasing and wearing her Michigan alma mater's blue and yellow for an entire month. After that incident, Ramona and Madrid's romance had risen to new heights, because thirteen months and a closet full of undesirable sportswear later, Madrid proposed to Ramona. Ramona was sure the proposal had something to do with the motto, "If you can't beat 'em, join 'em."

Ramona shook her head lightly in an attempt to drift back to her immediate environment. Glimpsing down at the odometer, then over at the clock, she noticed that the dials read 6:23 P.M. and 185 miles. "Better make a pit stop," she softly mumbled. She eased over to the right lane and exited at the next rest and gas area. Following the arrows for the food and restrooms, Ramona found a parking space and wedged Meka between a large Lincoln Continental and a Toyota mini-van.

Locking the car door behind her, Ramona raced inside only to find a long line for the ladies' restroom awaiting her. She deliberately concentrated on the stuffed animals perched in the tiny gift shop window as she prayed silently for the line to speed up. Noticing the fast food restaurant to her right, she decided once she had finished in the restroom, she would sit at one of the tables and eat her turkey and cheese sandwich. The line had finally reached the interior of the ladies' room, where Ramona's eyes scanned the cold, steel-colored lavatory.

Unconsciously, Ramona swayed back and forth, doing the little *I got to go* bathroom dance as she patiently waited her turn. Glancing around the room once again, Ramona caught the smile of a woman standing at the sink. Promptly she returned the smile to the little red-haired woman.

"You're almost there," the woman smiled, rubbing her hands together under the hand dryer.

"Not soon enough," Ramona replied. "This is ridiculous. Maybe I should try the men's room. They never seem to have a line out the door like we do. Why do you suppose that is?"

A few ladies in line laughed at Ramona's comment. The woman at the end of the line actually took Ramona's advice and slipped over to the men's room. Ramona could easily have done the same thing, except she was finally the next person in line for an empty stall. *At last,* Ramona huffed silently as she walked to the back of the restroom and into the handicapped stall.

A few minutes later, Ramona emerged from the stall only to find that the line had vanished. "Figures," she fretted as she stood at the sink scrubbing her hands. Outside, she began searching for an empty table in the crowded restaurant. After surveying unsuccessfully for a vacant table, she strolled over to the table where the red-haired woman from the bathroom was seated. The woman's broad smile was welcoming, which made Ramona's approach easier.

"Hello again," Ramona smiled. "Do you mind if I share this table with you?"

"Not at all," the woman happily replied. "I was just thinking about how wasteful it was for me to have four seats here when there are so many people looking for seats. I'm Dolores," she said, extending her hand. "Most people call me Dolly."

"Nice to meet you, Dolly," Ramona responded taking her hand. "I'm Ramona."

"Good to meet you. You look a lot less stressed than you did a few minutes ago," Dolly laughed, slinging her hair back over her shoulders. Her freckled face was warm, radiating the result of a recent trip to the Caribbean or the tanning salon.

Ramona's eyes immediately drifted from Dolly's chiseled face to the large pear-shaped diamond ring on her dainty ring finger. My God, Ramona thought assessing the ring from afar. It had to be at least two or three carats in size because the ring was considerably larger than the one-and-a-half-carat diamond wedding ring Madrid had given her.

Dolly caught Ramona staring at her ring and smiled. "Enormous, huh?" Dolly said, looking down at her ring.

"I couldn't help but notice it," Ramona bashfully replied.

"It's all right. I'm used to it," Dolly said, clasping both hands together "I have my late husband to thank for it."

"Oh," Ramona said, with widened eyes. "I'm sorry."

"Please, don't be. I've had a few years to cope

with my loss," Dolly smiled, perusing Ramona's hand for a sign that she might be a member of the marriage club as well. Noticing the marquise diamond sparkling on Ramona's finger, Dolly continued, "I see that you're married."

"Yes," Ramona exhaled. "I just hope I never have to switch ring fingers someday," she said, looking down at her hand.

"I know what you mean," Dolly chuckled, pouring more sugar into her coffee. "I'm so used to wearing a ring on my left finger, I'd feel bare without it," she said, glancing down at her own ring before continuing, "It's a difficult thing when you lose a spouse. My husband and I were married for twenty-two years before he died."

Ramona could tell by Dolly's expression that she was still grieving the loss of her husband. She didn't want Dolly to slip into a temporary state of mourning, so she quickly responded, "Twenty-two years? How wonderful. I hope my husband and I make it that long. Do you have any children?"

"One," Dolly said, lifting her eyes to meet Ramona's once again. "My daughter, Susan. Matter of fact, I'm driving to her school to pick her up for the summer. Mercy me, it was hard to say goodbye when she left last year. You know, Ramona, there are times when a parent is torn between wanting their children to stay close to home and wanting them to get out."

Ramona joined Dolly in laughter before replying, "I can imagine."

"Oh, no." Dolly smiled wider. "You must have children."

"Two," Ramona offered before taking a small bite of her sandwich.

"Boys or girls?"

"A boy and a girl."

"How old are they?"

"Nathan is four years old and Leslie is the feisty eleven-year-old," Ramona told her.

"I can remember those days like it was yesterday. The dreadful adolescent stage of parenthood. I tell you," Dolly said, pausing to take another sip of her coffee, "I wouldn't take those days back for nothing. During those days, it was a constant struggle to get Susan to cooperate around the house. And Norman, my late husband, bless his heart, didn't help matters by being so easy with her either. He would let her run all over him. I was the dreaded villain who had to keep her in line."

"Sounds familiar," Ramona chimed in. "Sometimes I wish my husband would be the one solely responsible for the disciplinary actions in the house. I get so tired of fussing that sometimes I just let things slip by."

"No, no," Dolly insisted. "You mustn't do that, Ramona. Believe me, what you allow your children to get away with now will haunt you in the future. Trust me. There's nothing wrong with fussing. Especially if you're trying to instill some moral fiber or survival skills. You have to hang on even if it means having the children angry with you. Of course, taking a vacation to escape now and then to replenish yourself is required." She winked.

"I guess," Ramona replied before taking a sip of her Pepsi. "That's why I'm here now. I needed to get away for a few days. I was about to explode and I knew that if I didn't step away to sort some of this craziness out, things could have really gotten out of control."

"Are you a working mother?" Dolly inquired.

"A domestic engineer maintaining a twelve-credit course load in a graduate program," Ramona sighed.

Dolly studied Ramona's full face for a few seconds before giving her a sorrowful gaze. "Don't worry, Ramona, you're not abandoning anyone by taking a little break away from home. I realize we just met, but I have a feeling that you're experiencing what all Americans, black or white, women or men, refer to as burn-out. It's normal."

Ramona sighed heavily. *Burn-out? To say the least.*

"That could be, Dolly. But my case feels exceptionally abnormal right now. Honestly . . ." Ramona paused, fighting back the urge to let loose the lump lodged in her throat. Had her frustration brought her to the point of tears in front of a complete stranger? "I know we don't know each other very well, but didn't you ever feel trapped in your marriage? Or like you should have remained single or childless at times?"

"Hell yes," Dolly smirked. "From the day I walked down the aisle and the day I entered the delivery room." She laughed some more. "Seriously, if I had to do it all over again, I would. But since there's no rush, and I've been down that path before, I may not remarry. And I definitely won't be having any more children. Beside all that, I don't believe there's a man out there that could replace my Norman. He was truly God's gift to me."

Ramona supposed that Dolly had slipped off into reminiscing about her late husband. This time she didn't try to rescue her. Ramona sat silently chewing on the remainder of her turkey sandwich while trying to think of another subject to discuss. Funny the way things worked out in life. She never would have imagined sitting in a rest area sharing her feelings about motherhood and marriage with a complete stranger. *Boy, I must really be drained.*

Ramona had been gnawing away at her meal in such concentration that she hadn't heard Dolly's question.

"Do you love your husband?" Dolly asked a second time.

"Yes. Very much," Ramona answered, surprising herself.

"Then work it out, Ramona. Love that weathers many storms is worth keeping. He'll come around," Dolly said, pushing her chair back and away from the table. "Especially after you return. They always do. At least for a while." Little streams of tears rolled down Dolly's cheeks as she stood up and gave Ramona a level gaze. "Just give them all the love and support you can, Ramona. They'll appreciate it one day, whether you ever know it or not. Believe me, when you lose someone unexpectedly, you hold onto every little thing you can remember. Enjoy your husband and your children while you have them. If things get a little tough, take a mini-vacation. If things get really difficult, take your concerns to God, then drag your family to church."

Dolly extended her hand once again, smiled broadly and said, "It was nice meeting you, Ramona. Have a safe and fulfilling journey."

Ramona watched Dolly walk down the aisle then out the door. Her words of wisdom left Ramona feeling like she and Meka should head back home. Ramona sat at the table slinging back the last of her Pepsi and considering Dolly's advice. She knew Dolly was right about one thing. Casting one's burdens on God and praying was another solution she hadn't thoroughly examined.

Standing, Ramona shook the crumbs from her sandwich off her lap. She gathered her trash and emptied it into the garbage can before leaving. Maybe that's what she and Madrid needed, she determined silently while walking toward her car. It had been many a Sunday since she, Madrid and the children had attended church.

They used to go to a service every Sunday in the beginning of their marriage. Initially, they both were adamant about giving the Lord glory and praise for blessing them with each other and their careers. But once the children came along, and their house and their busy schedules evolved, they lost touch with not only themselves but with God.

Ramona sat in the car gazing out the window. She noticed the line for gas had extended to the end of the exit ramp. Deciding not to chance that the line would get any longer, Ramona drove to the back of the line. Helen Baylor's "Live Testimony" serenaded Ramona while she waited for her turn to fill Meka's tank.

A few times she thought about turning around and going home. But Madrid's strident voice and threatening comments kept creeping into her mind. The line had moved less than two feet before Ramona had to stop again. This time she laid her head back against the headrest and closed her eyes. *I'm a good woman, a dedicated mother and a damn faithful wife who loves her husband. Any blind man could see that, and Madrid needs to realize that. All I want is for him to give me a little recognition, a few more compliments, and a little respect and acknowledgment for my household contributions like he used to before I stopped working. That's all.*

Ramona opened her eyes in time to see the car in front of her had moved to the furthest tank. Slowly, she inched Meka up behind the midnight blue Intrepid. *Must be a sales rep,* Ramona smiled. She remembered the Caribbean green Ford Taurus company car she'd had before giving up her career and identity to become an often overwhelmed domestic engineer-slash-sex goddess. God, how she often wished that she could trade in a few days of "Mommy, honey, please" for a few days of professionalism.

Looking around the gas station, Ramona wondered how many other women were experiencing the same thing. She knew she wasn't the only housewife in the world who felt like her self-esteem had crashed and burned, although she felt like it sometimes. *Yeah, well I'm not going to think about any of that stuff this trip. I'm going to have a good time and let my hair down. Nobody is going to crucify me for taking some time off the job. Hell, everybody else gets to have a vacation from work. Why can't I?*

Four

Ramona coasted into the city with Aretha Franklin's remake of Curtis Mayfield's "The Makings Of You," tingling through the speakers. She smiled faintly, absorbing the lyrics of the nostalgic '70s song along with the view of the five tall smoked-glass buildings facing her as she drove down Jefferson Street. The Renaissance Center was the highlight of Detroit's downtown area and often served as host to many conventions.

She held the remote button for a few seconds, rolling her window down part way. The brisk night air jostled the strands of hair hanging against her left cheek. Ramona welcomed the burst of freshness by taking a deep breath and inhaling the cool Detroit River air. Driving through Greek Town, she felt a sudden surge of excitement kick in as it hit her that she was home. "All Night Long" by the Mary Jane Girls suited her listening pleasure for the rest of the short ride to Indian Village, where Lalah lived.

This short trip will do me some good. It just has to. I need to be happy again, like I was not so long ago.

I want some of the burdens to be lifted. Everything seems like such a major chore lately. As unfortunate as it seems, even Madrid is becoming a chore.

Ramona flicked the headlights off as she pulled into the circular cobblestone driveway. The front of the old saffron brick home was concealed by a cluster of mature oak trees. A string of motion-sensitive lights lined the side of the driveway closest to the front of the house. She shut off the engine then glanced over toward the stairs leading up to the front door.

"Thank God they got rid of those hideous looking gargoyles," Ramona muttered under her breath before stepping out of the car. Standing on her tiptoes she rolled her shoulders forward then arched her back. Shaking her legs one at a time, she thought that the ten-and-a-half hour drive had not been as grueling as she'd anticipated.

She noticed the dim glimmer of light through the chiffon curtains in the living room window. *Good,* she thought, tossing her overnight bag and pocketbook onto her right shoulder. *Lalah's still up.* By the time Ramona reached the second set of stairs, Lalah had flung the front door wide open. There, at the top of the landing, Lalah stood looking richer than ever in a long, black silk nightgown, matching robe and black slippers.

"Hey now!" Lalah shrieked with excitement. "Good Lord! How long you plan on staying?" she joked, stepping down the stairs to greet Ramona with a hug before grabbing the bags off her sister's arm.

"I made it," Ramona said breathlessly, following Lalah up the rest of the cement stairs. "I see you finally got rid of those repulsive statues. Now, all we need to do is figure out what you're going to do about all these steps."

"I tell you what we're going to do," Lalah said, locking the door behind them once Ramona entered the foyer. "We can start by getting your breathless self in shape." She grinned perversely.

Ramona joined in the laughter, letting her bags drop to the salmon-colored granite floor.

"Lalah, you look good!" Ramona said, scanning her sister's lean, five-nine profile. "Your haircut is supreme! Who cut it, Jonathan?"

"Of course," Lalah replied, placing a slender cigarette in the corner of her mouth and lighting it. "You know, he's the only one I let put scissors to my hair. Yeah, and I scheduled you an appointment for Friday."

"Good. I'm sick of my hair. I can't do anything with it lately."

"Don't worry, 'lil sis. You're home now. We'll get you set straight before you leave," Lalah said confidently, turning away from Ramona to exhale the cigarette smoke.

"Still got that nasty habit, I see," Ramona said, waving her hands in an attempt to clear the smoke that was beginning to fill the foyer. "Did I ever tell you about the time when I was working for Pont Pharmaceuticals that I had the chance to witness a live open-heart surgery? The surgeon took special pains to point out the patient's blackened lungs. Need I say more?"

"Yeah, you've told me that story before. Some things never change." Lalah winked. "Now, what's all this talk about you being chunky?" She rubbed Ramona's shoulder, looking her up and down. "I don't see what you're fussing about. You may have picked up a few pounds, but you look beautiful as ever to me."

Ramona found herself blushing at her sister's unexpected compliment. She supposed it had a lot to do with the fact that she hadn't received one in so long that she wasn't sure how to take it. Maybe Lalah was being kind, considering that she knew how sensitive she was about her weight.

"Don't be fooled by the baggy clothes, Lalah. If I whipped off this whale of a sweatshirt and snatched off these not-intended-to-be stretch pants, you'd be singing a different tune. Trust me."

"Ramona." Lalah walked ahead of her toward the kitchen, her slipper heels clinking against the marble floor. "I just don't see what you're moaning about. The way you were complaining, I was expecting I wouldn't recognize you. If you gained twenty pounds, it's not that obvious. But what you need to do is lose those darn baggy clothes. It does nothing for you, Mona. I keep telling you that, girl," Lalah said, turning on the kettle. "You want some tea?"

"That sounds good." Ramona took a seat at the kitchen counter. "But regardless of the over-sized clothing, I still feel chunky and sluggish."

"I've got a bunch of teas to choose from," Lalah said, placing her cigarette in the ashtray and reaching up into the rose-colored oak cabinet. "Let's see, I've got Lemon Zinger, Earl Grey, peppermint, cranberry, Orange Spice, and raspberry. What kind do you want?"

"I don't care. You choose." Ramona looked around the enormous kitchen before resting her eyes on the glass room that had once been the breakfast nook but was now full of hanging, sprouting, wandering green plants. "Is this new?"

"What?" Lalah turned around to see what Ramona was talking about. "Oh, the green room? I added that on a few months ago. You like it?"

"I love it," Ramona said, awestruck.

"Wait until morning. It's so peaceful to sit and eat breakfast out there. You'll see. Anyway, about all this weight stuff. Honestly Mona, I truly don't see it. But if you keep wearing large clothes, you're bound to fill them out one day. Just be careful not to let that happen. You *do* look tired. You've got them dark circles under your eyes like mom." Lalah dropped the tea bags into the over-sized mugs then picked up her cigarette again. She took a few drags before asking, "Sugar?"

"Please," Ramona yawned. "I just need some undisturbed rest for a few days so I can soul-search. That's all. I can't remember the last time I took a vacation by myself. Come to think of it," Ramona paused, trying to recall her last solo vacation, "since I've been married, I've never taken time for myself. Imagine that," she grumbled, taking the mug from Lalah's hand.

"Thank you. What kind is it?" Ramona sniffed the hot steam rising from the rainbow-colored cup.

"Orange Spice." Lalah sat down next to Ramona and studied her sister's full face for a few seconds before carefully taking a sip from her own cup. "Are you happy, Mona?"

Ramona didn't answer immediately. Instead, she averted her gaze from her sister and looked around the spacious kitchen. Her eyes consumed the massive room, snapping mental pictures of the black-speckled granite floors and counters, the rose-colored cabinets accentuating the smokey-gray dishwasher, trash compactor, microwave, stove, double oven and refrigerator. Lalah had sure done a spectacular job remodeling the one hundred and forty-year-old Victorian, Ramona thought.

When Lalah purposely slurped the tea from her cup, Ramona's eyes returned to the counter where she and Lalah sat. She took a few more seconds and another deep breath, trying to formulate an answer to Lalah's question.

"Well?" Lalah queried impatiently. "Are you happy?"

"Not particularly," Ramona shrugged. There was another long pause before she continued. "I mean, it depends. Some days I feel like I'm flowing with energy and buzzing with happiness, but most days recently I feel completely drained, unattractive and lonely."

"Lonely? How in the world can you feel lonely with the children and Madrid in the house?" Lalah frowned.

"Because sometimes there's no one for me to talk to or lean on. Everyone comes to me with their concerns, questions, problems, worries, illnesses, and on and on. I have to be so strong for everyone else. That's what they expect of me, and that's usually what they get. But when it's time for me to shut down or chew on someone's ear, no one seems to be there. The kids are too young to understand, and Madrid is too wrapped up with his career and trying to be a popular dad to accommodate my needs lately."

"Does he *know* what your needs are? I mean, have you told him recently?"

"I'm sure I have in more ways than one. Either

I'm not doing an effective job communicating my feelings, or he's doing a grand slam job of minimizing them. He doesn't even compliment me anymore. Nor make love to me like we used to. Got to wait till three o'clock in the morning," Ramona mumbled under her breath. "Ridiculous."

Lalah didn't respond. She thought it best not to express her feelings yet. But oh, how tempted she was to tell her little sister a thing or two about men. The way she read it, Madrid was engrossed with himself and definitely ignoring her sister's cry for help, some attention, an occasional compliment and a reasonable love-making hour.

"What do you think it is, Lalah? It's like he's a different person than the man I married six years ago."

"Well," Lalah began hesitantly. "It's hard to say." She knew she had to tread lightly. "Six years is a lot of time, and all of us should be growing during such a stretch. What you have to ask yourself is, what makes you feel like he's changed so much, and whether or not you've changed, too?"

Ramona let out a lengthy yawn. Her eyes and her mind were wearied from the drive, so much so that all she could think about was getting some sleep. She was too exhausted to think—or feel—anything. Taking a few more sips of tea, she pushed away from the counter and stood up. "Where's your phone?"

"It's over there next to the cappuccino machine," Lalah said, pointing to the far end of the kitchen. "Calling home?"

"Yeah. I probably should at least let Madrid know I made it here safely. Although he may not want to talk to me considering how I left," Ramona said, picking up the telephone and punching in the eleven digits.

Lalah continued sipping her tea while eyeing her sister from behind. *No doubt Ramona's lost some of her zeal,* she acknowledged quietly. *She seems too damn complacent, less fiery. So uncharacteristic of Mona. Them kids—and Madrid. I tried to tell her, tried to warn her. Sorry-behind men.*

Lalah halted her self-talk when Ramona hung up the phone. "What did he say?"

"Nothing," Ramona replied with concern. "No one answered the phone and the answering machine didn't pick up either."

A streak of panic whisked through her. Where could Madrid be at 2:10 A.M.? The children should be asleep, and so should he, for that matter. She let out a deep breath then took her seat next to Lalah. Her mind went fishing for some explanation why Madrid had not picked up the phone and why the machine had been turned off. How was she to let him know she had arrived in Detroit safely? Wouldn't he worry about her? The warm touch of Lalah's hand atop hers made her jump slightly.

"Mona, he probably unplugged the phone and the answering machine knowing that you would react this way. Think about it. It's the wee hours of the morning. Honestly, where in the world do you think he and the children could be at this godforsaken time of the morning? He's gaming, child. Madrid is banking on the fact that you would call home when you got here. He was hoping by not answering the phone or letting the machine pick up, you would be sitting here questioning your decision about coming. Look at you." Lalah chuckled. "It's working, too. Damn, that boy knows you better than you do. Relax.

He's pouting now, thinking that he's doing something. But when he wakes up in a few hours realizing that he doesn't know if you made it here or not, his tune will change. He'll be forced to call you to find out if you're in Detroit or not."

"I'm sure you're right, Lalah." Ramona smiled faintly. "Knowing Madrid, he's trying to make a point. More than likely, he'll call and leave a message for me to call him. Then again, he was so adamant about me not going that he might not care if I made it or not. Lalah," she said, her face turning somber. "He also told me there would be no 'Honey, I'm home' crap if I left. He said I could stay gone forever."

"Child, please! He was just trying to scare you into staying. You did what you needed to do. Surely when things calm down, he'll get over it. And to hell with him if he doesn't."

Ramona yawned again. "Maybe." She still couldn't help feeling a little guilty about the way things happened. It also didn't help wondering if her decision to get away for some peace of mind had cost her her marriage. It was ludicrous, she resolved silently, shaking her head. There's no way this little excursion to her hometown could cost her everything with her husband. *Could it?*

"I'm telling you, Mona, if I had to do it all over again, I would never get married. I don't care what all these self-appointed, psycho-retarded therapists say about women wanting to be married. I'm going to tell you the God's honest truth. I wouldn't touch matrimony with a ten-foot pole."

"Lalah, please," Ramona said, rolling her eyes. "Sure, it's easy for you to say all that now, considering you and Gordon have been together forever and have everything you want. Why are you so down on marriage all of a sudden? You might feel a little different if you were one of the many single sisters out there in search of a *good* man and a compatible soulmate."

"I could care less, Mona. Besides, I don't need no damn soulmate. I need a playmate, a chess-mate, or a money-mate perhaps. But I don't need anybody cluttering up my soul," Lalah crassly replied.

Ramona studied Lalah's face for a few minutes. She never remembered Lalah being so cold, so cynical, about men or marriage. Apparently something other than time had polluted her conviction. But what? Who? Lalah appeared bitter and hardened. Perhaps she would share her feelings with her while she was home. Maybe, for a change, Ramona would be able to help her sister out, give her some advice or some words of wisdom. But right now all she wanted to do was drench her body with some sleep.

"I can barely keep my head from flopping all over the place. I'm going up to bed now. Don't wake me too early. I'd like to get more than four hours of sleep if I can," Ramona said, standing and giving Lalah a level gaze.

"Don't look at me like that. I haven't been the one responsible for keeping your behind up to the early break of dawn. You need to take that up with Madrid," Lalah grinned. She looked over toward the kitchen door. "Gordon's home."

"He is? How can you tell?"

"I hear the garage door lifting."

Just as Lalah stood up to follow Ramona into the foyer, Gordon walked through the kitchen door attached to the garage. His muscular five-eleven frame was draped with a well-tailored pair of dress pants and a heavily starched white shirt which accentuated his deep, date-colored complexion. The earth-toned silk tie was still knotted firmly around his neck. Dropping the worn, tan leather briefcase onto the floor, Gordon released his contagious smile.

"Ramona, how are you?" Gordon grinned, walking over to give her a brotherly hug. He swayed—his balance not as steady as he would have liked before his sister-in-law. "What brings you to town?"

"Oh, I suppose I needed a getaway," Ramona said, inhaling the aroma of gin that wafted through the space between them. She was first to break free from the embrace.

"Hey babe," Gordon said, attempting to kiss Lalah on the lips. When she turned and gave him her cheek instead, he reached over and tousled her hair.

"Stop it, Gordon," Lalah frowned, pushing his hand away. She eyed her husband suspiciously. A sour stench mixed with a sweet aroma reeked through his pores. "Are you drunk?"

"I don't remember," Gordon lazily chuckled. "I don't think so." He leaned forward like a drunkard.

Lalah sucked her teeth with disgust and walked away from him. She rinsed the mugs with warm water before loading them into the dishwasher. *Coming home smelling like whiskey and cheap perfume. Damn it, Gordon,* she hissed inwardly.

"Everything okay with you and the family, Ramona?" Gordon slurred. He took a minute to compose his stature, then continued, "You're looking awfully pretty. Madrid must be doing something right."

"Yeah, getting on her nerves like men normally do," Lalah commented.

"Now, honey, don't go tainting your sister's mind. I'm sure she realizes that women cannot live on careers alone. Huh, Ramona?" Gordon laughed wickedly.

"Sometimes I wonder, Gordon," Ramona teased with a slanted smile. She never remembered seeing Gordon so high before.

"Oh Lord, you and Lalah must have been having one of them 'why do women need men' talks. In that case, I can't say anything to help out my fellow brother." Gordon loosened his tie then pulled it to one side until it slid off.

"We weren't bashing you guys too bad," Ramona assured him.

"That's right, honey," Lalah said, winking at Ramona. "All I told her was that a man can be an ass sometimes."

Lalah and Ramona busted up with laughter for a few seconds as Gordon looked on, shaking his head. There was no way he was going to get into any kind of female-male relationship conversation with these two. Besides, he was too tired and tipsy to even care what the real reason was for Ramona's visit. The way he saw it, whatever the problem might be, he was certain that his wife wouldn't make matters any better. No, not with the way she bad-mouthed men. Gordon collected his things and weaved toward the stairs.

"Are these your bags, Mona?"

"They sure are," Ramona replied.

"I'll take them up for you," Gordon said grabbing the bags, struggling momentarily to catch his balance. "Good night, ladies. See you tomorrow."

"I'll be up in a minute, honey dearest," Lalah promised.

"I bet you will," Gordon snapped under his breath as he strolled up the spiral staircase.

"I guess we should go on up, too," Lalah said, threading her arm through her sister's before leading her up the steps. "I've redecorated the two guest bedrooms since you were last here. You can either sleep in the pink room or the black and white room. Which one would you prefer?"

"Hmm." Ramona paused purposely. "I think I'll feel like a little color when I wake up in a few hours. The pink room will do. That's if you don't have all that AKA pink and green junk hanging around."

"AKA junk? I beg your pardon. It's not like you didn't have the opportunity to make the right choice. Don't be angry because you chose to go astray and pledge that other sorority. Just remember, red and white equals pink in case you hadn't noticed," Lalah grinned. "Don't know why you didn't follow my footsteps anyway."

Because I wanted to be my own person for a change, instead of constantly being overshadowed by your striking beauty and popularity, Ramona answered silently. *I'm tired of always being referred to as Lalah's baby sister.*

The wide steps were covered in a plush, off-white carpet. Once they reached the top of the landing, Ramona peered back down over the wooden banister, which was open to the foyer and living room below.

Ramona found herself gasping for air when she reached her room, which was on the far right side of the huge house. *I need to get my tail in shape,* she determined silently, pressing her hand across her heart.

"Here you go," Lalah said, swinging open the French doors. "Are you okay?"

"I'm fine," Ramona responded weakly. "Really."

"Are you sure? 'Cause I can put on some clothes, comb my hair, put on my face, start up the Benz, drive *way* across town, park in the far corner of the parking lot, and carry you to the hospital if I must," Lalah said sarcastically.

"Funny," Ramona snickered. "I'll be okay. I wouldn't want you to have to go through all the trouble."

Ramona stepped into the guest bedroom behind Lalah. The room was incredibly beautiful—done in dainty shades of mauve and pink with thin stripes of green running down the wallpaper. The canopy bed was made of dark oak and sat about two feet from the floor. Several pillows in all shapes and sizes were scattered across the green, pink and silver multi-printed comforter. The highboy matched the queen-sized bed. Across the room, facing the large bay window, was a forest green chaise lounge with a pink shawl draped across it.

"This is beautiful, Lalah," Ramona gasped, struck with amazement as her eyes perused the room. "It reeks of tranquillity and calmness. I love it. Shucks, you might not be able to get rid of me."

"Glad you like it. This was my project a few months ago when I got bored with the other color scheme and furniture. So, I decided to give the room a face-lift. I knew you'd like it. This is probably my favorite room in the entire house outside of the master bedroom and the kitchen."

"I can see why," Ramona said, climbing onto the step stool then plopping down on the bed. "Nice and comfortable, too," she said bouncing up and down on the bed lightly. "This will work."

"All right then. You're all set. Don't forget the

bathroom is right over there," Lalah said, pointing to the door on the far right wall. "There are fresh towels in the cabinet under the sink and toothpaste in the medicine cabinet. I'll see you in the morning." Lalah turned to exit the room. "Right now, I need to go cuss my husband out."

Ramona was confused. "Cuss Gordon out? For what?"

"For strolling in here drunk as a skunk this time of the damn morning. That's for what."

"How come you didn't say anything when he first came home? Everything seemed okay between you two."

"Really? Well, I guess you would say that because you didn't notice that lipstick stain on the left side of his collar. Coming in here drunk and reeking of Paloma Picasso. Please, Mona. It was all an act on your behalf. He knew I wouldn't go berserk on him with you standing right there. He also knows stepping in this house after midnight, without as much as calling with some kind of lame excuse, doesn't cut it with me, either. But that's okay. I'm going to get his Cheshire-cat, grinning butt straight. If he's going to be out screwing around, the least he can do is pretend like he has some respect for me." Lalah scowled.

Ramona inhaled suddenly, gasping for air that had been snatched away momentarily. "Screwing around?" she asked in a shocked tone. "He's seeing someone else? No way!"

"Way," Lalah huffed. "But that's fine because I just met me a little tender myself." She grinned sheepishly.

"What?" Ramona shrieked, sliding off the bed. "You're cheating on Gordon?" She whispered, as if Gordon was standing outside the door. "I can't believe this, Lalah."

"Relax. Nothing has happened yet. But I'm sure, given a little more time, Drew and I could be having a little secret rendezvous of our own."

"Who the heck is Drew? Wait a minute, Lalah. Sit down." Ramona patted the bed. "We need to talk. What the devil is going on around here? I thought you and Gordon were the happiest, most stable, loyal couple on this earth besides Mom and Dad and me and Madrid." Ramona put her hands on her hips and glanced up at the ceiling before letting out a deep breath. "This is crazy. I come home to sort out my feelings about my marriage and I hear that my sister and her husband have redefined the vows. Ain't this something."

"Calm down, Mona. This has been going on for years. It's just that lately he's been less careful about hiding his actions."

She had to be kidding, Ramona thought. She stared at Lalah long and hard. Gordon had been having affairs for years? How come nobody had told her about it? How come Lalah was still married to him if that was the case?

Lalah could tell by Ramona's expression that she was having a difficult time processing the unsettling news. She let a few more minutes elapse before saying, "Mona, the world is not coming to an end. It's just moving a little ahead of you, that's all. Listen, we'll talk later this morning, once you've had some sleep. Okay? It's nothing to worry about. What's good for the goose is good for the gander. Remember that. Sleep well, sis." Lalah smiled, shutting the door behind her.

Sleep well? What kind of sign-off was that? Ramona frowned. How in God's good name could she sleep *period* with everything happening? She would never have envisioned her own sister trapped in an unfaithful marriage, let alone a disloyal accomplice.

This was not the kind of welcome-home embrace she wanted to deal with. Gordon messing around on Lalah? Lalah messing around on Gordon? Seventeen years of marriage down the tubes? Good thing they didn't have any children. How long had Mr. and Mrs. Trevell's charade been going on? And to think, they played it off so well in front of her. How many other times had they kept the mask up?

Lord have mercy, never in a billion years would Ramona have thought it would happen to her sister, the girl who had been adorned with such impressive titles as Ms. Popularity, Ms. Homecoming Queen and Ms. Detroit. Lalah always swore that if she ever caught Gordon cheating, she would divorce him immediately and milk him dry. So why was she settling for a dysfunctional marriage? Better yet, how could she compromise her values just to even out the playing field? *Good for the gander?* "Please," Ramona huffed under her breath.

Ramona kicked off her shoes, climbed back onto the bed, tossed a few of the many pillows onto the floor, then laid her head down. Maybe there was a reasonable explanation for all the madness. Perhaps it wasn't as bad or involved as it sounded. *Though Lalah is my sister and I love her dearly, Gordon is also a part of the family. Not to have him around anymore would be just as devastating.*

As long as Ramona could remember, Gordon Trevell had been a member of their family. Lalah began dating Gordon during her junior year in high school. Ramona would never forget the big deal in their household because Lalah was attending the prom with Gordon, who was then a senior. When he left to attend college at Central State University in Xenia, Ohio, Lalah immediately began making plans to attend Wilberforce University, which was located across the yard from Central State.

Three years after Lalah went off to school, she and Gordon were engaged to be married. Gordon graduated from Central State and returned home to attend Wayne State Law School. Lalah followed him home and got a job with an interior design company, finishing her last year of college at Wayne State before she and Gordon tied the knot. From the start of their relationship, Gordon expressed no interest in having children, which was fine with Lalah.

For years to follow, Gordon and Lalah were known around Detroit as Mr. and Mrs. Society. They always took elaborate vacations, hosted popular parties, purchased the best cars, clothes and other material pleasures. Not having children was the best decision they could have made, Lalah always said to Ramona. Lalah felt that children stifled a couple's growth in a relationship. From what everyone could see, Lalah and Gordon Trevell had the perfect marriage, one many people envied. Now, to hear that they both were going astray was not only shocking but unbelievable.

Ramona let out another yawn. Glancing at the clock, she noticed it was 3:22 A.M. *I should wash my face—take a shower. My body is so tired.* Ramona blinked her eyes a few times before her body began slipping off into a doze. Sleep had won her over for a change. She just hoped that sleep was the only thing that would win her over.

Five

The pleasant chirping of tiny birds perched on the window ledge, with the sun beaming through the blinds made for a beautiful morning. James Brown's "It's A Man's World" crooned through the clock radio speakers. Madrid wasn't sure he had read the time correctly. He blinked his eyes a few times then refocused on the electric blue numbers—6:18 A.M.

Quickly he glimpsed over to his wife's side of the bed. Empty. Madrid lay in bed, eyes fixed on the ceiling fan until James' voice trailed off. Then he threw back the covers and sprang up. Sitting on the side of the bed, he wondered how he was going to get through the day on just three-and-a-half hours of sleep. Mentally he began listing the day's activities, trying to prioritize as best he could. First things first. He would have to prepare the children for school, then call his office and reschedule the morning's interviews for later this afternoon.

Glancing at the nightstand where the unattached cords from the phone and answering machine dangled, he wondered if Ramona had tried to call him last night. He thought about plugging in the answering machine, but chose to reconnect the phone only. *That'll show her,* he thought. If she wanted to suddenly leave her family, there was no need for her to be concerned with the household's going-ons anymore.

Madrid stood up and slowly and made his way toward the bathroom. Before he reached the partially closed door, Nathan stumbled into the room. He had been sleep-walking again, Madrid assessed, picking his son up and laying him down on his bed.

"Little man, we're going to have to do something about your sleepwalking."

Nathan grumbled lightly but never opened his eyes. Madrid peered at him, smiling faintly. This sleepwalking thing was something he had been doing for the past few months. A few nights a week, Nathan would wake up and roam the hallway until he reached his parents' room. Ramona swore that he'd grow out of it. Madrid only hoped that it would be soon, because Nathan's wandering could develop into a dangerous situation. It was a good thing Ramona had stayed after him to put the gate across the stairs during the night.

Madrid rolled his neck around his shoulders under a hot, steaming shower. This morning, he didn't have the luxury of lingering under the gush of hot water like mornings past. Today, time was of the essence. He dried off halfway, tossed some lotion on his skin, rolled some deodorant under his arms, splashed on some cologne, then wrapped the damp towel around his waist. Scanning his closet for a few moments, he selected the olive green Armani suit, a starched white shirt and an earth-colored, floral silk tie.

Madrid slipped into his underwear before putting on his slacks and shirt. Now all he had to do was get Leslie and Nathan up and find a pair of black socks. Searching his top drawer for a pair of matching socks, he let out a frustrated breath. Figured. He couldn't find a matching pair of socks anywhere in his drawer.

Barefoot, he made his way downstairs and opened the vertical blinds to the family room before rummaging through the clothes basket, which had been sitting in the same place for the past two days. After a few seconds of digging, he found a matching pair of black socks. *Leslie is going to put these darn clothes away today,* he vowed, slipping his feet into the socks.

Madrid decided to let the kids sleep another ten minutes before waking them. He puttered around the kitchen making coffee, looking through the cabinets and through the refrigerator. *There's nothing in here already prepared,* he thought as he shoved containers from side to side, looking for God only knew what. The kids would have to eat something this morning, but what? Finally, he decided on oatmeal and toast. *This will have to do for now. I can always give Leslie some money for lunch,* he determined as he filled a large pot with warm water and placed it on the stove before heading back upstairs.

"Leslie, time to wake up," Madrid beckoned in his sweetest voice, standing in the doorway of her room. "Come on, baby girl. I know your bed is feeling real comfortable right now, but you've got to get ready for school."

Leslie stirred under the covers briefly before whining, "I don't want to go to school today. I don't feel good, Daddy."

"You don't? What's wrong, Leslie?" Madrid asked, concerned. He hoped that it wouldn't be something serious.

"I'm tired," she groveled some more.

"Tired?" Madrid nearly yelled, partly from relief and partly from annoyance. "Girl, you better get some energy and get out of bed. Come on, Leslie. We don't have all day." He stood watching her for a few seconds longer until she fumbled out of bed. Good Lord, he panicked, looking at his daughter and her hair, which was scattered all over her head. What the heck was he going to do about that head of hers? Once Leslie entered the bathroom, he went down the hallway to wake Nathan.

Madrid rocked Nathan softly. "Come on, chief. It's time to wake up." It was a lot easier for Madrid to convince Nathan to get out of bed than Leslie, probably because he was still young enough to be excited about starting his day.

At 7:23 A.M. Madrid and Nathan were downstairs waiting on Leslie. He had bathed Nathan and dressed him in a pair of jeans, high tops and a Cleveland Cavalier's sweatshirt. He would try his best to brush Nathan's hair and tame his large curls before they left for daycare. Deciding not to let the oatmeal get any colder, Madrid handed Nathan his bowl and then called for Leslie once more.

"Leslie! Come on down here and get your breakfast before it turns cold."

A few moments later, Leslie came bouncing down the stairs, hair looking wilder than before. "Sorry, Daddy. I couldn't find my other shoe," she said, sitting down at the table.

Madrid's attention was diverted by his daughter's wild hair. "What are you going to do about your hair, Leslie?"

"I don't know," she shrugged. "Mona always combs it for me."

"Jeez," he mumbled under his breath, careful not to let the kids hear him. Just what was he supposed to do now? Madrid could feel the anger stirring up again. "Well, eat your food, then we'll try to do something with your hair okay?"

The kids ate in silence while Madrid called his office. He checked his voice mail before leaving a message for his assistant, Bridget, telling her he was running a little late. Resetting the phone, he then placed a call to DeMar.

"DeMar," Madrid said, "Give me a call later at the office. I may need you to do me a favor. Buzz me." He wanted to know if DeMar could drop the kids off at school the next morning. He had an early meeting with a large chemical company that was considering using his firm exclusively for their telecommunication needs.

It was the biggest deal yet for his career and his corporation, CTT. If he was able to secure the contract, another huge promotion would definitely follow, monetarily speaking. The thought of adding a few additional thousands to his income would certainly be welcome. Especially if he and Ramona got a divorce.

The notion of a divorce sent a chill through his body. Where had that thought come from? Never before had the idea of divorce crossed his mind, not even during their past disagreements. But this time it felt different. This time she was challenging his manhood.

Madrid glimpsed at the microwave clock—7:38 A.M. "Leslie, are you done?"

Hesitantly, she replied, "Yes."

"Let's try to do something with your hair, all right?" Madrid said, picking up Nathan's brush and walking toward the table where Leslie sat with a long face, tears welling up in her eyes.

Madrid stared at his little girl's hair, trying to determine the best way to handle things. "A ponytail!" he sang gleefully, as if he had just invented a new style. "That's what we'll give you. Do you have a rubber band or one of those ball things you wrap around your hair?"

"There's some in the drawer," she said somberly, pointing to the drawer in the kitchen corner.

"Nathan, do me a favor and go get one of Leslie's hair wrappers for me."

Nathan slid down from his chair, darted into the kitchen, and found one of the hair bands with two blue balls attached to it. Running back to the dining area, he handed it to his father.

"Thank you, son," Madrid said. Taking a deep breath, he softly laid the brush on the crown of Leslie's head and began brushing her hair. After two strokes, Leslie screamed for mercy.

Immediately, Madrid snatched his hand away from her head. Bewildered, he asked, "What's wrong? What's the matter, Leslie?"

Tears were falling. "It hurts. My head hurts."

"But I haven't even begun to brush it thoroughly yet," Madrid said defensively. He could understand her hollering if he had been using all of his mighty strength to brush her hair, but he hadn't. He had approached Leslie's head like a servant about to place a crown on a queen's head. "For Pete's sake, Leslie, we have to do something with your hair. You can't go to school looking like this. Bear with me a little longer, okay?"

Madrid let a few seconds elapse, then approached her head once more. This time he was able to get in five or six strokes before she let out another yelp. He stopped momentarily to look at his daughter. Turning to face her, he knelt down beside her. "Leslie, Daddy doesn't mean to hurt you, but I have to do this, sweetheart. I'm almost done, all right?"

Leslie nodded in agreement, wiping her eyes. Madrid kissed her forehead. Nathan sat across from Leslie, feeling sorry for his sister.

"Daddy, Mommy says Leslie's tender-headed."

"Really?" Madrid smiled. He was impressed with the way Nathan had structured his sentence. "I'll be careful with your sister. Okay?"

"Be real careful, Daddy 'cause Leslie's crying. 'Kay?"

"Okay, chief," Madrid said, trying to wrap the little hair band around the thick cluster of hair he held in his left hand. He didn't know the first thing about combing Leslie's hair or how to work the darn hair band. Every time he tried to secure it, it popped loose. *Wish you were here to handle this one, Ramona. Mornings were much quieter with you doing Leslie's hair.* Madrid hadn't realized that his frustration was causing him to apply pressure to Leslie's head. Overwhelmed, Leslie snatched her hair free from her father's grasp and jumped up screaming.

"It hurts, it hurts," she cried hysterically.

"Okay, okay," Madrid said, putting his hands up in an I-give-up gesture. "Just wear it down for today. Gosh!" he huffed, walking around the dining table. *Mona, where are you when I need you?*

"Well, how 'bout you, Nathan? Can I brush your hair?"

"Yes," Nathan responded joyously, bouncing up and down in his seat.

Madrid loaded the children into the Jeep and took off toward Leslie's school. The hair ordeal had nearly wiped him out. He glanced at Leslie, whose attention was focused on the bustling streets. She looked like a junior version of Chakka Khan with her thick hair spread all over her face and shoulders.

Shifting the car into park, Madrid stopped in front of Leslie's school. Immediately his attention focused on the tall female figure whose eyes were also fixed on him as she sauntered in front of the Jeep with her purse in one hand and a little girl holding onto the other. Smiling, the woman nodded at Madrid. Madrid responded with the same trite movement. *Absolutely beautiful Nubian sister,* Madrid observed quietly.

Without paying much mind to Leslie, Madrid reached into his wallet and pulled out an Abe Lincoln, his eyes never leaving the woman who had strutted past him. "Here's some money for lunch, Leslie."

Leslie's eyes lit up as she took the five-dollar bill from her father. "Thank you, Daddy," she said, reaching over to place a kiss on his cheek. "Mona only gives me three dollars."

Before Madrid could respond, Leslie was out the door and up the walkway. And it was a good thing, too, because he wasn't sure if his daughter had noticed his reaction to the well-dressed woman. He watched as Leslie entered the building behind the mystery woman. It had been a long while since Madrid had been affected by a woman's presence in that way. Without time to linger outside the school in the hopes that the unknown woman would come back outside, Madrid threw the car into gear and pulled away.

Nathan was frantically pulling Madrid by the hand as he walked up the daycare stairs. "Come on, Daddy," Nathan directed. "Tony's going to get to the chest first if we don't hurry."

Madrid didn't bother to ask Nathan who Tony was. His guess was that he was one of Nathan's classmates who had a knack for arriving early and taking the best toys out of the toy chest. As soon as they walked into the lobby, Nathan took off down the hallway. Mrs. Fryer, an elderly graying woman and the daycare director, caught Nathan halfway down the corridor.

"Hold on, Nathan. Where are you running off to so fast?" she asked, bending down to greet him at eye level.

Nathan replied breathlessly, "To the toy chest, Mrs. Fryer, before Tony gets all the toys."

"Nathan, where's your mommy?" She stood up and took him by the hand back toward the front of the center.

"She's at my Grammy's house in 'troit."

Madrid met her partway down the foyer. "Is everything all right?" he questioned. "I'm Nathan's father, Mr. Shaw," he offered with an extended hand.

"Pleased to meet you, Mr. Shaw," Mrs. Fryer said, clutching his hand firmly. "Everything is fine with Nathan. Actually, he's one of our favorite students." She smiled and looked down at

Nathan. "It's just that today is Thursday and Nathan is not scheduled to be here today."

"Oh," Madrid said, embarrassed. "I didn't realize. My wife had to go out of town suddenly. I guess I got the days mixed up. Is it possible that you could squeeze him in this morning?"

"I'm sorry," Mrs. Fryer said apologetically, shaking her head. "We don't have the room. We have limited slots and so far today, none of the other children have canceled. We would be glad to keep Nathan, but we're at our limit today. I apologize, Mr. Shaw."

Nathan's face drooped with disappointment. Madrid let out a disgusted huff, directed not at Mrs. Fryer but at the situation Ramona had left him in.

"I understand, Mrs. Fryer. Thanks for your time. Come on, Nathan, let's go." Madrid reached out to grab Nathan by the hand. Nathan pouted and unwillingly took his dad's hand.

"We'll see you tomorrow, Nathan," Mrs. Fryer said sweetly. "I'll set aside a special toy for you, okay?"

Nathan nodded, trying desperately to keep up with his father's strides as they walked out of the Wee-Wacs Daycare Center. The brisk morning chill felt more like winter's wrath than spring's arrival. But Madrid needed the coolness of the morning breeze to calm his flustered face. *Now what to do? How am I supposed to hold my interviews this morning? Ramona! I can't believe you did this!*

Madrid buckled Nathan up and got into the Jeep. He sat staring out the windshield for a long while before glancing at the clock—8:50 A.M. There was no way he'd make it to Morristown for his 9:15 appointment. Irritated, he picked up the cellular phone and punched in his office number. Bridget would have to help him reschedule the interviews for Monday morning.

She answered the phone on the third ring. "Mr. Shaw's office."

"Bridget, good morning. This is Madrid. Something unexpected has come up. I need you to contact the three candidates and reschedule their interviews for Monday. Please give them my sincere apologies."

Bridget hesitated before replying, "No problem, Mr. Shaw. I should be able to catch the other two candidates, but your 9:15 appointment was waiting in the lobby at 8:30 this morning."

"You're kidding." Madrid said, eyeing the clock in the Jeep again. *Boy, this is an aggressive individual.* "Who is it?"

"Alyson Rivera."

"Bridget, will you apologize to her and see if she can come in late tomorrow afternoon or Monday morning? Tell her I'm real sorry."

"Sure, Mr. Shaw. Is everything okay?" Bridget asked with sincere concern in her voice. It was unlike Madrid to cancel his appointments on such short notice.

"Yes, everything's fine. It's just that Ramona had to go out of town suddenly and the daycare center can't take Nathan today and I can't find another sitter. And—" Madrid caught himself. He realized that he sounded like Bridget, who had on a few occasions called in sick because her son was ill or because the sitter couldn't watch him. The role reversal made Madrid uncomfortable; it was the first time he could actually relate to a single working woman's occasional dilemma with babysitters.

"Well, I'll pass on your apologies," Bridget responded aloofly. "I hope everything works out. Don't forget you have that big meeting with the chemical company in the morning. You'll be able to attend that, won't you?" she said slowly.

"Of course I'll be there tomorrow, Bridget. Don't worry." Madrid pushed the power button and rested the phone in its cradle. He didn't know if he liked having to explain to Bridget about not having a sitter. Or having to reassure her that he would be in tomorrow for the meeting of the century. It made him feel uncomfortable, like he was being scrutinized unfairly, as if he was lying.

Perhaps it was his previous skepticism when Briget had phoned in a few times with the same excuse that made him feel uneasy. Well, he had assumed she was making an excuse, but now he wasn't so sure. Madrid felt a surge of guilt for having thought those things about his exceptionally brilliant assistant. He would have to do something special for her to make up for it. More than that, he would learn to be more understanding in the future if the issue ever arose again.

He sat motionless for a few more moments, thinking about how to spend the rest of the day with Nathan. He couldn't recall a time when he had had to spend an entire day with his son. Normally, his schedule permitted him to spend a few hours after work a couple of times a week, or a few hours on the weekend. But not once had he ever spent a full day alone with his son, much less a couple of days in a row without Ramona nearby to help out.

"Fire truck, Daddy!" Nathan shouted, eyes wide with awe. "Look, Daddy, see?"

"Yes, I see, Nathan," Madrid replied. Then it

hit him. He would take his son by the firehouse to visit his buddy Saied and show Nathan a fire truck up close and personal. He and Saied had played on the same softball team and had developed a strong friendship over the past four years. Madrid was certain that Saied wouldn't mind if he brought Nathan by the station. In fact, it was Saied who had suggested it to Madrid on several occasions. Madrid looked at Nathan. "Would you like to go see a fire truck?"

"Yeah! Let's go, Daddy. We can catch that one," Nathan said, pointing to the distant fire truck while bouncing in his seat.

Madrid pulled into East Orange Station House Two. He spotted Saied, an average-sized, well-built, light-complected man, soaping down the rims of his black Explorer. Suds were everywhere. Pulling his Jeep alongside Saied, Madrid rolled down the window and said, "Taxpayers' dollars just running down the drain."

Saied lifted his head slowly. He stood erect, letting the excess water drain down his lower arm as he held the sudsy sponge. His uniform, a navy blue shirt with matching trousers, exposed his upper body muscles. A smile swept Saied's face as he walked towards Madrid's Jeep.

"What's up, Drid? How come you're not out there in the corporate world today?"

"Had to take a breather," Madrid replied, giving him the pound-up handshake. "I'm still doing what I can to make my contributions. Thought I'd bring little man by to check out the fire trucks," Madrid said, nodding his head at Nathan. "Is this a good time?"

"We always make time for our young little brothers. Hey, Nathan." Saied smiled. "Come on out so I can show you how the rest of us brothers live."

"Yeah!" Nathan screamed. He tried to jump out of his seat before unbuckling his belt.

Saied helped Nathan out of the car before rinsing the remaining suds off his rims. It was a good time of the day to take Nathan on a quick tour because the captain had made his weekly visit yesterday morning. The little firehouse was quiet and still for the moment. House Two was the busiest house in East Orange and very rarely did the crew have the opportunity to visit with guests. Even during the appointed days for tours, history had it that the station was always summoned to a call.

Before long, Madrid, Nathan and Saied had roamed the entire station, including the sleeping quarters, the make-shift gym which boasted a bench press and several free weights, and the concrete basketball area, where most of the brothers hooped during their free time. Wade, another crew member of the firehouse, had taken Nathan back upstairs to the kitchen while Madrid and Saied took advantage of the moment to indulge in a male rap session.

"This is a rarity for you, Madrid," Saied teased, resting a foot on the bench and leaning his forearm on his knee. His muscles cut through the blues.

"Yeah, I know," Madrid said, eyeing Saied. He had leaned back against his Jeep for support.

"You're taking off work to hang out with junior? What's up?"

Madrid paused for a moment. He never did believe in spilling too much to his buddies, figuring it best to drop as few hints as possible. "Mona and I are going through one of them cycles, I guess. She's in Detroit visiting her sister. Pulled out of here yesterday afternoon suddenly, leaving me with the children." Madrid shrugged. "I don't know about this one, Saied. It was real ugly."

"Sounds like it. Then again, you never can tell. Things always have a way of working themselves out," Saied said pensively.

Madrid reflected back to the tall, well-tailored woman he had seen at Leslie's school. But how could he even be daydreaming about any woman at a time like this? He let out a deep breath and mumbled, "In the midst of all this chaos with me and Mona, and getting the kids ready for school, some fine sister at Leslie's school managed to draw my attention. She looked as if she could use a man friend." Madrid smiled.

Saied looked at his friend long and hard for a few seconds. "Don't go there, man. It's dangerous. Trust me. Have your way with her, but only in your head. Besides, how would you know by looking at her that she could use a man?" Saied laughed.

Madrid knew he was taking a chance sharing his temporary lust with his buddy. Saied was so noble and honorable. Madrid found it hard to imagine Saied thinking about cheating on his woman, much less doing the deed itself. "All I know, Saied, is Mona better wake up and smell the brew, because with the shortage of men being what it is, she would have a hard time if she was out there again."

Saied laughed loudly, causing Madrid to look around to find out what had cracked him up. In a few seconds, Saied slowly returned to a state of normalcy.

"Look, Drid," he continued chuckling. "Don't

go swelling your head up with all these talk shows, lopsided statistics or new contemporary writers who swear it's so damn hard for a woman to find a good man. Hell, it's equally as impossible for a brother to find a good woman once he's ready to settle down. We have to sift through tons of women to find just one good one.

"Let's say we have five woman standing before us right now. Two of the lovely sisters will be qualified as female dogs by virtue of the statistics. One of the beautiful sisters will be filled with so much hurt that she's bitter beyond decent conversation. Another one of the princesses will be so damn desperate and accommodating to have a man, she'll let us get away with all kinds of crap, from supporting us to infidelity to God knows what.

"And the last queen may be the jackpot, barring the possibility that she might be so independent, self-righteous and demanding that she only has room for herself Or she may have been married before, and/or has a child. So where does that leave us? Back at the drawing board. Yeah, there's supposedly five women to every man, but look at the sifting we have to do, too."

Madrid took a minute to ingest Saied's theory. Thinking about DeMar and his often short-lived rollercoaster excursions with married women, committed women, desperate women, stupid women, and opportunists, he had to agree. "I guess you have a point. I never thought of it in that way."

"Well, maybe you should. This way it'll keep your head level and your heart humble. Don't let Mona go, Drid. She's a good sister from the old school. There's a lot of brothers who would gladly

trade places with you. You better store that somewhere in your memory bank."

Madrid buckled Nathan into the Jeep, thanked
Saied and pulled out into the light mid-morning
traffic. His mind was spinning—he needed to get
back into his pattern, his groove. This sudden jolt
in his daily routine had indeed caused him some
unwanted anxieties. But it also had become another test of strength, as well as a growth spurt.
Thinking about the morning's rituals and Saied's
theory, he knew that Saied was right about Mona
being a good woman from the old school.

Despite the current mountain standing before
him and Ramona, Madrid also knew he could
usually count on looking to his left or right and
finding Mona standing right beside him. But this
time she was wrong for the way she had handled
the situation, Madrid swore silently. Pulling onto
Route 280 and thinking about the days that lay
ahead of him, Madrid realized Ramona was right
about one thing. *Leslie does need to have her damn
hair braided.*

Six

"We've got plenty of time, Mona," Lalah squawked, pressing the accelerator down until the black Benz leaped into another gear. The early afternoon traffic was light. Lalah had both windows rolled down mid-way, inviting the mild temperature into the newly upholstered car. "You know Sophia doesn't get home till late in the evenings. And more than likely, Poppy is down at the senior center whipping up on some innocent soul in chess or checkers. We'll get to see them today. I promise."

Lalah put a long brown cigarette into the corner of her mouth before placing the hot cigarette lighter to the tip of it. She took a long drag. "Besides, it's more important that we add some updated pieces to your wardrobe. Or at the very least some new undergarments. It'll be quick, painless and with any luck, fun. First, we'll stop by Vicki's Secret, then race over to BeeBee's. Relax, would you? You never know what the day has in store for you."

"I am relaxed," Ramona said unconvincingly. She swept windblown strands of hair out of her eyes before viciously fanning away the second-hand smoke. It was yet another frustrating hair day for her. She couldn't wait until tomorrow to let Jonathan do something with her hair. And she couldn't wait until tomorrow to be done with Lalah and her maneuvering tactics tonight.

Deep down, Ramona knew she wasn't comfortable about meeting Lalah's potential future adulterer, Drew, for dinner this evening. What would Gordon think if he ever found out? How could Lalah be so carefree about it? Why would she even share this sort of thing with her? She wondered if Sophia knew too? Questions were racing through Ramona's mind at top speed as she revisited her earlier conversation with Lalah about her relationship with Gordon.

All Lalah cared to reveal was that Gordon had been a ladies man from the onset, but that lately he had been allowing his emotions for some twenty-two-year-old college student to overwhelm his good judgment. It was the threat that this mesmerized college student was pregnant with Gordon's child that had unnerved Lalah and caused her, for the first time, to seek comfort in someone else's arms.

Leaving had never been an option, Lalah further stressed. Especially since she had already invested seventeen years into the marriage, let alone, the lifestyle they had established together. Simply said, Lalah would be damned before she rolled over and let some sweet young thing have the entire pie that she and Gordon had sweated long and hard to make. After hearing Lalah's position and feeling the pain and anger she felt, Ramona thought it best to back off for the time being, although, she really wanted to talk some sense into her sister.

Staring at the unknown, unhappy faces walking through the mall parking lot, Ramona let out a discouraged breath. This was not what she'd had in mind when she set out for her peaceful journey. If she'd wanted to spend some time at a mall, she could have done that back in Jersey.

"What's wrong now?" Lalah said, shutting off the engine and hearing Ramona's exasperation.

"Nothing. I just don't see why we have to rush and pack everything in today. I feel like I'm running around with my head cut off. I could have done this at home, Lalah." Ramona stepped out of the car, fixing the ponytail that sat on top of her head.

"Yeah, but you wouldn't have, even if you had the time. I'm telling you, Mona, you're having the life sapped out of you. It's evident by the way you're dressing. And seeing you step out of the bathroom with them big granny bloomers on . . . well, I just can't accept that one." Lalah laughed loudly. "Let's go, woman. It'll be fine. You'll thank me for this later. Trust me."

Trust. That's a funny thing for her to reassure me with, Ramona thought, walking into the mall lobby. Public telephones lined the left side of the lobby. Ramona studied the silver and black phones and for a moment thought about calling Madrid. But Lalah must have felt her vibe, because she swiftly snatched Ramona by the arm and lead her to the east wing of the suburban mall.

"Listen, Ramona," Lalah whispered, still gently clinging to her arm, "if you're going to worry yourself to death about calling that boy, then you might as well head home right now. Remember, you're only here for a minuscule amount of time. All right?"

"Okay," Ramona said slowly, with a half smile.

"I'll relax. I just want to know how the kids are," she said, stepping onto the escalator.

Glancing down at her watch, Lalah replied, "They should be arriving home from school this time of the day. You can call them when you get back to the house. That's if Madrid hasn't phoned you first." Lalah winked as she stepped off the escalator.

The mall was buzzing with people, their voices echoing throughout the corridors. A fragrant mixture of aromas greeted the sisters as they passed the food court.

The popular lingerie shop was adjacent to Pete's Pies & Stuff, an addictive pastry outlet. Cutting across the marble floors, a group of boys, probably too young to be full-fledged adults, were overtly smitten with Ramona and Lalah. They whistled loudly and made some obnoxious cat calls. Lalah responded with a bashful grin, Ramona with a harsh rolling of the eyes.

"See, that's what I'm talking about, Ramona," Lalah said disappointingly, shaking her head. Ramona would have to do something about those passé clothes, Lalah vowed. The paisley-patterned shirt was lifeless, the blues now gray and the gray now white and the oversized jeans did nothing to enhance her sister's figure. Lalah looked Ramona over more intensely. *Pitiful* was the word that popped into her mind. Lalah's mission was simple enough—help her baby sister resurrect her once vibrant identity.

Lalah eyed her sister coolly. "Ramona, those little boys found you attractive, paid you a compliment to the best of their abilities, and all you did was bruise their egos."

"That's too bad, Lalah," Ramona snapped,

brushing past her into the peachy smelling store. Lalah's gibberish was starting to get on her nerves. "Whistling and making obscene comments is offensive and disrespectful. I don't care how unintentional it may seem. These young boys have no home training."

She really didn't care one way or another about some less than full-grown men making comments to her. Actually, the way she was feeling, a grown man couldn't have gotten away with much more. Ramona didn't want to be there anyway. She had come to Detroit to release and relax, not be overwhelmed by Lalah's fashion critique and expertise. There was nothing wrong with the way she dressed, anyhow. Madrid never complained.

She walked past the colorful silk and satin camisoles and teddies, pajamas and gowns, to the back of the store. The selection of bras and panties was almost dizzying. So much to choose from, so many kaleidoscopic patterns and styles. So beautiful and soft, Ramona thought, holding up a purple and red lace bra and panty set.

"That's what I'm talking about, Ramona," Lalah said sneaking up behind her. "You've got to get it together, child. Look at this." Lalah grinned seductively, holding up a black merry widow. "This, my dear sister, will work wonders for you. Might even get you some loving before three o'clock in the morning. Try it on. I'll look for some stockings."

For a while, Ramona just stared at the bodice. She had owned one of these a few years ago, a white one. But that was before the kids. In fact, she wondered where the enticing outfit had disappeared to. Reluctantly, Ramona located a sales representative and asked her to unlock one of the dressing rooms. What in the world was she going to do with this lingerie anyway, she wondered, stripping herself bare before her foe, the larger-than-life, streakless mirror.

She stared into the mirror, trying to find the right adjectives to describe her womanly body. Once considered slightly more voluptuous than a cinnamon stick but less than a candy apple, Ramona exhaled hard. Her breasts no longer peaked at full attention, their perkiness giving way slowly to gravity. The 26-inch waist she used to be so proud of had stretched to 31 inches, at least. A slight winter layer of excess fat rounded off her stomach.

Thank God she had been able to keep it flatter than it should be for a thirty-four-year-old woman who had birthed one child. Probably due to divine intervention, she reasoned. Lord knew sit-ups were never an enjoyable task when she used to work out.

Her thighs were still tight, but her buttocks, as she turned sideways to get a better view, were just starting their descent. Lalah was right. She was way too young to let herself go. Ramona walked closer to the mirror, staring into her smooth, even face. Intently, she glared into her pupils until her eyes dazzled her with their sparkle. *Who am I, really?*

Lalah knocked on the fitting room door just as Ramona finished fastening the last button on her favorite shirt. "I'll be right out," she responded, placing the merry widow on the hanger before opening the door.

"So?" Lalah paused, eagerly waiting for some feedback.

Ramona smiled. "I like it."

"Thank God," Lalah exhaled, handing Ramona a bunch of silk panties, a few camisoles, some satin pajamas and a slinky nightgown. "You're not done yet. Try these things on. I'll come back and check to make sure the sizes are okay." She pushed Ramona back into the dressing room. "Take your time and get a feel for the stuff. There's no rush. Be free."

"Who's gonna pay for all this stuff, Ms. Be Free?" Ramona bantered, sitting down on the satin-covered bench.

"I am, of course," Lalah said, closing the fitting room door halfway. "What are sisters for? And besides, you never know who you might run into."

Poppy John answered the door in a pair of cache pants and a burgundy and black checkered shirt. He stood no more than five feet ten inches tall and weighed no less than 180 pounds. Peering through his part bifocals, John Howard smiled at his youngest granddaughter standing on the other side of the wooden door. The wet Detroit weather had swelled the wood, and Poppy John had to tussle with it until it finally flung open. Chips of faded wood stuck in the doorjamb.

"Mona," Poppy John grinned, exposing his less than perfect teeth. At least they were his; he'd refused to succumb to the dental chair and purchase nightstand teeth, as he referred to dentures. "So good to see you, baby," he said, opening his arms.

"Poppy!" Ramona fell into his embrace. "How are you?" she sang in a jubilant tone.

"Fair to middlin'." He closed the door behind

her, "I suppose for a seventy-eight-year-young man, I'm doing swell. When did ya get here?"

"Late last night." Ramona followed him into the chilly, cigar smoke-ridden living room. Poppy John had taken a seat in his favorite worn blue Lazy Boy, which faced the white-brick fireplace.

Ramona took a moment to survey the simple room. Light blue chiffon drapes covered the two, colossal windows. The sky blue velvet sofa was still protected by the yellowing plastic covering. Nothing had changed in all these years, except the presence of her grandmother. Coral Howard's sudden death had shocked everyone in the family, though they should have suspected a heart attack brewing based on Coral and Poppy's years of unhealthy eating habits. Saturated fats at all hours of the day and night had taken their final toll on Coral three years ago.

"Where's my other wildcat granddaughter?" Poppy John questioned, twirling the cigar in the corner of his mouth.

"She's home fiddling around the house. I couldn't wait any longer to see you." Ramona smiled. He still hadn't lost any more hair on the sides; just the top of his head was bald. His ginger complexion still even, though his once plump face had thinned.

"Um hmm," he replied, studying his granddaughter some more. "How are the children? I thought you would have carried them along with you so I could see them."

"They're fine, Poppy," Ramona replied softly, shuffling her right foot back and forth across the carpet. "I needed a little time to myself. I thought about bringing them, but decided against it."

Poppy John chewed on the ragged end of the

cigar, puffing occasionally. Looking down, he fanned his left hand out and stared over his bifocals at his well-manicured nails. "That's not what Madrid told me," he said, taking a sneaky look at his granddaughter. She had on a black skirt and a white silk blouse with sheer sleeves that buttoned at her cleavage. Obviously Lalah's doing, Poppy determined. He wasn't really sure if he liked seeing his baby granddaughter this way. The hair resting on her shoulders was okay—a little on the wild side. She reminded him of Coral in that way. But the red lipstick was a bit much.

Patiently, he waited for Ramona's response. He was curious to know just what kind of bad habits she had picked up from Lalah in a twenty-four hour period. If she lied, he would know it off the back. He only hoped that she would not resort to such self-serving behavior.

Ramona wedged her hands under her thighs. The house was damp and chilly; she should have brought her jacket inside. "When did you talk to Madrid, Poppy?"

"Not long ago. He phoned over here when he didn't get an answer at Lalah's earlier today. He said he just wanted to know if you made it in safely or not. Apparently he was worried about you, girl. How you going to leave your family and not call them and tell them you made it in safely? That's not like you, Mona," Poppy scolded.

That sneaky . . . How dare he call over here, getting Poppy all worried, knowing that I probably tried to call him last night. But he was so busy playing games that he wouldn't answer the phone or let the machine pick up. He's got some damn nerve! Wait until I speak to him later.

"Poppy, I did call him when I got in. But he

didn't answer the phone." Ramona frowned. "I can't even believe that he thinks I didn't try to call. *He* was the one that forgot to turn on the answering machine and refused to answer my call last night."

"What's this I hear, you just left him and the kids? I asked him point blank if it was because of another woman. He said no. Then I said, well, are you beating on my granddaughter? He said never. So I asked him what good reason would you have to up and leave him like that? He said housework."

"What?" Ramona yelled, unable to mask her irritation. "I don't believe he even had the nerve to say that," she said, rising from the love seat and walking toward the black rotary phone.

"Hold on a minute, Mona," Poppy advised. "Sit down. I didn't mean to get you all worked into a tizzy. I was just concerned, that's all. He made it sound like you all were getting a divorce. And all I could think about was the children." He looked up at Ramona. "Go on baby, have a seat."

Ramona's face had turned fire-red. If she could have slapped Madrid for attempting to use her grandfather to manipulate her, that would have been all the better.

"Poppy," she started, exasperated, but settled down once she sat down on the tattered love seat again. "There's so much more to it. I didn't just leave him, like he's trying to make it sound. I decided to take a four or five-day trip home to Detroit. I can't believe . . ." She paused to shake her head. "That he would even have the *audacity* to make such a preposterous statement to you." She was getting all hot and bothered again.

"I kind of figured there was more to it than what he was telling me. It's really none of my business,"

Poppy quickly added, hands in the air. "The only thing I ever want for you and everyone else in the family is to be happy. Believe me, Mona, I'm not trying to meddle. What goes on with you and that boy is your own beeswax," he chuckled.

Ramona smiled, relieved that her wise, opinionated grandfather had let her off the hook. Deep down she knew he did want to know what was going on—well, so did she. After some laughter and some small talk, Poppy pulled out the old, torn photo albums, a ritual expected by Ramona and the rest of the family whenever they visited the modest brick home on Lynwood. Poppy's only way of holding onto his current life, it seemed, was by recollecting his life of years ago.

The stories kept spilling. New ones and old ones as Poppy slipped into one of his reminiscing trances. Ramona found herself experiencing Germany during World War II all over again, Poppy's first driving experience on his daddy's 100-acre farm, his cotton-picking woes in the heat of a sunny Alabama day, and his first glimpse of his beloved Coral. The stories seemed to be the only things that kept blood pumping through Poppy's veins.

Hearing the first bong, Ramona glanced up at the dust-riddled grandfather clock. Almost seven o'clock; she had spent a little over two hours with Poppy. She rose from the sofa. Lalah was expecting her at the restaurant by 7:30 P.M., so she had to get going. Greek Town was only a fifteen-minute drive. Poppy stood up with her.

Age had been pretty kind to Poppy, considering, Ramona thought. His shoulders had rounded some since the last time she saw him, but overall Poppy John Howard was still an exquisite-looking man by many measures. For the first time since her grandmother's death, Ramona was afraid of losing yet another grandparent. She couldn't bear to lose Poppy. Hugging him tightly, as if it might be their last time together, Ramona's eyes filled with tears. *Dear Lord, please look after Poppy. I love him so much.*

Poppy sensed Ramona's uneasiness and pulled away. His youngest granddaughter was the emotional one in the family; always had been. *Just like her Grandma Coral. Snot up a man's shirt without a second thought.*

"What are you laughing at, Poppy?" Ramona questioned, wiping the tears from her cheeks, unaware that she was destroying her neatly applied makeup.

"You, little lamb. God bless your soul. You're just like your grandmother." He paused to run his hand over his dampened shirt. "Full of flowing water."

Ramona laughed aloud. Her grandmother used to talk about how Poppy hated for her to cry on his shirts. "Madrid hates it, too," she said, smiling.

"Boy got good sense, that's why," he said, looking up at her again. "I tell you baby, that boy is a good man. Better than I've seen them in a long while. If he's out there bringing home the bacon and providing for his family, then you do what you must to keep him happy. Too many sorry, lazy, shiftless men out there in the world anyway. They would never be able to survive my generation of menfolk. They too girlie-like. Don't know what it takes to provide for a family, cherish and honor a wife. Sorry, just plain sorry," Poppy repeated, shaking his head.

"He's a man, Mona, taking care of you and

your children so you don't have to be out there working unless you want to. There's a difference. You could be with one of them men who expects his wife to work to make things easier for him, to gain more material crap. I don't care that you're one of these here independent, educated women. He's being a man by my standards.

"Now you be a woman and work it out before the devil get your mind all turned around and you lose what you have. And don't take no advice from Lalah. Or Sophia either, with all them damn uncombed, nappy twirls about her head. Blind leading the blind, that's what'll happen," he mumbled before continuing, "Don't go sending him into the arms of another woman, and don't you go traipsing into the arms of another man either. You hear me?"

"Yes, Poppy, I do. I do," Ramona acknowledged before opening the front door. "I love you, Poppy John." She kissed him on the cheek. "I'll be over tomorrow sometime. You can go ahead and dust off the chessboard," she teased, bouncing down the front steps, pumps clicking against the concrete.

"Baby, I know you didn't come all the way to Detroit to get your buns beat by your Poppy here. But if you insist." He smiled and waved. "See you tomorrow."

Once inside the car, Ramona let out a deep breath and turned on the radio. A nostalgic Whispers song came on. Poppy sure could be forthright, Ramona smiled, merging onto the Lodge Highway, heading downtown. She had fifteen minutes to get to the restaurant, find a parking space, and meet Lalah and Drew. Ramona sighed. How had she let Lalah talk her into meeting this

fool anyway? The whole covert plan was outland-
ish—Lalah lying to Gordon about what was on
their agenda tonight and Gordon probably doing
the same damn thing.

She found a parking space right in front of the
restaurant. Maybe a good sign, she thought, walking in. By the time the hostess approached her,
she had spotted the back of Lalah's head and two
thick-necked men sitting to the right of her.
Thanking the hostess for her help, Ramona
strolled toward the table.

The small supper club was buzzing with conversation and peals of laughter. It was a sophisticated
little joint and obviously popular, considering the
crowd, Ramona observed. The jazz quartet had returned from their break and was beginning an old
Bobby Womac tune when Ramona was halfway
across the room. *My favorite song,* she thought, following the lyrics. *If you think you're lonely now,* she
hummed under her breath.

The unexpected tap on Lalah's shoulder startled her. She turned around praying it wouldn't
be Gordon, and Lalah smiled when she saw it was
Ramona. She stood up immediately, blocking the
view of the men seated beside her, and embraced
her sister.

"You look good in black and white. I told you,"
Lalah winked, taking her seat.

"Thank you," Ramona blushed, walking
around to the other side of the booth, anxious
about meeting Lalah's soon-to-be lover. "This is
crazy," she murmured, a smidgen below a whisper. Taking her seat, mere discomfort swiftly
turned into bewilderment. Ramona's heart
vaulted into her throat when her eyes locked onto
the face across from her. Her hands began to

tremble and her right foot slid back and forth under the neatly pressed red tablecloth.

"Ramona, this is Drew," Lalah said proudly. "Drew, this is my sister, Mona."

"Nice to meet you," Drew said in a slightly squeaky voice, not quite expected from a man of his physique.

"Same here," was all Ramona could muster. *Lord.* She cringed, mesmerized by familiar features.

The waiter approached their table, and Ramona's eyes scanned the table, trying to get the scenario clear in her head. The waiter, ready to take their order, Lalah in her sequined red top and dazzling haircut, Drew with his adolescent voice—and Ronnie Ware! *What in God's name is Ronnie Ware doing here?*

Ramona's heart shifted into overdrive, thumping louder with each beat. Her eyes roved for refuge—away from Ronnie's face—and her mind raced through a series of questions. *Why is Ronnie here? Because it's a small world, that's why. Do I have lipstick on my teeth? How's my hair? Oh, Lord, I should have seen Jonathan today instead of tomorrow.*

Drew was talking about something in the background. Ramona heard his voice, but couldn't concentrate on it. Things were moving in slow motion, blotting out everyone at the table except Ronnie Ware.

A deep voice cut through Drew's babbling. Ramona's eyes came full circle and locked with Ronnie's.

"Hello, Ramona," Ronnie said slowly, letting her name roll off his tongue.

"Ronnie." A grin was beginning to raise the corners of Ramona's mouth.

Ronnie smiled warmly, exposing his straight, pearly white teeth. His mocha face was still smooth and hairless, and his mannerisms were still as sleek and cunning as a prowling panther, Ramona thought.

"You're more beautiful than I remembered, Ramona." He paused purposely before he continued. "Ever could have imagined," he murmured, sliding across the horseshoe-shaped booth toward Ramona.

"Thank you." Ramona blushed. *He thinks I'm still beautiful with all this extra weight and grandma hairdo?*

Drew was totally enthralled with Lalah and her cleavage. They had managed to strike up a two-way conversation, leaving Ramona and Ronnie to fend for themselves. Lalah stole a glimpse at Ramona, who was seated directly across from her. *Exactly what she needs,* Lalah smiled. *Exactly.*

Ronnie was seated right next to Ramona now, grinning, staring and plotting. His heavy floral scent spread freely, claiming its territory like a vacationing cat returning to an old neighborhood. His leg innocently brushed against Ramona's, where he let it rest for a few seconds.

A chill shot down Ramona's spine. Her entire body stiffened. She moved her leg away from his, then exhaled hard. *Lord, please don't let this man get at me. I'm here to relax . . .*

Ronnie reached over and planted a surprise kiss on her cheek—his lips lingering too long on her soft, warm flesh. "I'm so glad to see you, Ramona," he whispered, reaching for her hand.

Ramona smiled tightly. *I'm here to re-energize.*

He grabbed her hand and eased it to his mouth,

kissing it softly. "I've been thinking about you so often," he told her.

I'm here to reconnect with myself . . .

Ramona snatched her hand free. She closed her eyes for a brief moment, trying to gain some strength, some composure. A few seconds later, she opened her eyes, only to be met by Ronnie's intense gaze. *I'm here . . . oh, Lord, please!*

Seven

Friday morning

Twirling the blue pencil between his thumb and forefinger, Madrid arched back in the soft, burgundy leather chair. Slowly, he swiveled around to face the enormous window. One of the things he appreciated most about his office location was the plush, rich greenery of the landscaped fifty-acre corporate site. The meeting with the chemical company was less than an hour away. Landing the account would represent a monumental transition for the company, as well as his career. That is, if he could stay focused long enough to get through the grueling presentation and close the deal.

This morning had still been a new experience for Madrid, in his second day in the role of Mr. Mom. Somebody's law, other than Murphy's, had redefined the meaning of chaos. For starters, he had tapped the snooze button too many times, causing him to oversleep. Once awake, Nathan began whining about a stomachache. Leslie's last-minute notification that she had no clean clothes to wear didn't make things any easier, nor her incensed wailing when he attempted to comb her hair again. DeMar's late arrival to pick the kids up for school almost iced the cake, had it not been for the bumper-to-bumper traffic.

He rubbed his hand over the left side of his head, massaging the area delicately. The nauseating pain was more intense now. His abrupt separation from the woman he loved, lack of sleep, uncharted avenues regarding the children, and an increased work load were all responsible for his despondency. "Just try to get through the meeting Drid, then go home and relax," he mumbled aloud, tapping the pencil against his lip.

Late last night, he'd repeatedly combed through his presentation, assuring his familiarity with the graphs and numbers. It seemed like he had done a million of these presentations before without the slightest bit of hesitation. But this time, one unique part of his routine was missing—Ramona. She had been by his side for so many of his meeting preparations, he found it uncomfortably strange not having her near this time around.

Madrid's eyes wandered past the azalea bushes and anchored at the man-made pond enclosed by a Chinese garden. A few ducklings were waddling through the water as if they hadn't a care in the world. *I remember when I didn't seem to have a worry in the world, either. When it was just me, myself, and I for a long time. Nothing to worry about but getting through school and securing a career. No wife, no children, no drama, other than what I created for myself. I was free to be whatever I wanted to be, do whatever I wished, wherever I felt like it.*

Since Madrid's parents' death twelve years ago, he had become obsessed with a sense of wanting to belong, to be responsible for and have a family of his own. Though youthfulness and foolishness were the reasons for Leslie's unexpected birth, he always attempted to be a responsible, ideal father even before Leslie's mother died. With his parents' committed and dedicated marriage as a role model, Madrid, certain that he could follow in his father's footsteps, chose the marriage route, too. Naturally, it seemed like the only logical choice.

He and Ramona had been dating strong for eight months when he made his decision. She had been the first real woman to *open his nose wide*, so to speak. Ramona was also the only woman to love sports, stimulate his mind, awaken his dying spirituality, and enjoy sex as much, if not more, than him. The handwriting had been on the wall. The only sensible thing left to do was to make her his wife.

She was so surprised and embarrassed the night he proposed. The old stadium, where the Cleveland Cavaliers had hosted the Chicago Bulls for a playoff game, had been rocking. It was half time and the Cavs were leading the Bulls by eight points. Ramona had needed to pay a visit to the ladies' room, but Madrid had insisted that she wait till he saw if the guy standing on the court could make the shot from half-court.

Ramona, who had never been especially patient, slouched back in her chair, annoyed. But when she heard the stadium announcer call her name over the PA, she had quickly perked up— especially after hearing the announcer say, "Ramona Johnson, Madrid Shaw wants to know if you'll be crazy enough to be his wife."

Ramona nearly fell out of her chair in shock. Everyone seated in their immediate section began clapping and cheering when Ramona accepted and Madrid placed the diamond ring on her fin-

ger. Even the oversized replay screen caught a shot
of Ramona's flowing tears and Madrid's thirty-two
teeth. Pretty soon the entire stadium was chanting
and cheering for the newly engaged couple.

Madrid smiled briefly as he reminisced about
the creative flare he had used to reel Ramona in
as his life partner. But that was then and now was
now. Thinking about the recent events, as well as
the unreturned call he had left for Ramona last
evening, made him challenge his decision. Mull-
ing over his reasons for getting married and his
situation with Ramona lasted only a minute more;
Bridget was buzzing him on the intercom.

"Mr. Shaw, Mr. Axel phoned. They're ready for
you in conference room one."

Madrid swiveled the chair about face and leaned
toward the speaker phone. "Thank you, Bridget.
I'll be right down." Standing, he slid his arms into
his navy blue suit jacket, shaking his shoulders a
few times to smooth out the wrinkles.

Walking toward the wall mirror, he scanned his
attire. Straightening the knot of his striped power
tie, he let out a breath and mumbled, "Here we
go, Mr. Shaw. It's now or never." He grabbed his
laptop computer, a small box of slides, and the stack
of handouts, wrapped in the clear plastic covers.

He stepped into the lobby, shutting his office
door behind him.

"There you are, Mr. Shaw." Bridget smiled,
turning to face him. "Good luck. I'm sure you'll
win them over. I made a fresh pot of coffee in case
you want a cup to take with you to the meeting."

"Thank you, Bridget. I could sure use something right about now." He smiled tightly. "I'll
be out of the office after the meeting and won't
return until Monday morning."

"Oh," Bridget said with raised brows. "I rescheduled Alyson Rivera for this afternoon. Would you like me to call her and reschedule again?"

Not her again. Madrid sighed inwardly. He had canceled their meeting once already in a twenty-four-hour period. How could he do it again? Giving Bridget's question more consideration, he responded, "Yes, please. I'm no good for interviews today. Too focused on this meeting, and more than likely, my brains will be fried afterwards. I should probably give her a call. This way, she'll know that we aren't being inconsiderate. What time is her interview?"

"Three hours from now," Bridget said, looking up at the round gray clock on the wall. "Don't worry about it. I'll call her. You go to your meeting and concentrate on that. All right?"

"I owe you plenty, you know that, Bridget?" Madrid grinned, backing away from her desk.

"A twenty percent raise and a few extra personal days might do the trick." She smiled easily.

"Yeah, okay." He laughed. "You'd better get it in writing," he said between the closing elevator doors.

You bet I will, Bridget smiled to herself, looking for Alyson Rivera's phone number.

Wiping streaks of sweat from his face, Madrid stepped off the high-tech treadmill. He took in a deep breath, then released it slowly. Working out seemed to be the best alternative for freeing his mind, releasing the tension. He was certain the presentation had been a flop.

Although the chemical company had not refused the deal outright, their hesitation to make a commitment today spoke for itself. Madrid's inability to fully concentrate on the presentation appeared to be obvious to a few of the representatives. Not even the thick cup of java provided the focus he desperately needed during his spiel. On more than one occasion, Mr. Axle, the vice president of business development, had to step in and ad lib when Madrid stumbled through statistical data. It would be safe to assume he could kiss the promotion as director of business development goodbye. *Damn it, Ramona. Why now? Why would you do this?*

DeMar had called Madrid shortly after the meeting, curious about the results. Detecting disappointment in his brother's voice, DeMar offered to pick up the children from school, giving Madrid an opportunity to stop by the gym and release some steam.

Considering the way things went this morning, Madrid wasn't sure if he'd be able to maintain his current position, much less expand his department and hire someone new. Everything would be spelled out during the Monday morning staff meeting. Until then, all he had time to focus on was the kids. And Ramona's true intentions.

Ramona glided Meka into the driveway and turned the revving engine off. Blankly, she stared at the Nefertiti ornament clinking against the other keys dangling from the ignition. The swaying motion of the keys hypnotized her and she closed her eyes, listening to the jingling sound. Ting. Ting. Ting.

Fatigue assaulted her as if she'd run a race the day before. Even the relaxing prospect of the hair salon had proved to be inadequate. The excessive wait for Jonathan's chair to free up annoyed her. It hadn't seemed to matter that she had an appointment.

The salon had been cramped with big bodies, loud voices and ridiculously dated magazines. The only saving grace was the final outcome—the new haircut Jonathan had blessed her with after three hours of squirming impatiently in the salon. Jonathan's disregard for her time made her swear that the next stylist she visited would either commit to their scheduled appointment or she'd bill them for her wasted time.

Instinctively, Ramona reached for the pieces of hair that used to hang down into her face. The bothersome strands of hair were gone, and thank God too, because she had grown weary of her unmanageable hair, not to mention her matronly appearance. Thanks to Jonathan, her new "Honey Hush" hairstyle—short and tapered above the ears and the nape of the neck, with a little height on the top blending into a full bang—left her feeling mighty fine about herself.

The black Benz and midnight blue Jaguar sat proudly in the open garage like display trophies. Lalah had done well, achieving just about everything she'd set her mind to, Ramona surmised, stepping out of her car. But last night Lalah had gone too far overboard with her determined ways. The audacity of Lalah inviting Ronnie Ware to tag along with them during dinner.

Meeting Drew, Lalah's soon-to-be sidekick if Gordon didn't straighten up and fly right, or so she said, was an uncomfortable situation for Ramona. Drew and Ronnie didn't seem to have a problem with the set-up, and neither did Lalah.

The whole darn evening was just a nest of butterflies, fluttering around in her stomach.

Ronnie had looked handsome as ever and had been dressed to kill. She wasn't really sure how she felt about her college sweetheart when their eyes locked together, but he still had the ability to make her heart thump louder. Ramona let out a long breath, turning the key to the front door. When she'd left the house this morning, Lalah had still been asleep. Ramona was glad Lalah was home and awake. It would give her another opportunity to discuss last night's ploy.

Ramona entered the marble foyer and veered straight for the kitchen. Her ears were greeted with a fiery disagreement between Lalah and Gordon.

"I don't know why the hell you're getting all worked up, Lalah. You and your sister seemed to be engaged in some wee-hour entertaining of your own," Gordon huffed. "Little sister blindly following big sister, eh?"

"Gordon, if you've got something to say to me, just say it," Lalah spewed.

"My sources indicated that you two were cozily relaxing with some gentlemen last night at Floods'." He raised his brow, waiting for verification, clarification, or just a plain old lie. Nothing. "I could always strike up some conversation with Ramona for clarification," he threatened.

Ramona gasped. Gordon knew about their venture last night? How? Hesitantly, Ramona eased into the kitchen, where Lalah stood frozen at the sink. Gordon sat at the counter with the morning paper spread out and his coffee cup in hand. His bald head glistened in the early afternoon sunlight. He looked up suddenly, glaring.

"Mona." Lalah was dramatically exasperated. "I

didn't hear you come in." Her gaze locked with Ramona's.

Silence saturated the room. Ramona grinned tightly. Gordon sipped his coffee loudly and intentionally. He was looking straight through her, she was sure of it. His face reeked of disappointment. Or were her eyes playing tricks on her?

Lalah spoke first. "Your haircut looks good. It's gorgeous! Isn't it, honey?" Lalah looked at Gordon, attempting to save face. Lalah walked over to Ramona, inspecting the cut further, which highlighted her features.

"Yeah. Just lovely," Gordon sarcastically replied. He stared at Ramona with a furrowed brow, then said, "So Mona, you decided to follow your sister's footsteps, huh?" He shook his head and rose from the table abruptly. "Watch yourself. You don't want to make Madrid go into tachycardia." His voice trailed behind him as he walked toward the front of the house.

Ramona detected the hidden sarcasm. Yeah, so she had chopped off her hair like her sister, but was that really what he was implying? Her heart dropped for a split second. The last thing she wanted was to be judged by her brother-in-law.

"Yeah, yeah, Gordon," Lalah waved behind his back. He had already reached the front door and was partway out on the landing. "He's like most brothers, Ramona—think sisters have to have a head full of hair to be considered beautiful." She was still trying to pretend not to know what he was really saying.

Lalah laid her fingers gently atop her sister's new hair-do. "The new cut does wonders for your face, Ramona." Lalah smiled proudly.

"Thank you," Ramona said, moving towards the

kitchen table. She would let the real subject take a back seat for now—at least until Gordon was truly out of earshot "I was tired of all those wild strands of windblown hair. This will be easy and quick." She rubbed her hand across the nape of her neck, which had been tapered with magnified precision.

"I left seven inches of lifeless hair on Jonathan's floor," she chuckled. "But I love it! Now all I have to do is put on some of that MAC Russian red lipstick and that black merry widow," Ramona beamed. She was feeling more confident than she had in a long time.

Lalah stared at her baby sister happily. Ramona's self-esteem had taken a plunge since she had become a mother and a housewife. She was ecstatic to see Ramona's spirits flourishing again.

"There's more salmon fritters if you like," Lalah said, cramming more dishes in the already swollen dishwasher. "Gordon didn't eat that much."

"Is he gone for the day?" Ramona asked.

"Yup," Lalah replied, never lifting her eyes from the stack of dishes.

Ramona dropped her tattered Coach pocketbook on the counter, then took a seat on one of the cane chairs. Everything was so bizarre and superficial between Lalah and Gordon. *What in God's name is left for them to talk about? Are they both in denial, or have they lost that much respect for each other?* Lalah knew Gordon was hanging out last night, and Gordon had some kind of proof that Lalah was up to no good as well. Surely, it couldn't be completely acceptable for Gordon to pull into the garage simultaneously with Lalah at 3:30 A.M.? Or was it? Ramona wondered.

"So, how long you and Ronnie been concocting your scheme?" Ramona questioned, trying to restrain from sounding annoyed.

Lalah didn't respond immediately. Instead, she shook the dripping water off her hands and wiped them on a towel. Grabbing her favorite coffee mug, a horrid collage of colorful, unrecognizable flowers, Lalah sauntered across the room and sat down next to Ramona.

The fact that she deliberately took so long to respond to the question irritated Ramona, mainly because she was well aware of Lalah's habit of ignoring someone when she did not want to be confronted with information or answer questions. Too bad though, because Ramona was determined to find out why her sister felt the need to interfere with her personal life, going so far as to invite Ronnie Ware to dinner without her approval.

"I bumped into him last week. I thought I told you that," Lalah said.

"You told me you saw him and he asked about me. You neglected to tell me that you were scheming with him about meeting us for dinner last night!"

"I knew you'd be hesitant to go if I told you. No harm was done. Why are you so annoyed? It was a simple dinner, Mona. That's all."

"Really?" Ramona said, staring at Lalah harder. "Then why didn't you tell your husband the truth if it was just a simple dinner?"

There was that silence again. Lalah nervously swirled the tepid liquid in the mug. The comment was unnecessary, from where she sat. It wasn't her fault that her baby sister still had a minimal ache for her college sweetie. Her intentions were innocent enough. All Lalah wanted to do was see Ramona's face flushed with some temporary joy, no matter how indefinite, no matter the situation.

Lalah absentmindedly sipped cool, creamed coffee. She thought the liquid was still hot—her lips barely and cautiously touched the cup.

Lalah swallowed. "I apologize if you took things the wrong way. Forgive me."

Lalah's words were less than convincing—more artificial, very rehearsed. All that practice with Gordon, probably, Ramona figured. She was still unnerved by the whole ordeal but chose to let it drop.

"Everything is everything," Ramona rehearsed similarly. Marvin Gaye's "What's Going On" softly piped through the speakers tucked into one corner of the kitchen wall. *Precisely,* Ramona thought, tapping her foot to the sexy, soulful song. Seeing Ronnie Ware after several years had been surprising and invigorating all at once.

Years ago, when she was still single and independent, Ramona had often dreamed of a moment like last night—feasting her eyes about her old flame and burning him back into her life, her bosom. But that was a few years, a few inches, and a few pounds ago. Last night hadn't proved much. At least so she'd like to believe. Unless, of course, feeling a tingling sensation overtake her body didn't really count for anything.

Lalah called out her name a second time and Ramona flinched. Her thoughts had blocked out all else.

"Are you going to meet Ronnie for dinner tomorrow night?" Lalah asked. She walked back to the sink, dumping the cold coffee down the drain.

Ramona shrugged, knowing full well that Lalah didn't have eyes in the back of her head. Her mind raced for an answer—a truthful one. Strangely, the quiet made it even more difficult to think. Would she chance going to dinner with Ronnie alone, without another person to chaperon their evening, their conversation, their blaze? *Maybe not.* Lalah had obviously set out to do whatever it was she aimed to do. Like it or not, she had to make a decision in the next twenty-four hours.

Time ticked slowly, coming to a stand-still for all Ramona could tell. She wedged her hands under her thighs. Lalah wiped the stove down a second time, then a third. Stalemate. Ramona refused to yield, and while Lalah didn't ask the question again, she gave in first.

"Have you seen Sophia yet?" It was a superfluous question, but something to get the ebb and flow going again.

Ramona conceded. "Not yet. I'm on my way over there now. She's probably cursing my name as we speak." She dug her keys out of her pocket, slung her heavy bag on her shoulder and headed for the front of the house. "You meeting us over there?"

"Maybe a little later. I have a few errands. You going by Poppy's?" Lalah followed Ramona to the front door.

"More than likely. Knowing Poppy, he'll probably want to order some Chinese food to help wash down his bourbon and sit around and talk." Ramona smiled.

"Ain't that the truth," Lalah told her.

"I'll see you later."

"Maybe." Lalah grinned seductively.

Ramona shook her head—disapprovingly. "Sis, with Gordon on your tail, maybe you should cool it."

"Yeah? Well, maybe you should, too," Lalah responded with an arched brow, before swinging the heavy oak door shut.

Eight

Ramona pulled to the back of the narrow driveway, nearly colliding Meka's left mirror with the tiny, cottage-style brick home. The only complaint Ramona had about Detroit was some of the narrow driveways scattered about the city. Sophia's yellow Volkswagen Bug sat parked on the grass at an obscure angle, cutting off any hope of a true backyard. The garage apparently was still too cluttered with knickknacks to be considered useful, Ramona thought, shutting off the engine.

Pockets of long weeds intermittently woven with patches of green and blonde grass lined the side of the house. Ramona stood on the cement step and rang the side doorbell; Most Detroit folks used their side doors as the entrance, unless of course it was Poppy's house. He never believed in having his guests use the side door, partly because he didn't feel it was anyone's business, unless he made it theirs, to traipse through the kitchen and see what he was having for dinner.

The warped wooden door squealed open. Sophia unlatched the screen door then stood back.

"Well, if it isn't my favorite niece," Sophia teased. "I'm thinking to myself perhaps I'm the only one with a favorite anything around here. It is now Friday afternoon, an entire thirty-six hours since you've arrived, and I'm just laying eyes on you for the first time."

Ramona stepped inside and embraced Sophia with more than one of those fake, frosty, A-frame hugs. Ramona shut the door behind her and followed Sophia up the few steps and through the small yellow and white kitchen. Sophia was decked out in a rich, chocolate velvet turtleneck dress, princess-seamed with a long-sleeved bodice and full and low over the calf.

"Hello to you, too, Auntie," Ramona threw back. Poppy was right. Sophia did have a trillion reddish-brown dredlocks about her head. Ramona closed her eyes for a minute, inhaling a deep spicy fragrance.

"What's that perfume you're wearing, Sophia?"

"Joy. It's a new fragrant oil." Sophia smiled. "Like it?"

"Very nice," Ramona told her, sniffing the scent again.

"My sweetie pie picked it up for me."

Sweetie pie? Ramona mimicked quietly. She'd have to get the scoop on this lover boy later on, once the conversation got really flowing.

The two bedroom, one bath home fit Sophia's lifestyle perfectly, just as it had fit Grandma Coral and Poppy thirty years ago. The little house on Manchester had raised Sophia and her two sisters, Lalah and Ramona's mother, Jules, and their other aunt, Candis, who lived in Paris, single and childless.

Ramona took a seat on the mud-cloth print-patterned futon positioned on the right side of the over-stuffed living room. Sophia picked up the antiquated black telephone receiver and continued her conversation, snuggled across from Ramona in a burnt orange leather bean bag with her matching Nubuck wrap boots crossed at the ankles. Her conversation was low, more so than the light sounds of Miles Davis' trumpet buzzing through the speakers. Sophia pulled out a pair of eyeglasses and put them on before rattling off the information from the flyer on the floor next to her.

A soft yellowish glow barely lit the dismal room. A large family portrait of Sophia, her sisters, Poppy and Coral hung above the fireplace. Several unique pieces of African art lined the mantel, as did many artifacts collected by Sophia on one of her many visits to the motherland. More pieces of art, the incense burner and a photography book highlighting works by James Van Der Zee lay on the oak fossil, clawfoot coffee table.

Ramona absently flipped through the book, patiently waiting for Sophia to finish her call. Silently, she turned one page after the other, straining to read the words on the pages. She closed the large book and placed it back on the table. Sophia laughed.

"Finished already?" Sophia teased, hanging up the phone.

"It's too dark in here, Sophia." Ramona said, slouching back against the futon.

"It works for me." Sophia smiled. The brown freckles dotted her tawny complexion.

"When did you start wearing glasses?"

"What? These things?" Sophia pulled the round, gold wire-framed rims from her face. She rubbed her eyes for a few times, smearing her mascara. "Dr. Rashman told me to eat more carrots and take more vitamin A. Well, you know

how I am about carrots." She grinned. Just then
Quala, her four-year-old black cat, jumped onto
the other futon close to the large wood-trimmed
windows, purring loudly. Sophia ignored her.

"What did he say about reading in the dark?"
Ramona joked.

"This room is not dark, Mona. It's soft, it's calm-
ing—it's me. You know that."

"Yeah, I know. So, you still working at the
FFOC office?"

"Of course. Where else am I going? That office
needs as many young, educated, dedicated souls
as possible. I would never abandon For Folks Of
Color project."

Dedication. Definitely the word that burst into
Ramona's thoughts when Sophia's name was
mentioned. She was the only person in their family to make a career out of working for a non-
profit organization focused on collecting data,
names and signatures for legislative changes in
Detroit.

"When did you grow dredlocks?" Ramona
asked.

"Nubian locks," Sophia corrected. "I call them
Nubian locks instead of dredlocks, because
there's nothing dreadful about them."

Ramona took a moment to absorb the information, nodding her head. Randy Crawford's remake of George Benson's "Give Me The Night"
was ringing in the background. "So when did you
start growing Nubian locks?"

"About eight months ago. When did you go
short?"

"Today. I had an early appointment with Jonathan. Didn't seem to make much difference,

though, because I was in the salon damn near all morning."

"And knowing Jonathan, he probably charged you an exorbitant amount, too. How much did it take away from your checking account?"

Ramona laughed. She had never looked at it that way. "Seventy-five dollars, plus a five-dollar tip."

"Eighty dollars? Sister, you could have fed a homeless person for five days with that money. You'd look good with Nubian locks—you should try it. Not only would it save you from wasting money for them to cut and kill your hair with that chemical stuff, but it would free your mind and perhaps strengthen your soul. It's liberating not having to worry about my hair every day of the week, every month of the year. Furthermore it's easy. And with you being a mother and all, you could appreciate it."

Ramona nodded in agreement. Although, she would have to do some way deep-down soul-searching about going locks. Nubian or otherwise.

"Speaking of motherhood, how are my great nephew and niece? I'm surprised you didn't bring them with you."

"The kids are doing fine. Nathan is at that stage where he's getting so independent, he wants to pick out his own clothes and dress himself"

"That's good, Mona. If you encourage him to be responsible and a decision-maker now, it'll keep him from being needy later in life. How did you get Madrid to agree to keep the kids? He doesn't strike me as that liberal."

Ramona hesitated. Everyone had something to say about her, Madrid, and the kids. "He didn't really have that much say. It was kind of a spur of the moment thing."

"I see," Sophia said slowly. "Want a ginger beer or some seltzer water or something?"

"Water would be fine. Thanks." Ramona yawned softly.

"Come on in the kitchen with me. I told Frankie I would make dinner."

Ramona trailed behind Sophia, as did Quala, who got tangled in Ramona's stride. Sophia grabbed a small box and dumped the special blend, recommend by the vet, into Quala's bowl, then washed her hands.

"Get one of those seltzer bottles out of the fridge if you'd like. I'm going to get this black bean soup started."

Ramona did as Sophia suggested, then wedged herself between the rattan chair and the tiny wood table pushed against the wall.

"Is Frankie your sweetie pie?" Ramona asked after taking a long sip of the carbonated drink. Ramona watched Sophia fuss through the cabinets, searching for her spices. Her short, stocky frame would be enjoyed by all men, Ramona thought admiring her Aunt's shapely five-four figure. Frankie would more than likely be a tall, sleek brother.

"Frankie is a friend of mine you'll meet in a few minutes," Sophia replied matter-of-factly. "So, Mona, how come the spur of the moment visit home?"

"I needed a little break. That's all." She sipped some more of her seltzer.

"Madrid must be working your nerves pretty bad. How did he handle your sudden decision, really?" Sophia continued dicing peppers, garlic cloves and onions.

"Put it this way, he wasn't what you'd call supportive or overly enthused. I think he said something like I could keep my unappreciative behind gone. Something like that, but don't quote me," she said bitingly.

"Hmm," Sophia murmured. "Unappreciative, huh? Boy, I tell you. They sure got some nerve. They just can't seem to let things roll to their natural beat. They're so self-centered." She dropped the items in the simmering pot on the stove before sprinkling in the Cajun pepper seasoning.

Ramona looked perplexed. "Who's they, Sophia?" She was fairly certain she was implying "men" but wanted to be sure—wanted to hear her say so.

"Brothers, sisters, men, women, all of them who suffer from being control freaks. That's what it sounds like to me. Madrid is trying to control your actions, manipulate your decisions. Do you feel like you have the opportunity to make unconditional decisions with Madrid?"

"Yeah, most of the time. What you have to remember, Sophia, is that we are married. And when you become part of a unit, a decision made by one member of the unit usually effects the entire unit. Sometimes though, one of the members will have to forsake the stability of the unit temporarily, in order to keep it from tumbling altogether. In my case, I made a decision. I needed a break. I chose to take it at the expense of rocking the relationship. But the bottom line is, if I didn't make this decision, the unit would have cracked quickly. You feel me?"

"I feel you, sister girl. I just hope that everything works out evenly for all concerned. Things happen."

Sophia stirred the pot's contents for awhile, then took a seat at the table facing Ramona. "Have you seen Daddy yet?"

"Yesterday. I told him I'd be by sometime today to whip him in chess. I thought maybe the two of us could go over there later."

Sophia furrowed her brows. "Oh, I don't know, Mona. Daddy ain't that keen on me right about now." She rested her elbow on the table, placing her chin in her hand.

Ramona studied Sophia's warm face. Traces of worn bronze lipstick still outlined her lips. Sophia truly favored her mother, Coral, more than Ramona could remember. Probably had something to do with the hereditary aging process.

"Why would you say that, Sophia?"

"Come on, Mona. You can spill it. I know Daddy said something smart to you about me."

"No." Ramona frowned thinking over her conversation with her grandfather. "Not anything major. Though he did say something, and I quote, about all them damn braids in your hair."

They both let out peals of laughter. From the open window in the kitchen, a car door slammed.

"Poppy can't be that blasted upset about some locks. What else would he be bothered about?"

"Frankie," Sophia said somberly. "He doesn't like Frankie."

The doorbell sounded. Sophia pushed her chair back and stood up. Quala ran ahead of Sophia as the bell chimed again. Sophia's eyes were wide, locking with Ramona's for a minute pleadingly.

"Well, why the hell doesn't he like Frankie?" Ramona asked innocently.

"Because she's my lover," Sophia said, then turned and walked to the side door.

Astounded, Ramona repeated the words aloud. *"She's* my lover?"

Frankie waltzed through the kitchen door with a bunch of exotic flowers in one hand and a Hudson's department store bag in the other. She was a short-stacked sister with long, jet black hair—a true candidate for the next Miss America contest.

"Smells good, whatever it is," Frankie said handing Sophia the flowers. "I knew you'd look good in that color, Sophia."

"This is my niece, Ramona," Sophia said, nodding her head in Ramona's direction while she placed the tiger lilies in a vase and filled it with water.

Frankie smiled broadly, extending her hand. "I'm Frankie. Good to finally meet you."

Ramona, still recovering from the shock of Sophia's unexpected statement, struggled for words. She smiled tightly and grasped Frankie's hand. "Same here."

An unexpected pang of jealousy rippled through Ramona's heart. *Flowers—how nice. I can't recall the last time Madrid bought flowers for me.* She took her seat again and studied Frankie and Sophia's interaction. Frankie was so attentive and helpful, chucking off her suit jacket to pitch in and assist Sophia with dinner. There was a time when Madrid was that way, Ramona fretted. Then she thought about the compliment Frankie had paid Sophia about the color of her dress. Frustrated, she wondered why Madrid couldn't do something so simple as to compliment her from time to time. Was that so hard?

Ramona sat down on the cool wood and black iron bench. The news about Sophia being gay had frazzled some of her brain cells. All this time, all these many years, and no one had suspected or openly discussed it with Sophia. Why hadn't Sophia said something to her? It was hard to believe that Sophia had kept it a secret for so long.

Ramona tossed a few more pieces of bread to the pigeons circling the Renaissance Center. The breeze from the Detroit River calmed her spirit. From where she sat, she had a premium view of Windsor, the tiny little Canadian city adjoining the Detroit/Windsor tunnel from Detroit. She wondered what the people over in Windsor were doing right now. What family crisis surrounded their lives? Did Canadians have the same concerns and issues as Americans? Did white Canadians share the same plights as black Canadians?

She exhaled hard. A small yacht pulled into the harbor, momentarily obstructing her view of the three or four buildings she counted in the small Canadian town. Was there a confused soul sitting in the Windsor park square staring across the frigid river towards Detroit, counting buildings and thinking? She would never really know.

The only thing she did know was that Lalah was threatening to whore around with Drew, Sophia was doing a coming-out number, and Ronnie still seemed rather appealing, as much as she hated to confess it. How come Lalah hadn't mentioned anything to her about Sophia? She was sure she had known. How come Poppy, who always said what was on his mind, neglected to say anything about Sophia being gay? Surely two games of chess, dinner, and more reminiscent stories had provided enough time for Poppy to at least approach the subject.

Ramona's eyes followed the ripples left by the passing boat. Who could afford yachts in a day and time like this? She huffed. Her mind was zooming around in a million directions.

Frankie Givens—Sophia's companion, a petite 38-year-old, cocoa-colored sister dressed to kill in designer wear, long, jet-black hair hanging to the middle of her back. She was an attorney, a graduate of a top law school in Northern California. A divorcée, a mother, a sister. Articulate, intelligent and down right beautiful was the best way to describe Frankie. What did she see in Sophia ? What did Sophia see in Frankie that kept them from being with men? She had meant to ask them that question. But time had ticked past and before long, it was time to leave—to visit Poppy and settle the nauseating feeling rising inside.

Aunt Sophia, gay and sharing her kisses and her bed with another woman? Ramona shuddered. She was appalled, almost embarrassed, by her own feelings and beliefs. Though love was love, no matter who or what the lifestyle a person chose, right? But was this right? Overall, everyone would still love and support Sophia, whether or not they agreed with her choice.

Ramona sat searching her soul, her spirit, for some level of comfort with Sophia's news. And then there was Lalah and her soon-to-be trifling ways. It was just too much to bear on a four-day excursion.

Ramona had dialed home twice from Poppy's

house, and both times she got no answer and no machine. Damn Madrid for not turning on the answering machine! As soon as she got home she would call New Jersey Bell and set up voice mail. That way, the next time something like this happened, she would be able to leave a message—let everyone know she was all right and that she did care enough to call and check in on them.

She imagined that the kids were wondering what had happened to her. She had never left them for this long—ever. Would Madrid remember where Nathan's machine was, in case he suffered from one of his asthma attacks? Did he know where to find the number to the doctor's office if an emergency arose? Would he remember that Leslie was allergic to penicillin? Had he paid attention to anything around the house all these years? Suddenly panic streaked through Ramona.

Trembling, she retrieved her cellular phone from the bottom of her bag and dialed home. The connection choked off on the second ring. She re-dialed—busy. She hit the end button and tried once more. One ring, two rings, connection!

"Hello," the crackled voice answered on the other end.

"Nathan? It's Mommy. How are you?" She let out the deep breath she had unconsciously held in.

"Mommy!" he yelled into the phone. More crackling.

"Where's everybody?"

"Daddy outside fixing Leslie's bike. Leslie's watching TV."

"Let me speak to Leslie, sweetheart." Ramona

felt her stomach churning. The line got fuzzier with static. She heard Leslie's voice. "Leslie, can you hear me?"

"Mona? Mona, where are you?"

"Still in Detroit, honey. My phone is dying. I tried to call several times earlier today. How's everything?"

"Fine, Mona. When are you coming home?"

"Soon, baby. Soon." Ramona smiled. It was nice to be missed.

"When? We miss you." Leslie almost yelled into the receiver. Louder crackling erupted across the line.

"Sunday. I'll be home Sunday. Hello?" Ramona paused. Leslie's voice trailed in and out.

"Hold on, Mona. I'll get Daddy."

"Leslie, who's that on the phone?" Madrid's voice called from the background.

"It's Mona," Leslie happily sang.

"What does she want?" Madrid yelled back.

"Leslie," Ramona called. "Leslie, wait. I don't have—" Click. Silence fell. "Hello? Hello, Leslie?"

Ramona shook the phone frantically, then slid to the other side of the bench. Still, silence. She pulled the phone close. "Damn it," she hissed. The red light signalling a low battery was fire-red. Figures, she huffed. She had finally called at a time when guilt wasn't the motivating factor, and *boom!* Dead damn battery.

She fell back against the bench, clasping the phone and replaying her brief conversation with the kids. Madrid's question angered her. *The nerve of him asking what do I want? I want to speak to the kids.* And they missed her—that was obvious. Madrid still seemed to harbor some sort of grudge.

Forget him. A few more days with the kids would loosen him up. It just had to.

Madrid jolted into the house, wiping the oil from his hands on a rag. Pieces of grass were wedged into the indentations in his knees from bending down on the lawn.

"Where's the phone?" he asked. There were a few things he wanted to share with Ramona. Leslie handed him the phone. The line was dead. "Did she hang up?"

Leslie shrugged. "It sounded fuzzy, then the line went quiet."

"Oh, so she finally decided to call home?" he mumbled under his breath.

"Mona said she tried to call earlier," Leslie replied.

He said nothing, keeping his comments to himself. *Called earlier, my foot. We've been here damn near all afternoon.* His disposition turned frigid. There was no way they'd be able to see eye to eye ever again, he was sure of it. He could care less if she came back or not. Well, so he thought for the moment. Gone two days and this was the first time she'd called. Bologna. Pure and simple.

The children looked perplexed. They hadn't really spoken much of Ramona, handling her absence a lot better than Madrid had. They seemed to understand, even appreciate, Ramona's decision to take a few days away from them. *Kids,* he thought.

"When is Mommy coming home?" Nathan whined.

"Sunday," Leslie answered.

Madrid shot her a surprised look. *Sunday? Oh really? Just like that, she's going to walk in here and think all is normal?* Hardly. He was feeling cruel, but couldn't help it. Actually, it was probably a blessing that he hadn't spoken to her. There was no telling what he would have said in front of the kids. It bothered him that he was left holding the ball on such short notice, without being able to sound off.

He sat down on the sofa next to Leslie, and Nathan joined them. *The Lion King* was playing for the tenth time. Madrid pretended not to care. He would take advantage of the colorful, musical cartoon to calm his mood. Leslie sniffled back tears as a tragic moment for the little lion occurred.

"Daddy, are you and Mona getting a divorce?" a wide-eyed Leslie asked unexpectedly.

Madrid frowned. "A divorce? Where did you get an idea like that, sweetheart?"

Leslie hunched her shoulders upward. Nathan squirmed in his seat restlessly, trying to concentrate on the action in the movie. Leslie's conversation with their dad was annoying him. He couldn't hear.

"When I told my friend Kim that Mona went out of town and you were mad, she said that you'll probably get a divorce like her mommy and daddy."

"Leslie, I can't hear," Nathan sighed, sliding off the sofa and sitting down on the carpet, closer to the TV.

Madrid considered how to answer for several reasons: one, he wasn't aware how perceptive Leslie was about his and Ramona's relationship; two, the subject of divorce was not something he wanted Leslie to worry about; and three, he wanted to be able to warn her about sharing too much of the family business with her friends.

Even if he wasn't really sure what would happen to them, he didn't want to alarm her—though he didn't want to shower her with false hopes like he had when her mother, Jocelyn, was on her death bed. Leslie had been only six then. He remembered the scene so vividly; they were at the hospital in south Jersey, where Jocelyn had moved to be closer to relatives in Philadelphia. It was a cold winter Saturday afternoon in January and Jocelyn had been diagnosed with stomach cancer the month before. The doctors had predicted she'd live no more than three months; chemotherapy hadn't worked as effectively as the doctors had hoped and Jocelyn's will to live had diminished completely.

Madrid had held Leslie's hand while she stood by her mother's sickbed, looking more mature than a small child should. She had shown so much courage then, so much understanding. A bright and dignified young girl, Leslie had been fine those three days that Jocelyn was in ICU. But on the fourth day, when Jocelyn's skin was colorless, Leslie panicked and Madrid had never left her side as she broke down and wept uncontrollably. She'd clutched his hand and asked. "Will my mommy die?" Madrid, inexperienced in these situations and at being a well-versed parent, unconsciously blurted, "No, sweetheart. She'll be fine. I promise." As soon as the words left his lips, he'd known it was the wrong way to handle the situation.

Two days later, a day before Leslie's seventh birthday Jocelyn passed away in her sleep. The doctor had phoned him at home. He and Ramona had been married for two years, and she was pregnant with Nathan. He had expected the call but what he hadn't prepared for was how to face Leslie. At first, Leslie hadn't responded to anything; no emotional reaction had surfaced. She was composed until the day of the burial, when she walked up to Madrid after they had left the cemetery and yanked on his hand. He knelt down to meet her gaze.

"See, Daddy," she had said. "Mommy did die. But you didn't know that she was going to die. Did you?"

The question was still very clear in his memory. The pinch he'd felt had penetrated his heart, and almost completely taken his breath away. He'd only wanted to protect his little angel from the pain that inevitably awaited her. Over time, Leslie was able to come to grips with her mother's death and Madrid's broken promise.

Now as he searched those familiar inquisitive eyes that reflected her very soul, Madrid hesitated. He would not promise her something he'd be unable to assure—not anymore. He cleared his throat, then smoothed back the wild strands of hair in her eyes.

"Leslie, I can't guarantee you that Ramona and I won't get a divorce. Marriage is a lot of hard work between two people who love each other. Sometimes things happen between those people and one person has to get away for a break. That's all that's happened with us."

"Will she really come back, Daddy?"

Madrid restrained the immediate urge to respond in the affirmative. Instead, he said, "I believe she will, sweetheart. You said yourself that she'd be home on Sunday, right?"

"Right." She smiled, displaying the rubber band attached to her braces. "I love Mona, Daddy. She's my mommy now, right?"

Madrid took a deep breath, then exhaled. "Right."

Leslie had been through so much already at her tender age that he couldn't bear for her to have to deal with anything else that might cause her pain or rock her stability. *Parenthood,* he thought. *Should be a class offered on it somewhere.* But even if there was a class, certain situations could not be prevented or taught without jumping right in. Case in point, fathers who have to learn how to comb little girls' hair.

The phone jingled again. Madrid sprung up and snatched the cordless phone off the counter.

"Hello?" Part of him wished it would be Ramona. His heart raced as he waited for a response on the other end.

"Hey, what you doing?"

"DeMar?" Madrid replied, disappointed. "Didn't I just bid you farewell a few hours ago?"

"Yeah, so? I'm calling again. I forgot to ask you what your plans are for the basketball game tomorrow night."

"I'll be here with the kids watching the game. Why?"

"I have an idea." The unexpected pause in DeMar's sentence forewarned Madrid.

"Is that so? What's it going to cost me?"

"You need to stop being so damn tight, Drid. I was thinking about bringing two of my friends by tomorrow to watch the game on that large, surround-sound, thirty-inch TV of yours. We could chip in and buy some steaks to throw on the grill. What do you think?"

"This is a first. Hold on a minute and let me get my tape recorder," Madrid teased. "Since when did you start chipping in?"

"I'm serious, man. Listen to me, I'll bring the beer, chips, salad and stuff, and you can spring for the chicken or steaks. How's that sound?"

"Sounds like the see-saw still got my behind sitting pretty high in the air." Madrid paused, taking time to think over his brother's proposal and whether or not he felt up to entertaining guests. "I suppose I could handle it. Just the meat, right?"

"Just the meat, little brother. I've got the rest. See you about two."

Madrid placed the phone in the cradle, then went upstairs to bathe away the sweat and stench of a hard day's work. The steam from the blistering shower fogged the mirror as Madrid slowly undressed. *Body feels tight,* he acknowledged, stepping under the pouring showerhead. He turned the nozzle to the heavy therapy setting, then let the water pummel his shoulders.

He moved them stiffly at first, letting the heat penetrate the muscles. What he could use was one of Mona's powerful massages. His body ached, probably a combination of exhaustion and stress. And malnutrition, defined by most starving husbands as wives who have gone on a food strike; in his case it was due to a wife who'd taken a leave of absence. Since Ramona's departure, Madrid had done his best to fill in the menu with his rusty recipes.

He stepped out of the shower, allowing his soaked feet to saturate the little strip of carpet.

It was one of Ramona's many pet peeves to dry
off before stepping onto the rug. But that was
too bad, he dismissed, because she wasn't here
to care about a soggy bathroom throw rug.

Pizza had served as the main meal Thursday
evening. A mixture of cereal, fruit and toast filled
the kids' stomachs this morning and his famous,
faithful tuna casserole would satisfy their hunger
cries this evening. Madrid threw on a pair of
shorts and an undershirt and headed back downstairs to prepare dinner. The kids were engrossed
in another Disney classic.

Placing a full pot of water on the stove, Madrid
sprinkled in a dash of salt then turned the flames
up high. The macaroni would be done in an in-
stant, which left him little time to get the rest of
the ingredients together. The can of tuna lay on
the countertop. Madrid stood with the refrigerator door open, searching for something to season
the tuna casserole. It had been years since he last
made the dish.

"Let's see," he mumbled, pulling an onion,
some mustard, ketchup, cheese, egg, green and
red pepper out of the fridge. He scanned the refrigerator racks some more. What else should he
add? He frowned, reaching for the relish and mayonnaise. For the next fifteen minutes, Madrid
chopped and mixed and stirred a little bit of each
ingredient in the bowl with the tuna fish before
adding the macaroni. He dumped the mixture in
a glass casserole dish, slid it onto the rack and
turned the oven on to 375 degrees. Twenty minutes should be plenty of time, he determined,
cleaning up his mess.

Feeling proud that he had accomplished what
he deemed a major task—preparing a thoughtful

dinner for his children—Madrid called for the kids.

"Leslie, Nathan, go wash your hands. It's time to eat." While the kids raced to the bathroom, he heaped the hot casserole onto three plates. The kids sat down at the table looking like famished wolves. Madrid sat down with them and recited a quick prayer.

Nathan spoke first. "It stinks, Daddy," he said, turning up his nose.

Madrid chuckled softly. "No, it doesn't, chief. Just try it and see."

"Well, what is it?" Leslie frowned. "It looks disgusting."

"It's tuna casserole," Madrid said defensively. He couldn't remember Nathan telling Ramona that her dinner smelled bad, or Leslie being unable to decipher a main course.

"It looks nasty," Nathan whined.

"We don't like tuna, Daddy. Mona never makes us eat it because it makes me throw up," Leslie told him.

Madrid cringed at the thought. He took in a deep breath then exhaled. "Fine. How about hot dogs and beans then?"

"What 'bout some fried chicken and macaroni and cheese and corn like Mommy makes?" Nathan jubilantly suggested.

Madrid pushed away from the table, hurt that the kids didn't want his casserole. He cleared their plates from the table, still feeling a twinge of disappointment, and placed them in the sink with intentions of washing them later. Trying to make light of the situation, he smiled and teasingly said, "So, you all mean to tell me you'd rather have fried chicken or hot dogs and beans over my tuna casserole?"

Leslie looked at Madrid, then over at Nathan, who shrugged his shoulders. She lowered her eyes for a second before sheepishly looking back at Madrid.

"Or Spam," she replied, before laughing loudly. Nathan giggled along with her. Madrid stood at the dining table shaking his head while his children continued to laugh at him.

Spam, huh? He let his smile erupt into bubbling laughter. Mona should have heard them. Realizing how difficult dealing with kids single-handedly could be, he wished his wife was there to help—everything seemed to run a lot smoother and easier with Ramona around. No matter, he thought, still laughing, he was here, Ramona was not.

Madrid put away the dishes, turned off the lights and headed upstairs to his bedroom. The kids had retired for the evening, after settling on hot dogs and beans. He smiled—that was okay, because tomorrow would be much different, even better. The soot-drenched charcoal grill, his other old faithful, would once again help him prove to everyone that he was indeed the king of this castle.

He let out a long yawn. What good would a king be without a queen? He knew the answer but stubbornly blocked it from his mind. Pettiness. That's what it was all about, he determined, he and Ramona, her in Detroit, him here with the children. The cat and mouse thing. He walked over to the telephone, perched sideways next to the answering machine on the nighttable, cords still unattached and twisted together. Madrid let out a frustrated breath. His behavior—ridiculous. Hers—even more so. He kneeled down to plug the wires back into their respective places. How could two people well into their thirties resort to such childlike behavior? The green light flashed on, as the answering machine clicked a few times before the tape rewound. *Now there's no excuse, Mrs. Shaw,* he thought. *You're welcome to leave a message, as I'm about ready to hear one.*

Nine

Madrid hadn't slept very well, if at all. The phone hadn't rung all night, like he had hoped, even dreamed, if indeed he'd ever truly been asleep. It was 6:45 A.M., too early to be awake for a Saturday morning; 8:30 would have been more appropriate, he thought, rolling over. He'd imagined he'd heard a faint ringing in the distance during the night. Once or twice, he had reached out and lifted the receiver just to check, to make sure that Ramona wasn't on the other end waiting for him to pick up the phone. He had checked the ringer more than twice before retiring for the evening. The dial tone was audible and the answering machine was working, but no calls. Could he have slept through Ramona's calls? It wasn't possible. He hadn't dozed off longer than fifteen, twenty minutes at the most, all night long.

Things were abnormally quiet most of the night. Nathan hadn't stumbled into Madrid's room, Leslie hadn't made her many trips to the bathroom like usual, and Ramona wasn't there to throw her leg across his. Staring at the ceiling, he smoothed the wrinkled sheet absently.

Madrid's mind wandered through thoughts of Ramona. He envisioned that she would pull into the driveway, lug her bags to the door, then insert her house key only to find that the key no longer fit. The locks would be changed or, better yet, he and the kids had left her, as she had left them. That would be justifiably poetic.

Then again, she might walk into the room now, as he lay daydreaming, with a trench coat on, some two-inch cowboy boots, a suede cowboy hat and some scrumptious red lipstick. She would seductively slide out of the dark coat, standing before him naked and ready to make love to him. She'd apologize for her irrational behavior, of course. Then she'd saunter over, lay on top of him, cowboy boots and all, ready to take him, wrestle him down, till he gave in.

Madrid sighed. His manhood had taken on a different posture—a familiar position that only his wife could change. It was 7:45 A.M. and not a sound in the house. Experience warned him that the kids would sleep for at least another two hours. He'd head out to the yard and prune the hedges, maybe even yank some weeds, before making pancakes for them.

He lifted the phone again, listening for the dial tone, and thought about calling Lalah's house. But hadn't he been the last one to reach out? Hadn't he tried to reach Ramona at Poppy's house first? Yes, Ramona had called yesterday evening, but she'd hung up before he had a chance to speak with her. She could have called back. Truly, all that nonsense about her trying to reach him yesterday, what was that lie all about? *She probably did try to call home, but couldn't leave a message because the answering machine wasn't plugged in.* No excuse. She should have tried again.

Well, Ramona would have to call home or come

home sooner or later, he finally resolved. He pulled on a pair of battered, turquoise nylon sweat pants and his worn Satchel Paige t-shirt. His grandfather had given him the shirt fifteen years ago, along with some stories about how Satchel Paige was the greatest pitcher in the Negro league ever to throw the ball.

He rumbled through a dozen pairs of dress shoes and sneakers until he located his worn, holy, Converses. Grass stains and spots of mud decorated the once white sneakers. He tugged them on, purposely neglecting to tie the laces, and went downstairs.

The nylon jogging pants had gotten tighter around his waist and shorter at the bottom since he'd worn them last. He could understand the waist situation—picking up twelve pounds in the last few months could explain the tightness. But the high waters? How could that be? There was no way he could have added another inch or two to his already towering six-three height. Not at thirty-five years of age, anyhow.

From where he stood, the house looked wrecked. Maybe not a true mess, but certainly like Ramona had been absent. There was no way he'd entertain guests, men or not, with his home like this. He would summon the kids to help him clean the place after they had breakfast. Leslie would dust, Nathan would pick up toys, magazines and other little things. Madrid would handle everything else after he trimmed the bushes and possibly cut the grass.

Spring's morning dampness brushed Madrid's face when he opened the door. The grass probably could wait another week, but he'd tackle it today since there wasn't much dew on the

THE GRASS AIN'T GREENER

ground. The garage needed painting, he decided, walking toward the shed attached to the side of it.

He fumbled over the hose before flipping on the light. After locating the pruning shears, rake and lawnmower, he shut the shed door and paused before it, scanning the yard. *Wild.* That's exactly what the yard looked like. The rose bushes were pricking through the fence that separated his yard from his neighbor's. He'd begin with those, then work his way around to the front yard. The one thing he despised most about homeowners, himself included, were out-of-control lawns and hedges.

Madrid was already perspiring and his allergies were threatening to kick up. He sneezed a second time, then a third, which always happened whenever he cut the grass. The short blades of grass had finally been evenly layered and the bushes in the backyard precisely clipped. The front yard proved more bothersome. The street was fairly sedate until his neighbor from across the street, Mrs. Plunkett, drove past him and winked. She was always flirting with him whenever Ramona wasn't around. He smiled and waved back. Rumor had it that she was in her late sixties, although Mrs. Plunkett could easily have passed for her late forties. He prayed that age would be so kind to him and Ramona.

Madrid washed his hands in the kitchen sink, another pet peeve of Ramona's, and looked at the clock—9:47 A.M. He heard the upstairs toilet flush. *Leslie's up,* he thought, until he saw Nathan bouncing down the steps with one of those senseless Power Rangers gripped in his hands. Madrid hated the toys—whatever happened to G.I. Joe and his friends?

"Morning, Daddy."

"Good morning, Nate." Madrid smiled. "You hungry?"

Nathan yawned before responding. "I think so. But I don't want cereal. It makes my stomach hurt."

"It does?" Madrid said. "Well, we're going to have to do something about that. How about we have some pancakes instead this morning?"

Nathan's eyes widened with glee. "Yes! Pancakes! I'll go get Leslie," he said, racing back up the stairs with his pajama britches hanging down almost past his butt.

The phone rang; Madrid reached for it, but stopped when it fell dead abruptly. He lifted the receiver to make sure.

"Hi, B.T.," Leslie was saying on the extension in Madrid's room.

B.T.? Who the hell was that? Madrid stood silently, still holding the phone to his ear.

"Hi, darling," B.T. replied in his adolescent voice. He couldn't have been more than twelve years old, Madrid guessed, and obviously going through the hormone thing because his voice kept fluctuating up and down.

"You told me day before yesterday to call you around nine on Saturday. Were you asleep, sweetheart?" B.T. asked.

Darling? *Sweetheart?* Who the heck was this little dude talking to Leslie like that?

"No, honey," Leslie said in what sounded like a thirty-year-old woman's voice. "I was just about to take me a long bubble bath, then polish my toenails."

Polish her toenails? Since when did Ramona allow her to paint her toes? Madrid questioned silently.

"I saw you on the school playground yesterday during lunch, but I didn't have a chance to come over and say hello. Some of my boys and I were discussing some business opportunities. So let me start by saying hi," B.T. said, trying to sound sexy.

Madrid snickered. How corny. Did he sound that way when he was in the sixth grade, too? He could hear Nathan telling Leslie about the pancakes in the background. Leslie cut off his sentence and shooed him away.

"Get out of here, Nathan," Leslie threatened. "Don't you see I'm on the phone?" Nathan used some underdeveloped expletive before darting out of the room.

B.T. cleared his throat. "So, Truth tells me that you're seeing him. Is that real, Leslie?"

Yeah, Leslie, is it? Madrid wanted to know for himself. His daughter was much too young to be seeing anyone at eleven years old.

Leslie hesitated deliberately, then sighed. "Not really. He just says that because he's trying to stake his claim. You know, spray his territory."

Madrid's mouth dropped open. *Spray his territory?* His daughter wasn't nobody's wandering poodle, much less somebody's property. He couldn't take much more of the conversation— he would have to interrupt. B.T. spoke again before Madrid had a chance to break in.

"Truth don't know much about anything. He's got no game, no business mind, no street wits. You too good for him, Leslie. Besides, he's too young for you. He's in the same sixth grade class with you, right? Peewee," B.T. snuffed. "You need an older man at the middle school like me, a ninth grader. Someone to take care of you. Someone to teach you the ropes, someone who always carries a Trojan in his back pocket."

Leslie giggled senselessly. Madrid saw red.

"Leslie!" Madrid barked. "Hang this phone up right now! B.P., or whatever the hell your name is, don't call here again. You got that?"

"Dad!" Leslie said, petrified. "What are you doing on the phone?"

"Never mind what I'm doing on the phone, what are you doing on the phone? Matter of fact, hang the phone up and come downstairs right now!"

The line went silent. B.T. hung up first, then Leslie. Madrid was incensed.

"Yes, Daddy?" Leslie said from the landing. "B.T. is my friend." She was already defensive.

Madrid looked his daughter over thoroughly, noticing the two little chestnuts evident through her pajama top. Were those breasts she was starting to develop? Had Ramona discussed menstruation with her? Sex? He took in a deep breath and motioned for her to take a seat at the kitchen table. He remained standing.

"Leslie," he said softly. "I'm sorry for listening in on your conversation. I know that wasn't necessarily the right thing to do. Sometimes parents do things that don't seem right to you at the time, but in the long run it's in your best interest."

She stared up at him blankly, waiting for the rest of the lecture. She said nothing, refusing to acknowledge her father's apology. She was too embarrassed and mad. She felt betrayed.

"Who is this boy, B.P. or B.T.—whatever his name is?" Madrid finally said.

"B.T.," she corrected. "He goes to my school." She nervously twisted her hair, eyes averted.

"What's this B.T.'s real name?" Madrid took a seat down beside her.

"Barry Taylor," she confessed. "He's just my friend, Dad."

Dad? So now I'm just plain old Dad? What happened to, Daddy? Madrid kept silent. Already a sudden sharp, unexpected turn onto Preteen Avenue. *She's growing up too quickly. What can I do about it?* He sighed again.

"I understand that, Leslie. And it's good to have both girls and boys as friends. But don't you think he's a little bit too old for you?" He was trying his best to handle the situation, although he wasn't sure if he was doing a good job. For a split second, he wished Ramona was there to help him.

"Dad, he just turned fourteen last week. I'm eleven-and-a-half. I'll be twelve in nine months. It's only two years' difference, really."

"Actually, it's three years. In any case, he's too young to be carrying a condom in his pocket and telling you about it. What do you know about condoms?" Madrid leaned back in his chair, waiting for his daughter to answer. How much did she know about sex anyway?

Leslie shrugged her shoulders. Madrid didn't say much more after that; it looked like another botched attempt at handling a sensitive issue with Leslie. Ramona was so good at those things—so much better than him.

Madrid stood up. "Do you want some pancakes, Leslie?" He walked into the kitchen; perhaps she'd feel less intimidated if he wasn't sitting directly in front of her.

"Yes, please," she answered methodically. "May I go upstairs and wash up now, Dad?"

There was that *Dad* again. He much preferred Daddy. There was something innocent and youthful about it. If he didn't know better, it sounded like Father would be the next choice. Probably when she got her first real boyfriend and her first experience with . . . He couldn't bring himself to even think about that. Nathan's wild laugh snapped him out of the inevitable future.

"Dad?" Leslie asked again. "Can I go up and take my shower now?"

"Sure, sure. I'll have your pancakes ready when you come down." He mixed more batter in the bowl. "Your Uncle DeMar and two of his friends are coming over later this afternoon. I need you and Nathan to help me clean up the house, okay?"

She nodded and stood up, pushing her chair under the table.

"Oh, Leslie," Madrid called.

"Yes, Dad?"

"You're not really going to paint your toenails, are you?"

"No way, Dad," she giggled. "I just told B.T. that. It sounded cool. Anyway, Ramona won't let me polish anything but the furniture."

By 12:10 P.M. Madrid was exhausted. He couldn't recall working so hard since his high school years, when he'd held a summer job as a package boy at his father's plant. Sweat dripped down the side of his face as he placed the heavy grocery bags into the back of the Jeep. Sixty-four dollars spent for some packs of chicken and Porterhouse steaks.

For some reason, he still felt like DeMar had ended up, as usual, with the better part of the deal. What was he thinking, going to Pathmark on a Saturday morning? The lines in the grocery store were out of control, damn near down the aisles, not to mention how irritable everyone from the shoppers to the cashiers were. It would have been worse had he taken the kids with him, he thought, stopping at the traffic light. But since Leslie was eleven-and-a-half years old, as she so often corrected him, he figured he could chance leaving her and Nathan home for an hour or so.

Madrid stumbled through the door breathing rapidly, clutching three plastic bags by their scrawny handles. He dropped the bags on the kitchen counter and saw that Leslie was dressed and dusting the family room. Nathan was also fully clothed and picking up his toys and books.

"Did you bring us a treat, Daddy?" Nathan whined.

"No, little man, I didn't have time. But we're going to have some delicious steaks later. How's that sound?"

"All right," Leslie chimed in. Nathan veered toward the bags, peering hopelessly, wishing for a treat.

"We straightened the house so when Mona gets home she won't have to," Leslie said. "I folded the clothes in the basket for Mona, too." Leslie lowered her eyes. "Mona is going to come back, right Dad?"

"You said she'd be back Sunday," Madrid replied, smiling. "And she'll appreciate coming home to a clean house. It looks good, guys. Thank you. So go ahead and relax, Leslie."

Madrid rinsed his hands and wiped them on

the dishcloth hanging from the handle of the refrigerator. Snatching off the clear plastic wrap en-
casing the chicken and steaks, he washed the
meat thoroughly, patting it dry before marinating
it with his secret sauce.

The sauce would need at least two hours to
soak through the meat before putting it on the
grill or it wouldn't taste as good. He glanced at
the clock—12:50 P.M. It would be 2:50 before the
grill singed the meat. Tough—they'd have to wait.
After all, his reputation was at stake.

"I can vacuum if you want me to," Leslie told
Madrid. She was still feeling the urge to chip in.
The thought of Ramona not coming back because she and Nathan wouldn't do their chores
frightened her. She wanted to help make the
house sparkle for Ramona—so that she wouldn't
ever have to leave again.

"Thanks, honey, but I'll do it. Let me get the
meat situated first." He looked at her. "Did you
comb your hair?" He knew the answer before she
even spoke.

"Yes," Leslie lied in her best dignified voice—
although her hair was clumped together in some
areas and spiked in others like a porcupine.

"After I finish up here," Madrid promised.
"I'm going to damp mop the kitchen and bathroom floors, vacuum, and unload the dishwasher.
I want you all to straighten up your rooms if you
haven't already. Okay?"

The kitchen floor winded Madrid. He couldn't
believe how difficult it was to remove grit, grime,
cherry juice stains, pizza drippings and Lord
knew what else from the streaked tiled floor. The
floor in the half bathroom downstairs was less

overwhelming, although the ring inside the toilet
bowl required a little elbow grease.

Ten minutes and several adjustments into the
vacuuming process, he realized why the machine
refused to suck up the dirt; the bag needed
changing. He tossed and tugged, pulled and
yanked, until not only was the bag free from the
vacuum, but the contents of the bag as well. The
heap of dirt and dust on the carpet caused him
to curse Ramona aloud. *She should have known the
bag need changing!*

The tussle finally ended, Madrid stood in his
second favorite spot in the house—under the hot
shower nozzle. He would have preferred his first
choice—his king-sized bed—but it was 1:49 P.M.
DeMar and his buddies would be arriving any
minute. Madrid shut his eyes. The water soothed
him while he lathered his hair a second time.
Foaming soapsuds tickled his forehead as they
drizzled down toward the drain.

Images of washing Leslie's head floated
through his mind. Ramona should really be com-
mended, he acknowledged inwardly. How did she
manage to wash Leslie's hair anyway? In sections?
How often? How long did the chore take? Did
Leslie scream and yell the way she had with him?
He would do something about Leslie's hair
soon—real soon.

Stepping onto the green throw rug again, he
realized that it was still damp from last night's
shower. He dried his hair quickly, using the other
small hand towel to absorb the excess water.

The door bell chimed. Probably DeMar, Madrid
thought. He pulled himself together, quickly ignoring his appearance. Knowing DeMar's friends,
his worst appearance was usually far more appeal-

ing and appropriate than theirs. Madrid slid into
his creaseless jeans shorts, a partially pressed
white polo, and a pair of dull, worn leather loafers before hurrying downstairs.

DeMar had cajoled the remote control from
Leslie and was flipping channels savagely as the
children grumbled in protest. Madrid reached
the bottom step and rounded the corner, eyes
immediately fixed on the two guests sitting on
the love seat.

Madrid blinked twice. What was this? Not two
of DeMar's roguish, testosterone-bulging male
friends, but two fine, sensual women silently surveying their surroundings. They were obviously
of mixed heritage, Madrid observed, likely Puerto
Rican and black. He let out a quiet breath, suddenly self-conscious and somewhat uncomfortable about his appearance. He should have
pressed his shirt, maybe even put on his Roman
leather sandals instead. Too late now—the dam-
age had been done. Nothing like a first impression. He smiled stiffly, making his way into the
family room.

"Drid," DeMar sang, standing some two inches
shorter than his younger brother. "I want you to
meet my two friends." He pointed toward the
love seat. "This beautiful lady is Connie."

Connie extended her hand and smiled broadly.
Her lips were smothered with bright orange lip
color, accentuating her deep, copper-penny complexion. She was heavier and shorter than the
woman sitting to her left. "Pleased to meet you,"
she told Madrid. He shook her hand.

"The pleasure is mine," Madrid replied. Then
his gaze shifted to the other woman with the tight
posture and conservative apparel.

"Lovely children, too," Connie told him.

"Thank you." Madrid smiled easily then glanced at the kids. They were engrossed in some imaginary game.

"And this lovely lady is Connie's sister, Alyson. Alyson, this is my brother Madrid." DeMar enunciated more slowly than necessary.

"Madrid," Alyson repeated before standing. "Nice city. Our great-grandfather was from there." She shook his hand, eyeing him thoroughly.

Fine little thing. Madrid smiled, returning the firm shake. Definitely a businesswoman, he thought. The handshake was well rehearsed and strong. Her hands weren't as soft as Connie's, though her professional manicure was more precise. And so were a couple of other things, he acknowledged.

"No history there on our side of the family that I'm aware of," Madrid responded, flashing a brilliant smile.

Alyson gave him a curt grin, the kind meant to substitute for a sarcastic remark. She resumed her position next to Connie, giving her a sly nudge on the arm. Madrid looked at DeMar, who had turned his attention back to the TV.

"Daddy, tell Uncle DeMar to stop flipping through the channels so fast. He's not supposed to," Nathan said, plopping down on the floor in front of the TV, his lips poked out.

"He's an adult, Nathan," Leslie chimed in. "You can't tell him what to do. Right, Dad?"

"Right, honey," Madrid told her. "Give it a minute, DeMar. Don't worry, we won't miss the game."

DeMar was silent, his gaze fervently glued to the screen.

"Would you ladies like something to drink?" Madrid asked.

"Sure," Connie replied happily. "What do you have?"

Alyson didn't respond. Her attention had been drawn to the children.

Madrid moved into the kitchen. "I have Pepsi, iced tea, beer, wine coolers, water . . ."

"I'll have a wine cooler, please," Connie told him. "Alyson, what you drinking?"

"Water, please, for now," Alyson told Madrid before switching her gaze back to Leslie. Absolutely striking young child, she thought, but a little crazy about the hair. She looked like a wild shaggy dog.

"I know the pre-game show should be on now," DeMar said, pounding through the remote buttons. "The paper said 2:15, channel four. Or was it seven?" He flipped anxiously between the two channels. "Shaw! What time is the game supposed to start?"

"Three o'clock, I think. Check the preview guide on channel 35."

"Shaw?" Alyson said, with a furrowed brow and a slightly elevated voice. "Not as in *Mr.* Madrid Shaw from CTT Telecommunications Corp.?" She was on the edge of the sofa now.

"Ah, well, yes," Madrid replied, not sure what to expect.

Alyson sprung up from the leather love seat so swiftly that it squeaked. "I'm Alyson Rivera. The woman you've canceled with twice." She strode into the kitchen, staring at Madrid peculiarly. "If I had known the only way to meet with you was at your house, I would have worn a suit and dragged my credentials with me."

A crass remark, no doubt, but Madrid resisted the urge to become defensive. He let out a visible sigh and winced, drawing back his cheeks until his clamped teeth showed. "Alyson Rivera. Yes, Bridget did tell me you were inconvenienced. I apologize. Things got so involved at the office. There was . . ." He stopped. *Excuses are nothing but procrastination in an individual*—that's what his grandfather had told his father and his father had passed on to him. "I just couldn't get my bearings," he said. "No excuse for my lack of professionalism. I apologize, Alyson."

Alyson nodded, but she was detached and unmoved by Madrid's rambling, her irritation brewing deep down. She would try to tread more carefully, however—the possibility of landing the job had not been totally eliminated, unless Bridget had lied to him about their phone conversation.

"Finally! I found the pre-game show," DeMar was yelling from the family room. "You need some help getting things going, Shaw? My stomach's crying."

As a matter of fact Madrid did need help. He needed DeMar to explain the bizarre coincidence that his buddies were not only women, but one of them was interviewing with CTT.

"Yeah, you can start the grill for me," Madrid called back. "We'll be ready to eat in an hour or so." He put the containers of salad and coleslaw that DeMar had left on the counter into the refrigerator, rolling his eyes in agitation. DeMar was always so damn helpless. Really, not enough sense to put the containers into the refrigerator? *Come on,* Madrid thought, shutting the refrigerator door.

"You mean you haven't gotten the coals going yet?" DeMar was saying as he walked into the kitchen. "Where's the matches?"

"In the top drawer next to the stove. Where they've always been," Madrid told him. "Hey De-Mar, did you know about Alyson and CTT?"

"What?" DeMar replied, head buried in the drawer.

"See, she's been trying to meet with me about the project manager position and I had to re-schedule the last two days."

"Is that right?" DeMar offered, heading out of the kitchen. "Nathan, you want to help me get the grill together? You can load the coals."

"Yes," Nathan sang joyously.

Madrid fumbled about the kitchen for a while longer, while Alyson looked on.

"Do you need some help in here?" she finally asked.

"No, thank you," he said, handing her a glass of water. "Leslie, come here for a minute, please."

Leslie took her time reaching the kitchen, dragging her feet.

"Yes, Dad?"

"Take this wine cooler into Ms. Connie for me, will you? Thanks." Madrid handed her the cold bottle. Leslie grabbed it and disappeared again.

"Alyson, you never did acknowledge whether you accepted my apology or not. Have you?" Madrid questioned.

She had taken a seat at the counter, resigned to watching the man that she might have worked with. Elusive, that was the feeling she got about

Madrid Shaw. Evasive and elusive. She only guessed it had something to do with his position—his many years of climbing the corporate ladder, rung by rung.

"I accept your apology," she said, knowing full well she deserved much more than a rhetorical apology. Who knew? Perhaps it was just the blessing she needed to help restructure her career. She decided to go for it. "Perhaps you could share some details about the position."

"We're looking to expand our new product line into Mexico and South America," Madrid said. "We need somebody familiar with the telecommunications industry as a whole, someone with related marketing experience, and someone who can speak the language fluently to make sure the product is up and running. We need a dedicated individual to troubleshoot complex situations and make on-the-spot decisions if necessary." He had his back to her, basting the meat one last time.

This could be an in, Alyson thought, *perhaps an offer of some type.* She had never had an interview outside of a plush corporate setting. Golf had never served its purpose, even after she'd learned to putt through an eighteen-hole game. And the sauna would never have been appropriate with her being the only female. Alyson straightened her posture.

"I have my MBA from the University of Chicago. I worked as a project manager for four years with HP, assisting them with their operations in Puerto Rico, my home. I speak four languages, I'm available for site transfers, extended or permanent, depending on the company's needs, I'm drug free and I have numerous references. Besides that, I'm unattached—divorced. Nothing keeping me here."

Madrid turned to face her. *Four languages? MBA from the University of Chicago? Divorced?* She had all the makings of a senior project manager. At least she hadn't received her MBA from the University of Michigan—that would have choked him outright. The job should be hers.

His mind wandered. *She's a sister struggling to make it. She has all the right credentials. I'm in a position to help her. And after all, I deliberately left her hanging. This would be a good way to make amends. Nobody else seemed as eager and determined to come on board.*

"We're thinking $48-55 thousand plus perks, benefits and expenses. Four weeks vacation, a 401k dollar-for-dollar match up to ten percent and a signing bonus." He let the sentence hang in the air. It was her turn.

She grinned cautiously, still businesslike. One one thousand, two one thousand . . . She couldn't be too anxious. Fifty-five thousand? Not too shabby at all. *Good Lord, if they're willing to pay me that, his position must pay close to six figures.* Her heart beat louder, and she could feel her cheeks growing warm at the thought of an offer. Would he notice her flushed cheeks through her almond complexion? She hoped not. Ten one thousand. Time enough, she decided.

"What kind of signing bonus are we speaking of?"

Madrid grinned diabolically. Got her! He cleared his throat. "There's some heavy travel plans abroad, as well. Is that something that could hinder you?"

"Like I mentioned earlier, I'm a divorced

mother of zero. He couldn't respect or support
my contributions to the household, nor could his
children. Or my dreams to be an individual outside of the marriage."

"You divorced him for that?" It was an inap-
propriate question, he knew. He never would
have gotten away with that had he been sitting
behind his desk. Ramona flashed across his mind.
Would she divorce him for the same reason? After
all, wasn't that what their disagreement had been
about? Something about contributions and respect and support, and blah, blah, blah? It was
all so foggy now.

"Yes, I did," Alyson replied. "And I would do
it again if necessary. No offense. But I'm not an
advocate of marriage. Catholicism, yes. Marriage?
No more. And I don't care if I ever reconcile the
two." Her voice became more rigid. The question
had definitely been a wrong turn.

Madrid hurried back to the previous issue.
"About the signing bonus. I can only say once
you've officially accepted the position."

"Have I officially been offered the position?"
she replied with a raised brow, her eyes as dark
and keen as a cat.

"Why, of course." He smiled steadily. Ramona
would have done the same thing. In fact, she had
with her previous employer when they'd offered
her the promotion.

"Then of course, I accept." She let her tightened grin relax into a full smile.

Madrid grabbed the pan with the meat and
walked toward the back door, signaling her to
come along. Alyson got up and followed behind.
For some reason, she reminded him of Ramona.
The way she kept her reserve, her steadiness—it

was one of the things he loved about Mona. He reached the screen door and popped the handle open with his elbow. Looking back over his shoulder at Alyson he said, "Ten thousand dollars. Payable after the reference check and drug test."

Ten

Ramona glided the ivory chess piece to a screeching diagonal halt. The queen sat proudly on a light parquet square. The onyx king had been hemmed in by the ivory rook and bishop.

"Checkmate," Ramona announced. She leaned back in her chair with a conquering smile. It had been years since she had beat Poppy in a game of chess, and Poppy gazed at the board, stupefied. But competition didn't allow for playing favorites. Granddaughter or not, pupil or not, Poppy was thrilled that his granddaughter had been able to wheel her way around the board so successfully.

"Well, I do say," Poppy said. "Suppose I was 'bout do for a whooping, huh? All them years of teaching finally caught up to me. Good job, my lamb." Poppy shuffled his feet across the carpet a few times, as if trying to get his bearings before standing. His tattered, backless brown slippers were another of his trademarks. "Say, angel," he said, picking up his pipe from the ashtray on the mantelpiece, "you want some of Sophia's black bean soup? She and that friend of hers dropped me off some supper last night." Ramona stood up and trailed behind him into the kitchen.

"Sophia came by here with Frankie?"

"Yeah, that there is the girl's name. Frankie. What a weird name for a woman. A weird situation, period. I told her, I say listen here, I don't like bean soup that much, especially with no meat. She looked at me sideways, cut me one of them devilish grins and told me. 'Poppy, me and Sophia be sure to put you some meat in there next time.' That's what she went and said to me." Poppy tugged on the refrigerator door until it finally opened. He fussed something under his breath before pulling out the bowl of left-over soup.

Ramona watched him. She was worried about Poppy wandering around the house all by himself, getting into Lord knew what. Sometimes his thoughts seemed to scatter, then, like nothing had happened, he'd sway back to the conversation at hand. It was normal, Ramona supposed. Poppy was in his late seventies, after all. She took a seat at the old powder blue and white-speckled table with its strong steel legs. All these years and many dinners later, it still looked like it was right out of a 1950s TV show.

"This here icebox going to be the death of me," Poppy was saying. "I told Coral before she died that we needed a new icebox But she was so darn-blasted stubborn and cost-efficient, she refused. I suppose I'm just going have to boil her out when I see her up there in the clouds. I'm gonna say Coral, why the hell you leave me here with a damn icebox door that jam all the time? She never had no problems getting in and out of this piece of junk." He slammed the door shut.

"Poppy, you aren't going anywhere yet. You're

going to stay right down here with me, at least until I can whoop you in three or four more games of chess." Ramona snickered.

"Well, then. I suppose I'll be down here forever, cause it's highly unthinkable you'll get me again. In this decade, anyhow." They both laughed. Poppy filled the pot with some soup and placed it on the front ring of the enormous white gas stove. "Now there," he continued, pulling a chair out from the table and sitting down. "What you think of Frankie?"

Ramona rounded her eyes comically at Poppy. What he thought of Frankie was more the question. "How come you didn't say anything to me earlier, Poppy?"

He peered at her—a serious glare from over his spectacles—then shrugged. "Figured you'd find out sooner or later on your own. It's your aunt's place to tell you she's one of them homosexuals. Not mine."

"You could have given me a warning. I mean, here we are in the middle of a conversation in her kitchen discussing some person named Frankie. I'm thinking wow, Sophia's finally met a nice brother, she's going to cook for him, and *bam!* The doorbell rings and she drops the ball in my lap and says Frankie's her *lover.*" Ramona gazed past Poppy toward the kitchen window. The sun was beginning to position itself west. She raised from her seat and flipped on the kitchen light; a fluorescent tube hesitated for a few seconds then flickered on.

"Child, what you mean by turning on the light this time of day? It's only 6 o'clock. What you meaning to see at this moment?" Poppy huffed. He was on a fixed income, and to him turning on

the kitchen light in May before 8 P.M. was ludicrous. "It's a good thing you're visiting. I got a
good mind to tell you to turn that darn light off."

He looked up at the faded cover protecting the
long tubes of light, squinting over his eyeglasses
and turning his nose upward. "Got to wash that
thing. Coral would have had a fit."

Poppy shook his head and let out a defeated
sigh. "Do me a favor, angel, and check the soup.
Poppy getting too old, too tired, to be bothered
with other people's business. We're all where
we're supposed to be in our lives. You remember
that, you hear me, angel? Ain't nothing in life by
chance. God ties all our experiences together for
a reason. We just have to ask him for clarity.
That's all."

Lalah knocked on the bedroom door. Ramona
still hadn't finished dressing. She couldn't decide
between the red Tahari dress Lalah had laid on
her bed or the black and white sheer pantsuit.

"Come in," Ramona called. She was putting on
her last bit of makeup. Charcoal and chocolate
eye shadow highlighted by black liner comple-
mented her eyes, and a dab of rust cheek color
dotted her face. Russian red lipstick touched off
her lips.

"You're still getting dressed?" Lalah scolded
playfully. "We won't be on time at the rate you're
going. Let's move it. I don't want to be late meeting Drew because of your snail-moving butt." She
laughed. "Then again, I bet Ronnie won't mind
just as long as you show up."

Ramona purposely ignored Lalah's last comment. "You look astounding as always, sis."

"Thank you very much," Lalah said, spinning around, then bowing. "Green becomes me."

Obviously, Ramona thought. She couldn't remember a time when Lalah had humbled herself before a compliment, or in any way, except when she'd pledged AKA years ago. Pledging was a humbling experience for everyone.

"Come on, girl. Put some pep in your step," Lalah fussed.

"I'm doing the best I can, Lalah. Relax. Besides, shouldn't we at least wait until Gordon leaves before we step out?" She faced the large wall mirror, holding up both outfits.

"The red dress," Lalah offered. "You can look real Delta Sigma Theta-like tonight. Anyway, he says he's not going out tonight. Mentioned something about coming with us."

"Coming with us? God, Lalah, he must suspect we're up to something." She felt faint. "I don't feel good about this. What did you tell him?"

"I told him it was your last night here and it was going to be a girls' night out, just me, you and Sophia."

"Sophia? Sophia never hangs out. She's too busy heading up some political campaign or attending some ski trip or shoe sale. A nightclub? He's got to suspect we're lying."

"Ramona you're *so* dramatic. It's going to be fine. Now, would you please slide your behind into that dress? There's nothing to worry about, really. I told him we're going to Franklin's Place for a down-home soul food dinner first, then to hear some jazz. And if we're up to it, maybe The Currency Exchange for some dancing. I bought us seven or eight hours. He won't suspect a thing. Me and Drew will be doing our thing, and you've

got the car phone number. I'll give you Drew's
pager number too in case anything goes wrong
with you and Ronnie's date."

"It's hardly a date, Lalah!" Ramona responded
harshly. "It's just two old friends getting together
to share dinner and perhaps some jazz, that's *all.*
I hardly came here to go on a date. I came here
to rest, in case you forgot." She pulled on her
pantyhose fiercely.

"In case *you* forgot, Ramona, it's okay to have
dinner with a friend that seems to be very smitten
with you. I don't blame you for wanting to hear
more accolades—you deserve it. I mean, if Madrid is unable to give you the attention and affection you need, there's nothing wrong with
someone else doing it." Lalah winked.

Ramona expelled a deep breath before meeting Lalah's gaze. "You're right. Maybe I am getting a little carried away by all the wonderful
things Ronnie said to me the other night. Maybe
I even wish I was hearing them from my own husband. But the fact of the matter is, he's still a
very dear friend that I want to spend some time
catching up. That's all, Lalah, really. I love Madrid and there's no way that I would ever jeop-
ardize my marriage for Ronnie."

"Yeah, okay," Lalah said languidly, waving her
hand at her and taking a seat in the wing-back
chair. "You're too uptight."

"Lalah, I'm telling you now, don't have me out
all night. And I don't want to have a problem
finding you later. It's bad enough I agreed to re-
linquish my mobility to you and Ronnie. I'd probably feel much better if Ronnie came with me in
the Benz and you went with Drew—that way I
could have an out if I needed it. I don't like de-

pending on riding with Ronnie while you're traipsing off with Drew somewhere."

Ramona smoothed her hands over the dress, took one final look in the mirror, and descended the spiral staircase with Lalah beside her. She hoped that Gordon was in his room or his office—that way she wouldn't have to face him, or lie to him, if he asked about their plans. But no such luck—Gordon and that bald head of his were sitting at the kitchen counter reviewing some documents.

He looked up with heavy, arched brows from behind his black-framed bifocals, examining them. His eyes took in Lalah's physique from head to toe before his eyes shifted to Ramona. A heat flash attacked her. She was on stage, no doubt.

"You all be cautious tonight." Gordon spoke through pursed lips, eyes surveying Lalah again. "Perhaps you should grab a jacket, dear." There was that fraudulent honey-dear crap oozing again. "You might get chilly in that sleeveless top."

If Lalah had turned her back to him, he would have noticed the sequined top was backless, as well. But Lalah didn't turn, facing him steadily.

"I have one in the car," Lalah told him before opening the door to the garage. She motioned for Ramona to walk ahead. "Don't wait up. We'll probably stop off for breakfast before we come home."

A malicious smile spread Lalah's berry-colored lips before she shut the door behind her. Ramona turned to face her, speechless, but Lalah purposely looked away as they got into the car.

Madrid crumbled the aluminum foil into a tight ball before tossing it into the plastic garbage

can. Pow! Two points! DeMar lay sideways on the
love seat, cooing to Connie about God knew
what. He should have been in the kitchen helping
Madrid straighten up—in fact, Madrid thought
he could have helped out more today, period.

However, DeMar always found a way out of any
situation requiring work or money. The lightning
bolt had finally struck Madrid between the eyes.
DeMar was a parasite. How unnerving. Ramona
had tried to warn him many times over, but he
hadn't listened.

Leslie and Nathan had gone upstairs to prepare
for bed. Earlier in the afternoon, Connie couldn't
resist the temptation to comment on Leslie's hair.
"It's just so thick and out there," she had told
Madrid. "A lot of young girls come into the salon
with the same problem. Trust me, honey. I'm an
owner of a hair salon. Braids would tame it
down—do the trick," she suggested.

A few minutes later, Connie had committed to
braiding Leslie's hair in the morning. Bright and
early, she'd told Leslie. Four hours of sitting in
one spot to have her hair braided seemed cruel
to both Madrid and Leslie, but Connie swore it
would be worth it in the long run. Leslie had
hesitantly agreed.

Alyson stood beside Madrid in the kitchen, assisting with the clean-up. Her personality had
warmed as the day unfolded. It was probably safe
to assume it had a lot to do with her newly ac-
quired position.

"Will your wife be back soon?" Alyson asked Madrid, a question she'd been anxious to pose all
day.

"Yes," was all he cared to say. He placed the
left-over pieces of chicken in a Tupperware con-

tainer, then began the painstaking search for a matching lid, preferring not to engage in conversation about Ramona's whereabouts.

Alyson caught the drift, asking for another bowl for the remaining potato salad. They worked silently through the kitchen, slowly piecing it back together, although Madrid wasn't really comfortable having some other woman shadowing him in his wife's kitchen. But what the hell? It wasn't like Ramona was standing right there with them. No, in fact, she had chosen to leave them, taking off with some sudden, unexplained need to visit home.

Madrid exhaled hard. He knew Alyson was catching the brunt of his coolness, but that was too bad. His morning had started with the roosters and had stretched into a long, busy day. Retiring for the night was his only concern at the moment. He yawned a second time, mumbling a faint "Thank you" under his breath.

"You're welcome," Alyson told him before walking into the family room, where her sister and DeMar lay snuggled on the sofa. "I think we should be going now, Connie." Alyson slid her hands into the back pockets of her baggy jeans. "Madrid seems exhausted. We better go."

"Oh, ain't nothing wrong with that boy," DeMar slurred. "He doesn't mind us staying longer just as long as we let ourselves out." Part of his body hung off the side of the sofa. "Right, Shaw?" DeMar yelled toward the kitchen. Madrid didn't respond.

"Well, I don't know about you all, but I'm pretty tired myself. I've been up since the crack of dawn helping Mama get the house together. Come on, Connie." Alyson urged again. "Vamos."

Connie untangled herself from DeMar and got off the sofa, stumbling slightly from too many wine coolers. Alyson placed a strong hand on her arm in an attempt to steady her sway. "I've got you, Connie."

Alyson hooked her arm through Connie's arm and led her toward the front door. DeMar stumbled up and followed, leaning more to one side than the other.

"What a nice time," he sang out. "Thanks, Drid. We must do it again sometime. 'Specially with your watchdog gone," he snickered childishly before stepping outside. Madrid ignored the intended insult. Right then, he just wanted them gone. He stood in the doorway, ignoring more gibberish from DeMar before calling out to Alyson, "Are you driving?"

"Yes," she replied, never looking back at him—Connie's rubbery legs and heavy body needed all of her attention. "We'll be fine."

"Then I'll see you on Tuesday, Ms. Rivera. Don't be late," Madrid teased.

Her head held high, Alyson pretended not to hear Madrid's ribbing, chuckling softly under her breath. *Some nerve.*

Upstairs, Madrid lay in bed feeling the day's strenuous activities vibrating through his body. His lower back had that dull, throbbing sensation again and his biceps and shoulderblades yearned for an application of Ben Gay. He turned over onto his left side. His sleep would be undisturbed this night for sure.

DeMar's whispered comment earlier in the evening ruffled Madrid. DeMar said he was finally serious enough to marry. Why would he get married at this stage in his life? When DeMar was in his early thirties, Madrid could have understood. Although, back in the day, DeMar never mentioned marriage except in a derogatory manner. He always teased Madrid, saying, "Men who get married are punks. I'm never going out like that. Never."

But now he'd consider marriage? For what? Why would any woman really want to deal with his trifling ways? He no longer sported the young, rock-hard body that used to drive the women wild, his exercising routine getting lost somewhere between the Lindas and Sheilas and Debras and Cynthias. And the dark circles beneath his eyes were a clear sign that he had boogie-woogie-oogied till he just couldn't do it no more.

If he'd had more time, if he had been even remotely prepared, Madrid would have told his brother not to bother—that his life might be more fulfilling the way it was, with no special somebody to get involved with only to sit by later and watch them depart, ungrateful and unappreciative. Yes, he would have cautioned against opening his heart, allowing someone in to discover all the weaknesses, quirks and insecurities. He would have asked, what was the rush to marry now? He would have advised him that his system seemed to be working fine and perhaps he should leave well enough alone. But DeMar had not given him a chance, a moment to warn him, before he teetered down the clay-colored cement steps, sniffing behind Connie like some canine in heat.

Madrid sneezed forcefully, his ears popping and his rib cage bunching while he waited for the attack to pass on. Allergies—always hovering around this time of the year, bugging the mess out of him and Nathan.

Sliding the damp pillow from under his head, he reached for Ramona's. Tossing his pillow to the foot of the bed, he tucked hers under his head. The floral aroma of freesias and rubrum lilies tickled his nose—definitely one of her designer perfumes. He cuddled the pillow closer, burying his face further down into its softness as he would have done if it had been her breasts, inhaling more of her intoxicating scent. Oh, how he wished she was there. Even through all that had taken place over the past few days, Madrid still yearned for his wife.

Ramona stood still, clinching both elbows, drawing them closer to her rib. A chill shuddered down her spine—not from the damp, dewy night, but more of a nervous, uncontrolled twitch. Ronnie locked the car door then turned to face her, his broad body erect and bold, cloaked in a designer suit patterned with thin navy and lime green swirls.

"You're so gorgeous," he told Ramona in a smooth, soft voice, holding the door to the Ristorante open for her. He barely towered over her. "I always knew red was your color."

"Thank you," Ramona said nervously. *I shouldn't even be here.* What would people think, with her dodging off like she had, leaving her family behind to meet her ex-college sweetheart for dinner? But how was she to know she'd bump into Ronnie Ware during her excursion? Steadily, she sauntered ahead of him, hoping that the three-inch pumps she'd chosen would not make her knees wobble. It had been years, at the very least two, since she'd sashayed around in heels while being surveyed by some man.

Mr. Fudichelli, the maître'd, a short, stocky man with an unusually red, jolly face and an even more jovial attitude, led them to a tucked-away table near the window. The Detroit River was visible through the windows. The pianist sat in the middle of the rustic Italian restaurant, honoring requests from enthusiastic patrons. Just then "My Funny Valentine" flowed from the white baby grand. Mr. Fudichelli pulled Ramona's chair out from the tiny table for two. He slid her toward the table, then snatched up the burnt orange napkin dramatically, snapping it in the air before placing it on her lap.

Ronnie allowed the waiter to rattle off the evening's specials—chicken florentine, veal marsala and garlic shrimp in pesto sauce—before speaking, then ordered a bottle of vintage red wine, despite Ramona's protests. Swinging his jacket over the back of his chair, he crossed his left leg over his right and leaned back easily in his seat. Umm, umm, he thought, staring at Ramona with the familiar sparkle in his eyes. Still got that pretty neck, he silently admitted. He let his eyes scan the V-neck crepe and wool dress, pausing at her breasts before looking into her face.

"I love the new haircut, Ramona. Very classy." He grinned.

"Thank you. A far cry from the other night, huh?" She grinned.

"Um hmm," he replied with a suggestively arched brow.

Ramona immediately wedged her hands under her thighs and slid her feet across the white, plush carpet, her heart rate elevated. All the compliments were about to drive her crazy. She couldn't believe it—all those years ago she had dreamed of something like this happening with her and Ronnie. Only she hadn't pictured him looking so distinguished, so sexy, with a dash of salt-and-pepper in his hair. Sitting before him, she had to struggle to remember the reasons for their break-up.

The massive personality change during Ronnie's last year of college was one of the reasons for their split, Ramona recalled. He had become too obsessed with fame, glitz and glamour. His ego became unbearable and the increased battle with his womanizing intolerable. After graduation, he'd headed for Kansas City to play professional football, where he immediately met the woman who would later be his wife. It had been a long time since things had been like they were tonight.

"Everything on the menu is a true delight," he said once the waiter had walked away. He sniffed twice. "May I suggest the shrimp and crab with angel hair pasta? It has your favorite. Alfredo sauce, if I remember correctly." He smiled coyly.

Ramona glanced up from her menu just long enough to acknowledge his smile. His eyes were still dangerously alluring, though tired and puffy, leaving him looking more average than she could ever recall.

Of course, he would remember correctly. He had taken her to an Italian restaurant in Ann Arbor, Michigan, for their first date. She fell in love with both Ronnie Ware and fettucine alfredo that harsh, winter night. She focused once again on the Italian and English menu. The duck in lemon pepper sauce tickled her fancy.

"I've given up on alfredo sauce," she grinned

before closing the menu. "I think the duck sounds like the winner."

"Filet mignon for me, as usual." Ronnie closed his menu. Reaching across the table, he grabbed Ramona's menu and placed it atop of his. His caramel-colored hands were still two shades darker than his pretty-boy face. "I became a meat and potatoes man while playing football. I guess some things never change."

"Some things have changed. We've all gotten older," she laughed, and Ronnie joined her.

"And wiser," he finally said a moment later. "My divorce wised me up." He leaned back in his chair and eyed her more intently, waiting for her response, like a principal with a troubled student.

Ramona freed one of her hands from beneath her thigh and grabbed her sweating glass of water. Divorce—a distasteful word separating everything she would ever hold near and dear to her, if the word ever became part of her permanent vocabulary. She swallowed slowly, trying to keep her hand steady. The situation still too nerve-wrenching. She was here, after all, with a man she had once loved more than life itself.

He sneezed violently. "Excuse me, Ramona," he told her, before standing and walking to the restroom. The waiter returned with a bottle of wine and two wineglasses, asking her if they were ready to order. She sent him away, asking him to check back in a few minutes. She retrieved her compact from her purse to check her lipstick and hair. A smidgen more of the red lip color was needed. After applying the lipstick she clamped the compact shut, startled to find Ronnie standing before her.

"You're beautiful, Ramona. You don't need

makeup. I always told you that." He took his seat. "You're a natural, sweetheart. A marvelous woman that any man would be proud to wake up to every day." He pulled her hand to his mouth, staring all the while at the glistening diamond. He kissed the back of it gingerly, leaving his lips on her skin longer than necessary. She withdrew it easily, her cheeks burning with embarrassment and nervousness.

"Tell me, Ramona, are you happy?" He had leaned back in his chair confidently again. Her unwillingness to answer the question was overshadowed by the appearance of Mr. Fudichelli.

"What will it be for you two love birds this evening?" Mr. Fudichelli stood with his eyes fixed on Ramona. Ronnie ordered their entrees then waited for Mr. Fudichelli to disappear.

"Are you?" Ronnie asked again.

"Am I what?"

"Happy. Happily married?" he pushed.

"Yes, I am," Ramona said quickly, eyes locking with his, although she was afraid of what he might find in them.

Ronnie stared at her for a long while before speaking again. "Is he treating you right?"

"I wouldn't be with him if it was otherwise," she responded defensively.

"Why aren't you with him now?" Ronnie poured himself a glass of wine, purposely avoiding her eyes.

Ramona felt a churning sensation in her stomach. Why *wasn't* she with her husband now? Already an hour into his company and Ramona wished it were Madrid sitting across from her instead of Ronnie Ware.

She waited until after Ronnie had taken a sip

of his wine before answering, "Because I love him."

"Because you love him?" Ronnie repeated, wiping his nose with his napkin. "That doesn't make sense, Ramona."

"It's because I love him that I had to take this trip home. Give me time to freshen up, to re-energize myself so we can regroup, begin again—together. One hundred percent. We need this." Ramona grinned slightly, not totally sure that she had convinced Ronnie of her theory. Though there was one thing she didn't have to convince Ronnie of—that she would never leave Madrid for him. Never.

Ramona's stomach pouched out slightly, though she tried, unsuccessfully, to suck it in. But the heavily starched meal would not be controlled by an occasional tightening of stomach muscles. Ramona leaned her head back against the soft leather headrest, groaning internally. Otis Redding's greatest hits CD filled the four-door sedan. She looked out the tinted window, staring at the inner city scenery.

A dilapidated three-story warehouse intrigued her; the burned-out cement building took up the entire block. She imagined that it had housed a manufacturing plant, employing hundreds of Detroit residents at one time or another. As they rounded the curve, the luxury sedan swerved suddenly, throwing Ramona against the car door. She stole a peek at the speedometer before repositioning herself in her seat—63 miles per hour. Too fast to be speeding around the bend.

"You okay?" she asked Ronnie. His disposition

had drastically changed since the three glasses of
wine and three over-long trips to the bathroom at
the restaurant. Had he even heard her? The music
couldn't be that loud, Ramona surmised. "Sittin'
on the dock of the bay . . ." Ronnie was totally
engulfed, singing and smiling and sniffling and
wiping.

Ramona reached over and pressed the arrow
button on the stereo downward. Ronnie's head
still bobbed back and forth to the old tune; he
hadn't even noticed the volume had been altered.
If he had, he surely would have put a plug in his
singing voice.

"Ronnie, is everything all right? You're not falling asleep behind the wheel on me, are you?"

"Everything is fine. Relax, Mona. I got this!"
he replied, reaching down and pushing the volume upward again.

Ramona furrowed her brows. *I can barely hear
myself think. Wish he would slow down before he gets
a ticket.*

"We can go to Belle Island!" Ronnie yelled over
the music. "It would be nice to park there and
talk like we used to." He looked over at Ramona,
eyes lowering toward her breasts. In that quick in-
stant the car swerved again. "Whoops!" he
laughed hard. "Better keep my eyes on the flat-
lands. Them mountains can get you in trouble."

Ramona was annoyed. There were no doggone
mountains in Detroit—just down her dress. The
night was beginning to take on a peculiar feel.
She gazed out the window watching trees and
houses flying by at an alarming rate. The music
had escalated to eardrum-piercing level. *Madrid
would have never been this inconsiderate,* she murmured inwardly. Having had enough, she turned

toward Ronnie. "Can you please turn the music down?"

Ronnie quickly honored the request. "The sound system is contagious in a Lexus," he explained. "A song starts playing and feeling good to me and I just want to turn it up more and more." He looked at her, hoping for some hint of understanding. Seeing none, he said, "Sorry, Mona." It was his term of endearment for her, too.

"Mona, you are so beautiful. I wish to God I never let you go. I was young and stupid. Can you ever forgive me? I can barely forgive myself. See, you would have stuck by my side. No matter what. Injuries, operations, money problems—it wouldn't have mattered to you. Nope, you're what every man asks for in a woman but can't keep once we get you. I know I hurt you and I'm sorry. I was young, Mona—so young. I still love you though, Mona."

"Call me Ramona, please." That was all she could bring herself to say. She hoped she hadn't come off too bitchy. But all that loud behind music and the constant rambling about his mistake—blah, blah, blah—had made her irritable. Screeching around corners doing thirty miles above the speed limit didn't make matters much more comfortable either.

She could appreciate him wanting to showboat his car; it was a natural thing with men. Even Madrid went through a similar phase when he purchased his Jeep, enticing her to accompany him on some pretend errand for a supposed fifteen minutes, which usually turned into two hours of joyriding. But this, tonight with Ronnie, was ridiculous.

"I think we should head over to the club now.

I'm sure Lalah and Drew are waiting." She really didn't know that for sure. What she did realize was that she no longer wanted to be in Ronnie's presence. Not anymore—there was something peculiar about his behavior.

"Ahh, Mona . . . I mean, Ramona," he said pulling the car over to the side of the road before flipping off the lights. The engine idled softly—almost too quietly. "It's only 10:15. I thought we were supposed to meet them around 12:30. What's the matter?" He unfastened his seatbelt and leaned his broad body toward her.

Ramona moved farther into her corner of the car, shrugging her shoulders and sliding her hands under her thighs. "Nothing. I'm just tired of sitting. My knees are bothering me," she lied. It was the only rational reason that came to mind. "I'm ready to stretch out a bit. That's all."

Ronnie shot a glance at the backseat, then back to Ramona. "You could always stretch out back there." He grinned diabolically.

Repulsive. Ramona averted her eyes, staring once again out the tinted glass. God, she wished she was laying in Madrid's arms right now. She let out a frustrated breath. Ronnie sniffled some more.

Ramona shifted her gaze toward him. Damn! He was right up on her, garlic breath and all. She tried to turn away, but it was too late. His pencil-thin lips clamped down on her face, catching her bottom lip. His hands, calloused from too many plays up the field as a running back, grabbed around her shoulders.

She withdrew violently, and her right shoulder slammed into her car door with a loud thump.

"Stop it, Ronnie! This is not one of our college

outings! I'm married, in case you've forgotten."
She tucked her arms under her bosom. Ronnie
yanked back his hands.

"You mean, in case *you've* forgotten, sweetheart.
I'm not the one married and out on a date with
someone," he said tartly.

Had she been brave enough to look him in the
face, she would have seen the famous Ronnie
Ware dagger-at-your-throat stare. But sudden embarrassment and swift revelation that indeed she
shouldn't be here had made her heart somer-
sault, and Ronnie's tone alarmed her.

"Spoiled damn brat! That's what you've been
all your life, Ramona Johnson." He laughed wickedly, for what seemed like way too long, before
reaching into the glove box.

Inside lay a shiny silver metal piece with a black
rubber grip for it's handle, next to a small packet
of tissues. Ramona's mind reeled. A gun? What
was he doing with a gun? She could feel her
blood pumping wildly as memories surfaced.

*Madrid and the kids—Nathan's fourth birthday
party. Happy birthday, dear Nathan—cake all over his
face, all over the floor.* Her reverie ended when she
saw what Ronnie was doing.

As he tore open the sealed plastic package, Ramona saw tissues. Was that all he was after? Just
plain old tissues? Ramona rolled her eyes up, trying to slow her heartbeat. She had to find Lalah
and get back to her house.

Ronnie tossed the sodden tissues out the window. *Litterbug,* Ramona thought. Then he pulled
out a small, gold foil package, and unwrapped it,
using a tiny straw to sniff some of the foil's contents up his nose.

Ramona gasped. "Ronnie! What are you—"

Ronnie sliced off her sentence with a piercing glare. He tossed the empty foil out the window, then flipped on the car lights. The engine's hum was so silent, it might have been off completely. Ramona wanted to bombard him with a series of questions: What was that? Drugs? Why are you doing it? How long have you been doing it? She decided against it, considering the awkwardness of the moment.

"Let me take your whining butt to your big sister," Ronnie sniffled. "And to think you consider yourself an adult. A mother, even. Please!" Purposely, he turned up the stereo's volume. So loud was the bass, that Ramona felt the vibration in her chest.

Ronnie merged onto the main street, the car accelerating so quickly it reached 75 at what felt like warp speed. Gravity held Ramona's head against the leather headrest; they were racing through the city streets at 83 miles per hour.

Time to pray. Ramona shut her eyes and dialed God up immediately. *Hello, God. Were you busy? Yes, this is Ramona Shaw. Umm, I know that I'm not where I'm supposed to be about now, but could you do me a favor and see to it that this fool sitting to my left doesn't do anything that would cause me not to be where I'm supposed to be tomorrow. Thank you.*

She was about to add an "amen" when, over the loud squeals of James Brown, she heard police sirens. Ramona reached for the volume. Streaks of red light ricocheted through the Lexus' black interior.

"Ronnie," she said softly. "I think the cops want us to pull over."

Ronnie looked into the rearview mirror, then back over his shoulder. Unexpectedly, he floored the gas pedal and leaned back as the automobile zoomed from 83 to 95 miles per hour in a flash.

"Ronnie, please! You're scaring me!" Ramona was frantic. This was not the way she was supposed to go out of the world. God wouldn't let it happen. Misty-eyed, Ramona gripped her armrest and pleaded again, "Lord Jesus! Charles Ronald Ware, what are you doing?" She thought about grabbing the wheel, but that would have only made matters worse.

The car hit an unexpected dip in the wide four-lane street, then bounced in the air, lingering indefinitely before landing. The high-speed ride continued for ten minutes before the street threatened to end; Ramona saw the telephone poles and trees that would cause their demise if God didn't send Michael or Gabriel down to stop Ronnie.

The sirens grew louder. Ramona knew by the variation in the red strobe lights piercing the windows that there were several cop cars tailing them. The closest tree seemed much to close for them to stop and walk away unscathed. Tears burned down her cheeks. This was it, she was sure.

"Stop the car!" Ramona yelled, bracing her legs against the floor and her arms against the dash. Ronnie must have pressed the brakes—the car skidded straight before spinning out into a wild circle. Ramona clamped her eyes shut and whispered to God, "Our Father, who art in heaven, hallowed be Thy name . . ." The car slowed—but the tree still hadn't moved.

Eleven

Madrid had dreamed twice since he'd been asleep. The first dream centered around enormous, full-bred bull mastiffs with foaming mouths terrorizing the city. Not such a big deal, considering he had been sitting on top of a skyscraper, watching the whole thing through binoculars. Crazy. The second dream was less bizarre, but more disconcerting. The scene was clearer—Ramona was on a stretcher, doused with blood, and there was Leslie crying, standing by a grave with two headstones. One with her mother's name, the other with Ramona's name scribbled across the gray stone.

Madrid jolted up, heart thumping rapidly and perspiration dripping. Fuzziness clouded his mind. He sat erect in his dark, cool bedroom, loneliness lurching, pupils still adjusting. Where was Ramona anyway? After a few deep breaths in the dimness, he got his bearings. He glanced over toward Ramona's side of the bed. Still empty. He cupped his face with his hands. The house reeked solitude like a neighborhood church on a late, late Sunday night. Just then, the faint sound of a distant siren whistled in the wind. An ambulance. He was sure of it.

A chill raced down his spine and his toes curled against the icy bathroom tile as he staggered toward the sink. Montclair tap water—Essex county's best. He filled the plastic cup a second time and quenched his throat once more.

Unable to doze off again, Madrid turned on the gooseneck reading lamp attached to the oak headboard. He picked up his if-all-else-fails book, *Parting The Water,* which always stood on his nightstand next to his leather King James' Bible. He thumbed through a few chapters until he found the spot where he had left off during another sleepless night. Seemed like he'd been reading the historical book recounting black history for years.

It was nights like these—that thank the Lord didn't happen very often—he was glad to have the book handy. A few pages into the chapter, his eyes began to droop. A wide yawn, almost forming a perfect circle, followed. He looked up at the phone momentarily, wondering, wishing, waiting for one woman to call—his woman.

Madrid's mind wandered. Would Alyson Rivera have done this to him? Leaving him stranded with the children to boogie off to another state? It was a sure bet that she would have, considering her attitude about relationships. Yes, he was certain Alyson would have done exactly the same thing Ramona had. Perhaps she would have gone even further and initiated divorce proceedings. But Ramona would never divorce him. Would she?

Tomorrow was Sunday. Ramona should return to her rightful home. An uninvited smile swept across Madrid's face at that thought. A cough from afar caught his attention. The cackle seemed strained and beckoning. Was it Leslie or Nathan? He sat up straighter in bed, ears stretched, anticipating another sound that would tell him which child was in trouble. A few seconds elapsed before Madrid swung his feet to the floor and journeyed toward his children's rooms.

Leslie's bedroom door was closed tight. How many times had he warned them to keep their doors open so that he could hear them during the night? But how many times had Ramona disagreed with him, saying something about it being a fire hazard?

He pushed open Leslie's door, and it creaked noisily. Mona's voice badgering him to oil the doors played through his mind. He would have to throw some WD-40 on the hinges in the morning.

Halfway into Leslie's room, he stumbled over something and Leslie stirred under the massive mound of covers. He stood, studying her for a moment, until he heard the lullaby of her breath. Everything fine here—and the door would remain open for the rest of this night.

There was that raspy noise again. This time Madrid recognized the sound—it was Nathan wheezing. Madrid rushed into his room and flipped on the light. Nathan sat in the middle of his bed holding his throat, eyes bulging, gasping desperately for air—a blue tint replacing the color faded from his face.

"Nathan! Oh God," Madrid cried aloud. He lunged toward his son in one swift step, lifting him up. "Leslie! Leslie, wake up!" he called frantically.

"Hold on, son, I'll get the machine going." He carried Nathan into the hallway. His wheezing was harder now.

"Relax, son. Try to relax." Madrid cuddled him closer. "Leslie!"

Leslie wandered into the hallway half asleep, rubbing her eyes. "Daddy?" she called out, squinting. "What's wrong? Is there a fire?"

"No. It's your brother. We need to plug in his machine. Quick! You plug in the machine, I'll find his medicine."

Leslie searched through the upstairs hall closet. Not there. She dashed down the steps and turned on the lights, searching the hall closet where the coats hung. The nebulizer was a lightweight machine with a humidifier and an attached mask for quick relief of sudden attacks. It was simple enough to use—plug in the machine, pour in the medicine, and place the mask over Nathan's face.

She ransacked the closet a second time. Still nothing! She left the door open and ran to the kitchen pantry, swinging the door open wildly. Spaghetti, canned corn, Cheerios, laundry detergent, Pepsi—no machine! She left the pantry door open and ran back toward the dining area, bumping into Madrid.

"Have you found it?" He sat Nathan on the breakfast nook table.

"No! Mona always leaves it in the closet."

"Never mind! Put some shoes on and grab a jacket," Madrid ordered.

Madrid charged through the sliding glass doors into a mobbed battle zone. Jumbled sounds and noises overwhelmed his ears, and the rank smell of perspiration, blood, and home-applied medicinal remedies instantly swarmed him.

In the stale-smelling waiting room, he saw a frail young boy with a compress held to his head by his mother; a woman with an ice pack on her foot; a screaming baby unable to articulate his pain; an angry drunk in need of the three S's; two teenage boys speaking in their native language; and a delirious old lady singing off key.

Madrid strode to the front desk. The nurse, a petite woman with long, dangling braids and flawlessly applied makeup, hurried from behind the desk alarmed by Nathan's bluish hue.

"What happened here?" she asked Madrid, taking Nathan.

"Asthma attack," Madrid told her, hurriedly following her. "We didn't have time to use the nebulizer."

"How long has he been like this?" she asked, placing Nathan on the gurney.

"Ten, twelve minutes. I'm not sure. Is he going to be all right?"

"I'm sure. Just give us a little room to work," the nurse said, removing Nathan's nightshirt. "You can wait outside with your daughter." She didn't wait for a reply, instead summoning another nurse before closing the curtains.

Disoriented—that was the only way to describe Madrid's emotions as he stood frozen outside the curtain. He would never forgive himself if something happened to Nathan on account of him not knowing the whereabouts of things in his own house. Not being able to match a pair of socks on a daily basis was one thing, but not knowing the location of his son's lifeline was a totally different matter. It wasn't until Leslie pulled on his sleeve a second or third time that he was reminded of her presence.

"Is Nathan going to be okay, Daddy?" A hint of concern heightened Leslie's voice.

"Why, of course, sweetheart. The nurses and

doctors will take good care of him." He looked up at the round, white-faced clock—12:33 A.M. He would have to phone Ramona. He peered down at Leslie, who had taken a seat on the footstool.

"Will you be a big girl and keep an eye on Nathan while I go phone Mona?"

"I'm a big girl already, Dad." She smiled, braces glittering in the fluorescent light.

"I'll be back in a minute." Madrid walked into the lobby, searching for a pay phone. Hopefully Aunt Lalah would understand the late-night call. After all, it was her sister's son, her nephew, that this call would be about.

Gordon grabbed the remote and turned down the volume to the television. Brian McNight was just finishing his love ballad on *Saturday Night Live*. The phone rang a second time. Gordon reached toward the nightstand, glimpsing at the digital clock. Awfully late for a call this time of night. Probably one of his clients needing some expedient weekend advice. He cleared the late-night frog lodged in his esophagus.

"Hel-lo," Gordon said in a strong voice.

"Gordon, it's Madrid. Sorry for calling so late. Did I wake you?

"Madrid? Naw I was watching a little late-night television." He sat up in bed. "How's things?"

"Not too good. I'm here at the emergency room with Nathan. He had an asthma attack tonight. It's pretty serious."

"Oh, no. Is he going to be all right?"

"That's what I'm waiting for the doctors to determine. I thought it best to let Ramona know.

You know, just in case it's a little more serious than I thought. Is she asleep?"

Gordon scratched the top of his hairless head, a habit whenever he had to stall for time, a symbol that his opponents in the courtroom kept an eye out for. He stopped scratching for a brief second, then resumed. Madrid couldn't see him anyway.

"No. She, Lalah and Sophia went for a girls' night out," Gordon said. "I expect them anytime. Can I have her call you at the hospital when she gets in?" He wished there was something he could say to his brother-in-law other than that his wife was not there.

Madrid was silent. Not there? Out with Lalah and Sophia while her child almost died? Madrid felt a severe headache seizing the left side of his head. So, that was what this trip was all about? An opportunity for her to run the streets with her family members while he tended to the kids? Wasn't she supposed to be getting some rest, replenishing her body and soul, or some crap like that?

Madrid's blood pressure began to percolate. *That's just fine, Mrs. Shaw.* He was overreacting, he knew, but he couldn't help but feel justified with the way things had transpired between them. Right now his only concern was Nathan's health. If hanging out in the streets of Detroit was more important than the welfare of her family, so be it. Madrid sighed hard. Gordon dared not speak first.

"Well," Madrid said somberly. "Tell her to call me at home whenever she gets in."

"How long do you anticipate being at the hospital?" Gordon felt compelled to try and smooth things over.

"I don't know. Half an hour, two hours, depends. Doesn't matter. She can call us at home if she finds the time. Thanks, Gordon. Sorry for disturbing you."

"Not at all, Madrid. I'll tell Mona as soon as she gets in. Take care of my nephew." Gordon hung up the phone, then turned off the television. *Saturday Night Live* hadn't been all that funny tonight anyway. He wondered when Ramona and Lalah would be home, and where they were for that matter. What if he had an emergency tonight, as Madrid had? Would he have been able to find his wife?

He picked up the phone and dialed, waiting patiently for the connection. Three rings, four rings, five . . . No answer. He reset the phone and pressed redial. Certainly the girls would be on their way home soon, or in the car to answer the phone. Two rings, three rings, four. He dropped the phone back on the hook. It was 1:00 A.M.— the dee-jays should be winding down the dance crowd now. He would try the car phone again in forty minutes or so. If all else failed, he would hit the streets to find them himself.

The champagne-colored Lexus had finally rested in the middle of some forsythia bushes, the engine still idling softly. Ramona sat clutching her face from the fear of a head-on collision, her heart rate elevated towards stroke level. Strobes of red light bounced off the tinted windows and sirens wailed piercingly.

A husky voice came over the police speaker. "Step out of the car now!"

Ronnie screamed hysterically, "I can't go to jail! I can't, Ramona! You don't understand!" He reached for the glove compartment. Ramona snatched his hand away, peering into his eyes, which no longer boasted luster or twinkle.

"What the hell are you doing? Haven't you had enough drama for the evening?" she snapped. The policeman's voice repeated the directions for them to get out of the car. Ramona could see other officers edging toward the front of the car with their guns drawn. "Whatever your problem is, Ronnie, don't make it worse by fighting these guys." She caught a glimpse of one of the officers. "Remember Rodney King?"

Ronnie looked out his window, noticing a lanky female cop with locks of blond hair dangling from her hat walking toward the front of the car. He turned to face Ramona, nodding "yes." He remembered brother King and his arrest.

"Then I suggest we step out of the car." Ramona pressed the electric locks and opened the car door. Ronnie followed suit.

"Put your hands up!" yelled two of the officers before swarming on them. "Now!"

The lady cop slung Ramona around harshly, then pushed her up against the car. She patted her down roughly, then said, "You like cops and robbers, eh? Then we'll see how much you like a night in jail."

Actually, Ramona did like cops and robbers, but she chose not to respond to the officer's statement. Instead she wondered how on earth she'd be able to reach Lalah now. She took in a deep breath and focused on Ronnie. She was frightened and worried for him, a black man captured by some white officers after leading them on a high-speed chase. She prepared for the worst, her mind conjuring up a gruesome scenario. She braced herself, waiting, expecting an altercation that never happened. In spite of the situation, Ronnie was standing erect, calmly talking to three of the police officers.

They were huddled together like high school chums—Ronnie and the three stooges. He said something, smiling, and the officer to his right laughed. Ramona wished she could hear their conversation. The shorter officer took Ronnie's license and walked back to the police car to call it in, while the skinny cop began searching the interior of the car. Another officer walked back to the trunk, his eyes fixed on Ronnie.

"Hey, Poncho," he yelled to the cop inside the car, "unlatch the trunk for me." The trunk popped open, and the thick officer smiled at Ronnie, who returned the gesture confidently.

Ramona couldn't see the contents of the trunk, but whatever they had stumbled on had excited the officers.

"What the—" The officers raced to his side as the cop behind the car exclaimed. The police-woman clamped the handcuffs on Ramona, pushing her to the back of the car so she too could assess the situation.

"Good Christ Almighty," the skinny officer said with bulging eyes, lifting up a bag.

Ramona knew her mouth had dropped open, but couldn't retain the involuntary action. Her eyes had stretched so wide she felt her veins straining. Disbelief and denial raced through her. *No way!* her mind screamed. Ronnie? This? How could she have been riding the streets of Detroit with Ronnie, her ex-college love, an ex-professional football player—a drug dealer?

"Don't touch it! Leave it," the older cop ordered. "Poncho, get on the horn and radio the narcs."

There were approximately twenty-five sandwich-sized bags filled with white, powdery stuff. Ramona was going to be sick. A bout of dizziness engulfed her, and her heart rang violently in her ears—she fought hard to remain standing. She looked at Ronnie, whose grin was replaced with fear. If she had been given the chance, she would have slapped the mess out of him right then.

From the time she was placed into the backseat of the police car until now, where Ramona sat in a tiny room at the police station, everything was a blur. Ronnie's whereabouts were long past visible and way past her caring. How in God's great name could he have been so stupid? Why would anybody drive around the city with cocaine, the equivalent of five or six kilos, in his trunk?

A police officer, a brother of enormous weight and proportion, came in and shut the door behind him. A deep, wide scar traveled down the right side of his blue-black face, and a black cotton patch covered his right eye. A thick mustache lined his thin lips and curled at the end, like whiskers. They've got to be kidding, Ramona thought. He looked like a character out of Robin Hood. She chuckled inconspicuously, or so she thought.

"I'm Officer Tulane," he told Ramona, sitting down next to her. She began to shake from the silent giggles trying to get loose.

"Something funny to you, Miss . . ." He paused to flip through a few sheets of white paper. "Shaw. Is that right?" His voice was as tiny and inviting as the boxer, Mike Tyson.

"Yes, that's correct," Ramona replied in her most businesslike tone.

"Well," Officer Tulane said, "this ain't a laughing matter. We got you and Mr. Ware locked down for drug trafficking. How's ten to twenty years strike your funny bone?" He smiled wide purposely, showcasing his not-so-pearly teeth. He had to use whatever scare tactics he could to gather information on Ronnie Ware, even though his gut told him Ramona was simply in the wrong place at the wrong time.

Ramona eyed him cautiously, the tickle instantly gone from the corners of her mouth. She averted her eyes, taking in the placidity of the steel gray room. An old tune that helped her to block out childhood chastisement, which was exactly what this felt like, crept into her head. *I don't mind if you say that you're going away . . . just don't want to be lonely . . . I'd rather be loved and . . .* She listened to the lyrics in her head until the cop's voice reminded her of her whereabouts.

"We're willing to work something out with you. All we need is a little information." He leaned further into her personal space, lowering his voice to a drawling whisper. "All I need to know is where you and Mr. Ware were on your way to."

Ramona glared at him. Where were they on their way to? The club, Canada, home, the hotel—how the hell was she to know where Ronnie was heading mentally? One thing she did know was that she didn't have to answer any questions if she wasn't officially being charged. Or maybe that was something she'd heard on *NYPD Blue.*

"I'd like to make my allotted phone call," Ramona finally said.

Officer Tulane leaned back in his chair and studied her for a second. A bright sister, he surmised. Even knew enough to request her one phone call. He stood up so abruptly, the chair scratched the tacky linoleum floor.

"One phone call," he threatened Ramona with a pointed index finger. "That's all you get. So you better make it worthwhile, 'cause you might be here all morning." He swung open the door and stepped out. Ramona watched expressionlessly.

She had just a few minutes to gather her thoughts—make her decision. One phone call, that's all that would be granted. She sighed deeply. One call, one time, one person. Who would she phone? She closed her eyes just as she heard the sound of the door hinges again. It was Officer Tulane, she was sure. She heard him wrestle with the wires as he placed the phone on the table.

"Okay, Mrs. Shaw. Here's your chance," he told her. He sat on the edge of the table with one foot in the empty chair and his arms crossed.

Ramona opened her eyes. One call, she thought again as she scooted her chair closer to the table. What was Lalah's car phone number again? She concentrated as she picked up the phone. Or did Drew's pager number start with . . . She hesitated.

Perhaps she should call Gordon. But that would blow her and Lalah's cover. She thought about Sophia. No, she was out with Frankie tonight. Maybe Poppy would crawl out of bed at this time of the morning to rescue her. Oh God, who should she call?

Ramona glanced up at Officer Tulane, imagining what he would do if he was in her position. Who would he call? The disgruntled look on his face warned her that his patience and her time was running out. She looked down at the number pad, took a deep breath, and punched in the phone number. The line on the other end began to ring. One ring, two. In a situation like this, there was really only one person to call. Third ring the charm—at least she hoped.

Lalah stood over the bed, looking down at Drew. Her face registered irritation and disgust at the sight of him drooling in the depths of sleep. She couldn't believe it. After all this time and all the hype, this was what it finally boiled down to? A bottle of wine, a few heated kisses, six or seven strokes, and then this—a tired man with a horrendous snore, dead asleep? She was disgusted.

She zipped her dress, stepped into her heels and snatched her purse off the dresser. She had fifteen minutes to make it to the club before Ramona began a conniption fit. Grabbing her parking ticket, Lalah headed for the door, but not before turning to view Drew's limp body once more. She rolled her eyes, then shut the hotel door behind her. Never again with him, she vowed. Never.

The valet who had parked her car less than two hours ago took her ticket. This time her mood not so festive. She waited with galvanized patience, wondering why she was really there with another man to begin with. The valet cruised the Benz to a near-perfect stop in front of her. Drew would awake later in the morning looking for her and, she supposed, a ride home. She offered a faint smile to the young brother who stepped out of her car.

"Here you go, ma'am," he said, holding the car door open for her.

Lalah reached into her purse and pulled out a five-dollar bill, handing it to the young man.

"Thank you," the boy said, tucking the bill into his red vest pocket.

"You're more than welcome, young brother. Keep up that beautiful smile. It'll get you far," she flirted, sliding into the seat and swinging her legs into the car.

"Oh, by the way, ma'am, your car phone was ringing when I pulled up from the garage. I didn't bother it, though," he told her.

"Oh, really? Well, thank you for telling me. Have a good evening," she said before pulling out of the circular drive. She had ten minutes to get to the club. She just hoped Ramona and Ronnie would be waiting.

Madrid took Nathan to the master bedroom and gently laid him down on Ramona's side of the bed. Leslie had already staggered to her room and dropped off into a deep slumber, her date with the comb and brush just a few hours away.

He eased Nathan's tiny Batman slippers off, deciding against changing his pajamas for fear of waking him. Nathan had been through so much tonight. First, the asthma attack, then the emergency room physicians, who had probed and poked and prodded him until he fell wearily asleep behind the dull powder blue curtains. A feeling of inadequacy overwhelmed Madrid. He just might be able to protect Nathan from most things in life. But from his own biological quirks? Unlikely.

Madrid sat on the edge of the bed facing the window, the moonlight glowing softly on his flesh. A moth trapped inside the vertical slats flickered

against the windowpane with a sickening rhythmic tap. Yesterday's socks lay balled in the corner
across from his nightstand, next to his sneakers.
The answering machine's light, representing that
a message awaited, had not illuminated during
his absence. And even now, in the calm, quiet of
the night, the phone had not jingled.

The past few days had not been very kind to him.
Challenging, even rewarding at times, but certainly
not kind. Madrid had made a promise to himself
that he and the kids would go to church on Sunday.
Now that decision appeared less do-able. He flipped
off his loafers and leaned back against the headboard, resting his weary body. Yawns exploded twice
more. Seven hours of undisturbed sleep was what
he needed to replenish his energy.

Madrid's body yearned for sweet sleep but his
mind churned aimlessly. He stared at the fuzzy
numbers on the clock; Ramona should have
phoned by now. It was damn near 3 A.M. He
didn't remember Detroit as a city that never slept.
His brow furrowed, his mind working. Reflex told
him to dial his sister-in-law's home again. Madrid
picked up the phone, paused a few seconds, listening to the even hum of the dial tone, then
placed it back in the cradle. *No.*

Gordon certainly would have given Ramona the
message by now. He wouldn't call her again—it
was her turn to put forth the effort. Thank God
Nathan was okay, Madrid praised silently. And he
had done the responsible thing by apprising Ramona of the situation. Pride swiftly turned to frustration—agitation—damnation! Where the hell
was his wife anyway?

Twelve

Gordon marched into the tiny, oxygen-deprived office in a pair of jeans and a Central State University sweatshirt. His bald head gleamed under the flickering overhead light. Never in his twenty years of practicing law had he been called in the middle of the night to retrieve a family member from a police station. It would be an unthinkable act for any of his Morehouse, Yale, or MIT-graduate relatives to be caught in a godawful police station. For *any* reason. He peered down at Ramona, scowling.

Embarrassment and humiliation prevented Ramona from greeting Gordon aloud. Instead, she hunched her shoulders and shifted her eyes to the overly waxed floor. Gordon had been her only logical choice—he was the only person who understood the inner workings of the law and what might happen to her. She knew when Gordon answered the phone that she indeed had throttled her and Lalah's alibis.

Gordon had done well not to ask too many questions over the phone, his instinct guiding him to get to the police station straightaway to clear things up. Funny thing was, he never did ask if Lalah was with her once Ramona explained "they" had been stopped and wrongfully charged with drug trafficking. She supposed he assumed she'd meant her and Lalah.

Now, as Officer Tulane stepped in behind Gordon, she knew he had clarified that misconception. Why else would Gordon be standing before her looking swollen and red? The drive home with him would be treacherous, emotionally speaking. Especially since Gordon would probably demand that she explain what the sam hill was going on and where the hell Lalah was.

"You're free to go, Mrs. Shaw," Officer Tulane told her.

Ramona dared to look up. She regretted it the moment she saw the wide, angular smirk plastered on Tulane's bizarre face. She stood slowly and took her purse from him, slinging it across her shoulder, trying her best to display an outraged sense of inconvenience. But she feared expressing it—the mere thought of having to verbalize anything paralyzed her. Shame, disgrace, humility—she felt all of them. She walked toward Gordon, not quite ready to meet his gaze.

Gordon reached into his pocket and handed Tulane a card that he took and jammed into his trouser pocket. Gordon extended his right hand and Tulane gripped it firmly.

"Thanks again, Tulane. Like I mentioned earlier, if you ever need anything call me. I'm reachable practically any time of the day or night," Gordon said sarcastically, glaring at Ramona, who kept her eyes focused on the window.

"Why thank you, Gordon. I'll keep that in mind for future reference. Yup,"—he paused to give Ramona a level gaze—"wrong place, wrong time. You're pretty fortunate, Mrs. Shaw. It's not uncommon for us to charge the female friend, too, in a case like this. I guess this was just one of those times when someone was actually innocent," he chortled. "Now I suppose you better head on out. I've still got Mr. Ware to deal with. You sure you don't want us to entrust him to you, Gordon?" Tulane chuckled, placing an unlit cigarette in his mouth.

"You can fry his butt for all I care. There's nobody here obligated to care that much for him," Gordon replied. Ramona could feel the arrows flying her way. "I'm sure he's got some lawyer on his payroll."

"Yeah, but none with your kind of reputation," Tulane egged him on as he clumsily searched for a light.

Gordon refused to be entertained. It was too early in the morning for wise remarks. The only thing he felt like doing right then was sleeping—not laughing. He looked at Ramona. "Let's go, Mrs. Shaw," he ordered, moving around her like an irritated, prissy feline. He held the door open for her.

Ramona walked through the door thinking that Gordon sounded so official, she wanted to puke all over the linoleum floor. Not since she was a young pre-teen, when she had teased Gordon for days after seeing him fondle Lalah's breast on the back porch, had she heard him sound so agitated, so annoyed, so plainly pissed off. And even then it didn't sound as disturbing as it did now. She dragged her feet purposely, yawning as if the tedious walk and her expressed tiredness would make a difference in what awaited her. All the while, her mind worked overtime, trying to finagle a way out of the mess she and Lalah had created.

For the first five minutes, they rode in deafening silence. No radio, no street sounds, no words—just the soft sounds of raindrops pelting against the roof of the car. Ramona stared out of the Jaguar's tinted window absorbing the sights. Gordon had inadvertently taken the scenic route, cruising down Seven Mile Road. The street was quiet and darker now that the neon signs once highlighting Church's Chicken and Bee-Bee's Bar and Grill earlier that evening had shut down. Tiny raindrops streaked the windows, making Ramona's vision blurred.

The traffic light seemed spitefully long. Ramona wondered if Gordon would have waited as patiently for the light had he been by himself. What was he so busy thinking about? Did he suspect anything? She sighed quietly. She would give anything to have Gordon acknowledge her presence. A car eased up beside them. She scanned the unfamiliar make of the car, then smirked inwardly. Typical Detroit style. A popular tune by some rapper thumped through the damp night air. Even with the windows shut tight, she could hear the bass. It was so loud and thick that the back window of the half Maxima-half Benz limousine rattled.

The hybrid automobile sped off. Gordon remained steady, his eyes focused straight ahead. The windshield wipers clicked to their own rhythm. Ramona prayed silently, asking God to please forgive the situation and to please let Lalah be home by the time she and Gordon pulled into the driveway. The way she figured, Gordon would for sure cuss Lalah out—or maybe not. Depended on how bad he wanted to keep the appearance of a wholesome marriage intact.

She heard a grunt—Gordon clearing his throat.

She wondered if he was going to ask questions about Lalah's whereabouts and her involvement with Ronnie Ware. The anticipation ended. Gordon spoke, but his words were not at all what Ramona expected.

"Your husband called tonight. He had to take your son to the emergency room," Gordon said.

"What? Why? What's wrong?" Ramona gasped. *Your husband called? Your son to the hospital?* Graphic images, tragic scenarios, dominated her thoughts. Nathan—a gashed-open head, stitches, a broken arm, a hit and run—what was it? The guilt trip surfaced immediately. *Should have never left him alone—without me. Oh, God.*

"He had a severe asthma attack. Madrid had to rush him to the emergency room. He called you from there," Gordon replied flatly. He made a sharp left turn onto his block.

"Why didn't he use the machine? Good gracious, can't he even find one damn thing without me? Did he say he tried the machine?" Her voice was strident.

Gordon slowed the car, then made the right into the circular driveway. "He didn't mention anything about a machine, Ramona. He called to make you aware of the situation." The garage door opened slowly. Gordon paused, leaving his foot on the brake.

"Is Nathan all right?" she asked frantically, unlocking the door.

"I don't know, Ramona!" Gordon snapped. "He's your husband, that's your family! All I know is, your husband called *you* regarding *your* son while you and Lalah were out gallivanting with some other men. That's what the hell I know!" He sped the Jaguar into the open garage. Then

stopped abruptly, just short of hitting the wall.
Lalah's car was nowhere in sight.

Ramona could have done without the self-righteous preaching. Especially from a man who had
been accused of impregnating a woman half his
age. *He's got his damn nerve.* She stepped out of
the car; Gordon was already at the kitchen door.

He reached for the garage door button just as
a set of headlights shone into the garage. It was
Lalah. Gordon shook his head disapprovingly,
spun around and walked into the kitchen—but
not before he slammed the garage door button
with his palm. Ramona stood stiffly, watching the
headlights move closer and the garage door shutting.

Ramona was sure the garage door would crush
the hood of the Benz. Apparently, Gordon
couldn't have cared less, and Ramona felt the
same way. If Lalah had never rekindled her asso-
ciation with Ronnie, if she had stopped being so
busy for once in her life, none of this would have
happened. She followed Gordon inside, where he
stood tall, erect and ready for battle as he waited
for Lalah, who was cussing from the other side
of the kitchen door. Too bad, Ramona thought,
looking for the cordless phone, which was not in
its normal place. She had a more pressing matter
to deal with—Nathan.

"Where's the phone, Gordon?" Ramona demanded. She was no longer in the mood for his
comments. Brother-in-law or not, she was an
adult.

"In the living room, upstairs, how the hell
should I know? I hardly use it anyway," he spewed
back at her.

"What's your problem, Gordon?" Ramona

asked, tossing her purse on the counter and placing her hands on her hips—preparing for battle.

Lalah busted through the kitchen door, smack in the middle of what would go down as a historic family episode. She glanced at Ramona, then at Gordon.

Gordon looked at Ramona with a piercing gaze, his forehead wrinkled in the middle and his eyebrows furrowed so low they almost touched his eyelashes. Lalah's presence was unimportant at this moment. "I don't have a problem! What's *your* problem? I'm not the one who got arrested tonight for drug trafficking. I'm not the one who left a family in one state while coming to another to screw around on my spouse. So, what's your damn problem?" He was seething now.

Lalah shot a look at Ramona, then at Gordon. What had she walked into? What the hell had happened in seven hours? The room sweltered with anger. Baffled, she spoke next. "Mona? Is that true? You were arrested for drug trafficking?"

Ramona glared at Lalah with dagger eyes. She had some damn nerve re-iterating the statement. "What part of the statement was unclear for you, Lalah?" Her question sharp and mean.

"There's no need to be sarcastic with me, Ramona, all right?" Lalah threatened. "I'm just trying to find out what happened, that's all. Sophia and I searched for you at the club and didn't see you. I was worried." Even now Lalah was trying to save herself from being found out by Gordon.

"Save the bull, Lalah!" Gordon told her. "Why don't you just finish filling in this tale of two trifling sisters." His voice thundered. He stood with his legs slightly apart, knees bent, rubbing his left arm constantly.

"Excuse me?" Lalah said innocently enough. "What are you talking about now, Gordon?"

"You heard me. I *said,* why don't you fill in the part of the story where you were off sucking face and God knows what else with your little Johnny, while your sister here tried to follow your sorry footsteps?"

"Gordon, I'm not going to get into this with you now. I'm tired. I've had a long night." She went to saunter past him, but he grabbed her by the arm and slung her around before letting her go.

"You listen to me, Ms. Thing. You might be fooling yourself thinking you're covering your tracks, but you're not. If you want to 'ho around with some little punk, you'll do it outside of my house. If he's that important, pack your stuff and move to the gutter with him. But I'll be damned if you're going to do it under my roof!"

"Your roof?" Lalah scowled. *"Please,* I ain't going a damn place unless I feel like it. And speaking of 'ho-ing around, Gordon, what's good for the rooster is good for the hen. You feel me?" She'd pointed her finger in his face.

Lalah was treading dangerous ground, Ramona could feel it. The whole thing seemed like a dream—a familiar one. Should she step in now? Should she leave the room and let them hammer it out in private? Yes, that's what she would do. Besides, she had to call home. She looked at the clock—4 A.M. Gracious! She hadn't been up this late, or early, depending on how one looked at it, in many moons. Ramona picked up her purse; she would go upstairs to use the phone. No more

use for her down here, and no more opportunity
to spew angry words at her brother-in-law whom,
aside all else, she truly loved.

"I'm not walking around the city streets pregnant by a man half my age," Lalah yelled at Gordon. At that Ramona looked over at Gordon,
whose face had drained of color. *Lord, Lalah why
did you go there?* "I'm sick and tired of your late-
night housecalls, your user-friendly ways with the
women, your limp—"

"Lalah!" Ramona cut in. She couldn't handle
seeing her sister disrespect Gordon so—or face
her own mirrored reflection in Lalah as she spitefully lunged at her husband.

"Shut up, Mona!" Lalah yelled, rolling her eyes
at Ramona. She was hysterical now. Like a pris-
oner pent-up in solitary for too many years suddenly free—wild. "If *your* house was in order you
wouldn't be standing in mine right now." Her
eyes met Gordon's again.

"You want me out of here? Then give me a
divorce. I'll have you so spent by the time I'm
done with you, you'll have to work from scratch
again. To think you'd be so stupid as to get someone pregnant. After all I worked for to help you
make it—to help *us*. You think I'm going to stand
by and watch you give all I've sweated for to some
little trollop?" She chuckled. "You crazy as hell!"

If they had paid closer attention, if Lalah
hadn't been so carried away with anger, if her
pitched voice hadn't soaked up all the attention,
they would have detected that something was
wrong the minute Gordon's posture changed. His
body had slowly crouched forward, his face
twisted in to a pained grimace.

Surely his right hand reaching for the left side

of his body, his chest, should have warned them. But it was too late. Gordon's knees buckled, then he crumpled with a loud thump to the granite floor.

It seemed to happen in slow-motion. Lalah knelt down beside him, her eyes wide, pleading. Ramona stood frozen in awe, her fingers splayed across her mouth, as she watched Lalah from the opposite side of the kitchen, the space between them seeming farther than ever before. Ramona saw Lalah muttering something but the sounds were muted—at least for a split second before a yelp snapped her back.

"Ramona, call an ambulance! I think he's had a heart attack for real this time." Lalah lifted his heavy head. "Oh, Gordon," she whispered over and over again, placing his head in her lap. "It's going to be all right. You just hold on."

Gordon was gripping his chest and gasping for air, his eyes fixed in one morbid position—upward. His skin felt like that of a sodden eel.

Ramona turned to pick up the cordless phone, before remembering it wasn't there. She raced through the long foyer, her heels clacking against the marble floor, before jogging up the steps to the first bedroom on the left. She yanked the receiver off the cradle and dialed.

"This is the 911 operator. What seems to be the problem?"

"My brother-in-law." She paused, winded. "He's had a heart attack."

"What's your name?" he asked her. She was rocking from side to side, nervously.

"Ramona. I'm at my sister's house." With each word her heart rate quickened. Hysteria was due to set in next. She rattled off the address, listening to the operator type in the information.

"Where is your brother-in-law now, Ramona?"

"He's lying downstairs on the kitchen floor. Lalah's with him."

"Is he breathing?" the operator asked.

"I'm not sure . . ." She began to weep. "I'm upstairs. Could you just send the ambulance!"

"They're on the way, Ramona. Is there a phone downstairs that your sister can pick up? I need to speak to her, or someone with him. We need to know if he's breathing. Can you find that out for me, Ramona?"

Beads of sweat were beginning to roll down her face and under her arms. "Yes," she told him, "I'll try to find the cordless."

"Don't hang up," the operator ordered her. "Just yell down to your sister and ask her if he's breathing, okay?"

While Ramona and Lalah were still yelling up and down the stairs, the ambulance finally arrived. Seconds later, the EMTs had Gordon on the stretcher with an oxygen mask strapped over his face and Lalah riding beside him.

Ramona was too unnerved to attempt the drive to the hospital. She woke Sophia instead.

"What?" Sophia's voice was groggy.

"Gordon's had a heart attack. Lalah left with him and the ambulance. I can't drive, Sophia. I just can't." She was crying again. "Can you come?" she sniffed. "Take me to the hospital to be with Lalah and Gordon?"

"I'm there!" Sophia told her, then slammed the phone down.

Ramona sat in the chair, crouched in the fetal position. What was the meaning of all this? Tonight with Ronnie and the cops, and now this? She wept inaudibly, her shoulders shaking.

Sophia ignored the speed limits, reaching Lalah's house in just nine minutes when it should have taken more like twenty. Frankie sat in the front seat beside her, rubbing her right shoulder as they drove. "He'll be fine," Frankie told Sophia in a misty voice. "Don't worry, we'll get through this."

Sophia pulled Frankie's hand from her shoulder and held it, smiling. "Sure we will. Gordon and Lalah will get through this, too. And we'll call Poppy as soon as we get to the hospital." Sophia glanced in the rearview mirror at Ramona.

Ramona did what she had done best that night—stared out the back window at the empty dark streets. The perfectly manicured lawns and brick homes with large front porch awnings were more visible than they had been earlier; Sophia had no tinted windows in her early-model Volkswagen. The cloth covering, used to hide the ripped leather seats snagged at Ramona's stockings.

"I told you to get a cellular phone, Sophia," Frankie said. "I'll pick you up one next week. You just never know when an emergency will come up like this. Besides, I wouldn't want you out here all by yourself, unprotected. It would kill me if anything happened to you."

"Nothing is going to happen to me, honey. Quit worrying so much," Sophia told her.

Ramona shuffled in her seat, shifting her gaze back out the window. She didn't want to hear this lovey-dovey talk between Sophia and her so-called partner, significant other, or whatever the hell Frankie was supposed to be. What was Frankie doing here anyway? This was a family crisis. She wondered if they were in each other's arms when she called. Thank God she saw the sign for the hospital—just three miles to go.

"Mona, you all right back there?" Frankie asked, looking over her shoulder. Her hair was twisted up in a bun.

"Are you and Sophia all right?" Ramona snapped, eyeing Frankie intensely. She could see Sophia staring at her through the rearview mirror. "I mean, really. The way you two carry on like high school sweethearts. It's nauseating."

Frankie turned away, quickly glancing over at Sophia, who kept her gaze straight ahead. Of all the people in her family, Sophia had half-expected her niece to understand, if not accept, her sexual preference. She stole another peek at Ramona from the rearview mirror. Ramona glared right back, frowning.

"Ramona," Sophia said slowly. Her voice was low. "Are you angry with me for choosing Frankie as my partner—my way of life?"

Ramona hesitated. She had expected to have this conversation with Sophia sooner or later. Was she angry? Hell, yes. Did that anger prevent her from loving her aunt? Never. But she did want to know why she chose a gay way of life. Hadn't Coral and Poppy raised her the best they could? Hadn't Victor Lang want to marry her from the first day he'd laid eyes on her? Didn't she want to have children of her own someday?

Ramona shut her eyes and sucked in a deep breath before answering, "Yes, I am angry! Very much so. I'm also confused, hurt, and embar-

rassed. You name it, I'll claim it." She didn't
mean to sound so tart. It was just that her cup
had runneth over with stress tonight: being arrested and questioned like a common criminal,
hearing about Nathan's asthma attack, witnessing
Gordon's heart attack, and wishing that Madrid
could offer the kind of love and affection that
Frankie seems to have for Sophia.

"Sounds homophobic, if you ask me," Frankie
muttered.

"Frankie," Sophia warned, glancing at her.
"Relax a minute, would you?"

"Maybe if you kept your eyes on the road, I could
relax," Frankie huffed. She could hardly contain
her emotions. She had been through so much with
her own family members, her co-workers and old
acquaintances, that she couldn't stand to hear any
derogatory comments from Sophia's relatives as
well. She turned to face Ramona.

Sophia should keep her eyes on the road, Ramona thought. They weren't actually in the clear
as yet. It had stopped raining, but the sounds of
water splashing beneath the tires and against the
oily streets still signaled a road hazard. They'd be
no good for Gordon or Lalah if they ended up
in the emergency room, too.

"Ramona," Frankie charged. "You think you're
so much better because you're in a relationship
with a man? You think it gives you the right to
be judgmental? You think God will overlook your
blemishes 'cause you married a man instead of a
woman?" Her voice was strong and strident.

"Frankie!" Sophia yelled. "Leave it alone, will
you? She's my niece. I'll handle it. Ramona, you
need to understand that regardless of whatever
your psychology books teach, or whatever your

problem might be with my lifestyle, Frankie and I love each other and plan to be together. Get over it!"

Sophia looked over at Frankie, then into the rearview mirror again. Ramona turned her attention back to the trees on the side of the road. Thank God this was their exit for the hospital. The drive had been longer than she'd wanted and the car hotter than hell. Sophia rolled down her window partially and the morning breeze swept through the car, taking with it the aura surrounding them.

They rode in silence the rest of the way. Frankie was feeling good about Sophia speaking up for her, Sophia was feeling a little bad about scolding her niece, and Ramona was feeling displaced and unsettled. There were still more obstacles to overcome: Nathan's state of health, Gordon's condition, and her marriage to Madrid.

Sophia parked the car near the emergency room entrance. It looked like a slow night for a Detroit emergency room, but it had been a busy night for Ramona Shaw. She stepped out of the car and realized as her foot hit the concrete that her feet ached. And so did her heart. She missed her family and needed desperately to be held, to be kissed, and to be loved by her man—the best way he could.

Thirteen

Madrid picked up the phone on the third ring, fumbling as he placed the receiver to his ear, his eyes still closed. A sharp pain traveled from the back of his neck up to his right temple.

He cleared his throat, answering, "Hel-lo," in a deep, raspy voice.

There was a pause. "Madrid," Ramona whispered softly. "It's Mona." If he could have seen her face, he'd know how elated she was to hear his voice—sleep and all.

He switched the phone to his other ear, rolling onto his back. Streaks of faint moonlight shone through the blinds, illuminating Nathan's undisturbed slumber.

"Hey," is all he said. He glanced over at the clock—5:10 A.M. Was Ramona just now getting his message?

"How's Nathan? Is he okay?" she questioned, twining her fingers in the chrome-colored phone wire until she made three ringlets around her index finger. Lord how she wished, as she shifted her weight again, that hospitals still had those old, tight-fitting phone booths with the rickety doors and the tiny seat meant for people with no butts. She stood in her stockings on the cool tile with her pumps on the little chrome shelf under the phone. Her feet were so swollen, she was sure she'd never wear shoes again.

"He's fine. Doctors gave him a shot," Madrid said, his voice level and aloof. "What time is it?" he whispered. He didn't want to awake Nathan.

"I don't know," she sighed heavily. "I lost track. It's been crazy here . . ." Her voice trembled.

Madrid used his elbows to push himself up until his back was resting against the headboard. He didn't like the sound of her voice. He knew his wife well enough to detect when something was wrong. He had hoped for a time like this, when she would call and he would be available to talk to her—to give her a piece of his mind for taking off and leaving like she had. But as he listened, tuned into her soul, the wish dissipated. For the moment.

"What is it, Ramona?" he said after a few silent seconds in the dark. He flipped on the reading lamp, as if it would shed some light on Ramona's situation. A page for Dr. Renee Dorian to pick up the courtesy phone could be heard blurted in the background. "Where are you?"

"Gordon had a heart attack."

"What?" Madrid was shocked. He thought about Gordon for a few seconds, forming a picture of his brother-in-law—bald, tall, brilliant, wealthy . . . "I just talked to him not long ago," Madrid told her as he looked at the clock. Actually it had been awhile back. "How is he?"

Ramona shifted her weight onto her other leg. "He's got some clogged arteries. Atherosclerosis. They're prepping him for surgery."

"Sweet Jesus," Madrid mumbled. "How's Lalah holding up?"

"Oh, well you know Lalah. She's wiping her tears and re-applying her lipstick," Ramona laughed. Madrid joined in, seeing a vision of Lalah discussing Gordon's plight with the doctors while holding a pressed-powder compact to her face. They laughed a good while, probably longer than the joke merited, but it was a much-needed ice-breaker.

Ramona wiped her eyes. Although she appreciated the laughter at Lalah's expense, the truth of the matter was that Gordon was still not out of the woods. She felt the tension again. "Lalah feels pretty bad. She and Gordon were arguing when it happened," she told Madrid.

Madrid paused, smile fading—that could have been him lying in the hospital, preparing for open-heart surgery. He wondered what Gordon would do if he couldn't practice law anymore, if he was confined to a strict diet and a grueling workout schedule. He sighed hard, the tightness on the right side of his head intensifying. "Are you going to stay for the surgery?" he blurted out.

"I'm not sure. Sophia and Frankie are here, and Poppy is on his way."

"Who's Frankie?"

"Sophia's friend," she sighed again. "That's a long story. Anyway I think it best that I get back and check on Nathan."

"He's fine. I'm quite capable," Madrid said disdainfully. No need for her to worry about Nathan now. Everything had been handled.

Ramona sensed his attitude immediately and felt the need to ask, "Did you try the machine first?"

"We searched everywhere and weren't able to find the damn thing." Madrid scowled, rubbing his temple with the palm of his hand in tiny circles, trying to ease the mounting pain.

"It was in the wash room," she said defensively. "It's been there for the last few days."

"Well, it should have been in the closet like it has been in the past. He could have died tonight," Madrid said.

"Died? That just goes to show that if anyone ever bothered to visit the wash room besides me, you all would have seen the machine in there."

Madrid sucked in a deep breath, increasing the pressure of his palms on his temple. Probably a migraine, he determined. He let out the breath. Three days later and still it was just like yesterday, with the familiar tone and accusations.

In the silence, Ramona closed her eyes, concentrating on the air and space between them. Right now she would rather be seated on one of those aqua plastic chairs only two feet away from her; if only the phone would reach that far. Opening her eyes, she saw Lalah and Sophia gathered in the waiting room and she wondered where Frankie was.

Ramona exhaled and spoke first. "I guess I better go find out about Gordon."

There was a moment of hesitation on Madrid's part, he was like a highway driver deciding whether to take the rapidly approaching exit. He let out another strained breath. "Tell Lalah I'll be praying for Gordon. Keep me posted."

"I will," she said, looking down at her swollen feet. "Well . . ." She stopped. There was more she wanted to say, or at least hear. She wasn't quite sure which, but she knew that she missed something about him. "I should be home soon."

"When?" Madrid said quickly.

Was that suppressed excitement Ramona thought she detected in his voice? She felt a slight twinge. "Later today," she cautiously replied—not sure if Madrid really cared about her return. Especially since he was *quite capable*, she thought.

"Later today?" he asked, looking at the clock again. "It's 5:15 in the morning already. Are you planning to get some sleep before tackling the eleven-hour drive?"

"Actually, it's about nine hours," she corrected. "I'll get in a few hours of sleep before leaving. If I leave around noon, that will put me at the house about nine or so tonight."

"Ramona, we need to settle some things when you get back here." The line fell silent again. "Don't forget to fill up with gas before you leave the city. It'll keep you from having to stop too many times on the road. You know, with it being late and the rest stops and all. Anyway, just be careful," he finished.

"I'll be careful. Thanks." She paused. She wanted to tell him something—wanted to get something off her chest, too, but chose to reign in the desire. "See you."

" 'Bye," he said and hung up. He looked down at Nathan, who was resting peacefully—with the shot of Benadryl, he would have slept through World War III. At least the kids would be excited to hear that Ramona was coming home. He, on the other hand, wasn't sure how he felt.

Ramona sat across from Lalah and Sophia, who were hunched together like conspirators. No acknowledgment of her presence was given, their attention purposely focused on the TV perched up in the corner, where some animal kingdom program was on. Ramona flipped through the tattered choice of magazines. A dated *Reader's Digest* won over the romance novels and AAA motor guide magazine. They were the only people in the waiting room. Ramona hoped the family therapy article would intrigue her, but after five or six sentences, her brain shut down.

"How's Gordon?" Ramona asked, breaking the nagging silence. If she hadn't known better, she would have thought Lalah blamed her for Gordon's dilemma.

"They're not sure if he's going to make it," Lalah replied, her eyes never leaving the TV. "It's a dangerous surgery. I shouldn't have stressed him out." Her voice trembled as she glanced over at Ramona. "Did he know, Ramona? Did you tell him where I was tonight?"

Ramona frowned, insulted. How could Lalah think such a thing?

"Gordon didn't ask me any questions about you. Of course I didn't tell him anything. Why would I?" she asked defensively.

"Because you're so damn self-righteous," Sophia snapped.

"What do you mean 'self-righteous,' Sophia?" Ramona demanded.

"You know exactly what the hell I mean," Sophia told her. "You're too judgmental."

Ramona glared at Sophia. She looked over at Lalah, who was eyeing her suspiciously, too.

"And I suppose you feel the same way?" Ramona asked her.

Lalah crossed her left leg over her right, reaching into her purse for a cigarette. She put it in her mouth and lit it—defiantly ignoring the *No Smoking* sign.

"There's no smoking in here, Lalah," Ramona said, annoyed. She didn't feel like breathing in the secondhand smoke.

"See, that's exactly what we're talking about," Lalah told her. "What do you care if I smoke in here or not? There's no one else in here but us." Lalah twisted her mouth to the side and exhaled the smoke. "You're my sister, Ramona, but you do need to learn to relax."

"Or mind your business," Sophia said crassly. "It's annoying. Always has been."

"Someone needs to keep a level head in this family. If grandma were still living, I wonder if you'd both be sitting here trying to shift the blame for your own dilemmas onto her?" Ramona said derisively.

"Well, she ain't here! And you aren't her," Sophia yelled at Ramona. "The problem is, you've been trying too hard to be like my mother, bless her heart. We're not your responsibility, Ramona. Concentrate on your own household."

"Excuse me, Sophia, if I speak my mind sometimes. Just understand this," Ramona said with a pointed finger. "I love you and Lalah both very dearly. But if I don't necessarily agree with or feel comfortable with some of the choices you all make, I'm inclined to say something. I'm not going to harp, or nag on and on, but I will speak on it once. We wouldn't be here had it not been . . ." She tapered off.

"Been for what?" Lalah jumped up. "Been for me? Is that what you meant to say? If you hadn't been so mesmerized by a few compliments and whispers of bull in your ear by Ronnie, we all wouldn't be here. Gordon wouldn't have had to bail your butt out of jail, and he would have been home safely waiting for our return. You're just as much to blame for this situation. Let me know if you plan on going home to Madrid and fessing up to what really happened to you tonight."

Ramona stood up, her heartbeat accelerated to a dangerous level. She couldn't remember the last time she kicked Lalah's behind. But if her older sister didn't put a lid on her mouth, she was going to give her a good old-fashioned whooping right here in the waiting room. How dare Lalah try and twist the whole thing around? She could feel beads of perspiration dot her forehead. All she could do now was ask God for the strength not to pounce on Lalah and Sophia.

Frankie walked into the waiting room, almost on cue. She stood in the doorway watching, waiting for the sparks to become full-blown. Sophia stood up, too. Regardless of how angry she was with Ramona, she didn't want her nieces fighting.

"Poppy's here," Frankie finally said. "He's in the bathroom now. I suggest you all put on some better-looking faces." She turned and walked out of the smoky waiting room.

Ramona dropped her shoes on the floor and stepped into them.

"Where are you going, Mona?" Sophia asked, motioning for Lalah to take her seat again. Lalah did, grudgingly.

"I'm going to have Poppy take me back to Lalah's so I can get a few hours of rest before I get on the road."

"You're not going to wait for the outcome of the surgery?" Sophia was shocked.

"You can call me at Lalah's. Or I'll call over

here before I hit the road." She was at the door already.

"Come on, Mona. We didn't mean anything hurtful. We just spoke the truth like you. No need for you to rush off—we're family. We need to stick together." Sophia smiled.

"Oh, I'm not worried about our difference of opinions. Madrid left a message with Gordon that Nathan had a severe asthma attack." She paused.

"What? Is he all right?" Sophia asked.

"Madrid claims that he is. But I need to get home and check on the kids and figure out my own relationship, like Lalah said."

"Mona, I didn't say it to be vicious," Lalah told her. "I just . . ." Tears began flowing. "This doesn't make any sense, us fussing unnecessarily while my husband lays practically on his deathbed and my only nephew was stricken with a severe asthma attack." Lalah stood and wiped her eyes, walking toward Ramona and Sophia. She reached out for them both and they all fell into an embrace. "I love you both, you know that," Lalah told them. "We're family, right?" She sniffled.

"Right," Ramona agreed.

"Good," Sophia said. " 'Cause I sure don't want to start all over again with another set of half-crazed women." She laughed.

"Ramona, don't worry about things here," Lalah told her, pulling away and wiping her eyes. "Gordon's stubborn self won't be going anywhere." Lalah smiled. "You get home and kiss my niece and nephew for me. And put a little sexual spanking on Madrid. That's all he needs." Lalah rounded her eyes comically. "Just slide into that black merry widow we bought and ride his ass all the way into the sunrise."

Ramona giggled. Lalah chuckled, careful to keep a steady hand while reapplying her pressed powder. Frankie stood in the doorway flashing a wide smile at Sophia, feeling the return of tranquillity.

Ramona was relieved. If only she had a camera. Instead, she snapped a mental picture of the three of them. She tried hard to fit Frankie into the scheme of things, into Sophia's life permanently. She vowed to keep an open mind. Poppy stood in the doorway, behind Frankie, smiling and observing the scenario. Ramona could have kicked herself for not bringing a camera on the trip. But she would never forget this moment—ever.

Five hours wasn't adequate rest for the drive Ramona was about to make at 10:47 A.M. But it was plenty time to get out of the motor city before Sunday church-goers bombarded the streets on their way from service to the fancy brunches scattered about the city. There was no word on Gordon's condition as yet—a good sign, she prayed as she dialed the number to the hospital. Surely her deep sleep wouldn't have prevented her from hearing the phone.

The line rang four times before the hospital operator answered. "St. Joseph's Hospital, how may I help you?"

"I'm trying to reach the ICU waiting area. Can you ring me through, please?"

"Just a minute," the operator told her, then placed her on hold. Symphonic music hummed in the background.

"Dear Lord, please let Gordon be all right,"

Ramona prayed aloud while she waited to be connected.

Finally a woman answered the phone. "ICU."

"Yes, my name is Ramona Shaw and I'm looking for my sister, Lalah Trevell. Is she there?"

"Hold on a minute and let me check," the woman told her, placing her back on hold. A new song played in the background, George Winston's "December" album. "Mrs. Shaw, your sister will be right with you. Can you hold just a few more minutes?"

"Sure," Ramona agreed. "Maybe you can tell me how my brother-in-law is doing?"

"He's still in surgery. Hold on, here's your sister. I'll transfer the call to that phone over there," the lady told Lalah.

"Hey, Mona," Lalah said, exhaustedly.

"What's the word?"

"None, as yet. They're still in surgery," Lalah yawned.

"Good Lord, why so long?"

"It's a complicated surgery, Mona. Not to mention that Gordon and the doctors were totally unprepared."

"I know, I know." Ramona exhaled. "How are you?"

"Oh, I'm holding on as best I can. Sophia, Frankie and Poppy are all here talking my damn ear off." She laughed.

Ramona smiled. Lalah would be crowned the family comedian for the rest of her life. It was good that Lalah wasn't by herself, that the family pulled through in times like these to support one another.

"Heading home?" Lalah asked.

"Yup. Just woke up a few minutes ago. Figured

I better call and find out what's going on before
I leave."

"You sure you got enough rest? I couldn't handle it if something happened to you, too," Lalah
said somberly.

"Yes, I'm sure," Ramona told her. "If I get
sleepy, I promise to pull over and get a hotel
room or something. Stop worrying."

"Child, I have to worry sometimes. Hell, with
you and Madrid and now Sophia and Frankie,
you're trying to put me in an early grave," Lalah
snickered.

"Speaking of Frankie, how come you didn't tell
me about Sophia? You run your mouth about
everything else under the sun, but you forget to
tell me something as monumental as that.
Geesh!" Ramona teased. "At least I would have
been better prepared."

"Why should you have been prepared? Hell,
nobody prepared me for the fact that my Auntie
Sophia is gay. Why should I have robbed you of
that joyous feeling when you found out? Furthermore, I had dilemmas of my own."

"How are you going to handle that, if the girl
is really pregnant?"

"It's probably true." Lalah exhaled. "Though
if it is for sure true, I'll give Gordon a few weeks,
possibly a few months, to get his strength back
before I kick his crippled ass."

"Lalah!"

But Lalah didn't care about Ramona's conster-
nation. Instead she laughed heartily and hard,
harder than Ramona had heard in a long, long
while. Ramona snickered along, too.

"Mona, you better get going. I'll leave a message with Madrid as soon as I hear something, all right?"

"I'll call you from my cellular phone, if I'm not too far out of the area," Ramona said. There was a moment of silence before Ramona spoke again. "Lalah, would you like us to pray together like we used to with Grandma?"

"That would be so nice, Mona. Why don't you begin?" Lalah said, shutting her eyes in preparation. An image of her grandmother flashed before her eyes. If their Coral had still been alive, half the things that were taking place in their lives wouldn't ever have manifested. Coral Johns would have seen to it, as Ramona had tried to.

Praying with Lalah had done something to rekindle Ramona's spirit, too, she thought as she showered. Feeling rejuvenated, Ramona shut off the steaming water and stepped out of the tub. She choked back the temptation to step into her worn undergarments, instead selecting the brand new green silk bra and panty set from Victoria's Secret. Although her old cotton bloomers would have made for a more comfortable ride, she had promised Lalah and herself that she would try to be more conscious about her appearance.

No longer facing a dreaded foe, Ramona peered into the mirror and for the first time in a very long time, she appreciated the face staring back at her. Her new haircut would quickly become her trademark, as well as the new natural shades of makeup. She applied the last stroke of mascara before applying the bronze matte lipstick. Dangling earrings, definitely a different thing for her, set off her new look. She raced through the room, tossing and packing old clothes and more new clothes into her two pieces of luggage.

She scanned the room for evidence of forgotten items, her eyes stopping at the bed. She should make it, but tomorrow was Monday and Lalah's housekeeper would be in to change the linen and clean the house. It was a hands-down decision, but Ramona chose to make the bed anyway. She snatched up her bags, struggling down the spiral staircase. She placed the bags in Meka, then returned inside to grab a few snacks for her trip. The refrigerator was bare to the bone except for a few bruised pieces of fruit. Ramona picked through the shelves to gather enough edibles to sustain her during the drive.

Meka was still in need of a waxjob. But Ramona was in need of much more than that—she needed to get home and save her own family, if it wasn't already too late. The gas needle stood at twelve o'clock; she would have to stop before leaving the city. The clock read 11:24 A.M. Good timing, she determined. If traffic was kind, she would pull into her driveway around 8:30 or so. Her heartbeat skipped with excitement. It would be good to see the kids, to wake up in her own bed, to sit on her own toilet, to eat her own cooking. And of course, to jump Madrid's bones.

Fourteen

Madrid was not the least bit perturbed when Connie phoned at 9:40 A.M. to change her hair appointment with Leslie to two o'clock. It gave them all another hour and a half of sleep and there was still—he glanced at the microwave clock—another hour before she was due to arrive. The kids were sprawled out on the family room floor, watching some Disney cartoon for the first or tenth time, he wasn't quite sure. He stacked the breakfast plates and glasses in the dishwasher and let it rip while he swept the kitchen floor. Again, it was hard to see how messy it had gotten in a measly twenty-four hour period.

The kids were elated to hear of Ramona's return. In fact, they were so jubilant, they thoroughly cleaned their rooms and put on their cutest outfits in preparation for the homecoming. Leslie had even offered to help Madrid fix dinner a second day in a row. Wow, Madrid thought. And all this owed to Ramona's return. He'd have to make a mental note of how the kids reacted the next time he returned from a business trip.

Tonight was the night to place the used newspaper bundles outside for the garbagemen to collect and recycle. Madrid searched the kitchen

drawers for a large rubber band or some string—
the wandering neighborhood cats and stray dogs
set the rules about loose newspapers left unat-
tended overnight. He stirred through the papers
in the drawer nearest to the kitchen counter.

The letter A, scrawled in bright purple ink
above "The Real Art of Communicating: Learning to Talk, Learning to Listen, Learning to
Hear" caught his attention. The first typewritten
paragraph on the sheet of paper was set off with
a footnote credited to Drs. Derek Hopson and
Darlene Powell Hopson. The name of their book,
Friends, Lovers and Soul Mates was apparently one
of many contributing factors to the paper.

One of Ramona's papers, Madrid thought, unconsciously taking a seat at the counter before
continuing to read the paragraph. . . . *No matter
how long you are together, exchanging confidences and
negotiating conflicts will require effort, but the time
spent in unproductive or destructive struggle is greatly
minimized as your mutual respect deepens and commu-
nication skills improve* . . . Is that so? Madrid
thought, reading on.

He sat in that position, for an hour, completely
mesmerized by the psychological jargon and
claims he'd always abhorred, until he was familiar
with *passive, aggressive, passive-aggressive,* and *asser-
tive* approaches in communicating. Drawing the
paper closer, he read until he saw his personality
unfold before him. *Aggressive* had definitely been
his style of communicating both in the work force
and at home. *And here I thought this stuff was a
bunch of malarkey.* Madrid chuckled lightly. *So,
Mona, this is what you had been going on and on
about when you tried to tell me I wasn't listening to
you. Interesting.*

The doorbell chimed. He didn't want to succumb to the visitors waiting outside his front door; he was focused on the new bit of information he had unveiled regarding his behavioral pattern. He looked up at the clock. Where had the time slipped away to?

Before answering the door, he marked his place with the felt pen dangling from the notepad, then replaced the paper in the drawer. He'd finish the reading later tonight—before Ramona returned. He realized that he hadn't bothered to have much interest in Ramona's schoolwork before now.

It surprised him to see DeMar standing next to Connie when he looked through the peephole.

"Back again?" Madrid said, smiling at Connie before looking at DeMar.

"Sí." She grinned, stepping into the foyer, holding a small, square tin can. "In my culture, *la familia es importante,"* she said, eyeing DeMar.

"I didn't mean you, Connie, I meant this brother here," Madrid said, referring to DeMar, who was surprisingly low-key.

"I missed you. What can I say," DeMar told Madrid, closing the door behind him. "You have what I want to have—a family. Haven't you and Ramona figured out by now that's why you can't get rid of me?" He laughed.

"Oh, is that it?" Madrid joked, walking toward the family room.

"Uncle Dee," Nathan called out. "Come here! The Indian lady is singing and dancing on the TV."

DeMar and Madrid exchanged quick glances and Madrid shrugged his shoulders. "Disney for ya," Madrid told DeMar.

Connie was already seated next to Leslie. She couldn't wait to tame the young girl's hair. Leslie had greeted Connie when she walked in the room, but that was about all. Leslie gave no indication that she was remotely prepared for the task that lay ahead of her—ahead of them both.

Connie sat quietly for a few more minutes, while Madrid and DeMar talked in the kitchen. "What you watching?" she finally asked, trying to break the ice with Leslie.

"Pono-hont-is," Nathan replied impatiently.

Leslie didn't respond. But oh, wait until Connie places her hands on the child's head, Madrid thought, walking back into the family room. She'd have plenty to say then.

"Leslie," Madrid said. "Connie's here to do your hair. How long you think it'll take, Connie?"

Connie studied Leslie's hair, as she had done off and on the night before. Connie said, "No more than three hours, I would say. Depends."

"On what?" Madrid cried out. "Good Lord, Connie—three hours seems like plenty of time."

Connie brushed past Madrid towards Leslie. "Leslie," Connie said in a smooth, reassuring tone, as she led Leslie by the hand toward the kitchen table. "I promise it won't be so bad."

Leslie wasn't convinced. "Three hours is *so* long," she whined. "Do we have to do all of it today?"

"I'm afraid so. You want to be pretty for school tomorrow, right?"

Leslie took a seat in the chair and Connie took a colored picture of a famous teenage rapper from the tin can, placing it on the table in front of Leslie. "See how pretty she looks with her hair

braided? You're going to look better than that.
You'll see." Connie winked.

Leslie eyed the picture intensely. She was familiar with the popular female vocalist. "Yeah, but
she's got on makeup, too."

"That's the difference, little angel." Connie
smiled, looking into Leslie's eyes, and gently cradling her chin between her thumb and index finger. "You're so pretty, you don't need any
makeup at all—ever."

Leslie grinned widely, letting her crescent-
shaped smile show her braces. She felt like someone had taken a feather and tickled her tummy
from the inside. Prettier than the singer in the
picture? Her rounded shoulders suddenly became more square as she replayed Connie's comment in her head.

Connie cautiously tugged at the thick locks of
hair, careful not to be too harsh, though some
amount of force would have to be used if she was
ever to divide the hair into four parts. For the
first few minutes, tears trickled down Leslie's
cheeks. She wiped them away as fast as they fell,
concentrating all the while on Connie's compliment, and the thought of not having to go
through the hair ordeal for at least the next few
months. This was worth it, she thought, swiping
the last tear away.

Noticing Nathan's droopy eyelids, Madrid laid
him on the love seat and covered him with the
worn burgundy and tan afghan Ramona's mother
had given them as their first anniversary gift.
"That damn shot is still having a lingering effect
on him," Madrid said protectively, gazing down
at his sleeping son.

"What shot?" DeMar asked, before dropping down on the sofa.

"He had an asthma attack sparked by some kind of allergic reaction last night. We didn't get home till three this morning," Madrid said, sitting down on the opposite end of the sofa. "I was scared as hell, too. He couldn't breathe, I couldn't find his machine—it was crazy."

"Thank God he's all right," DeMar compassionately replied. "I tell you, bro, you never realize how precious life is until it's threatened or snatched away."

"That's exactly what Dad used to say all the time." Madrid chuckled, reminiscing about his deceased father and his neverending clichés."

"It's been many moons now, but I miss that old geezer, too." DeMar beamed. "Remember the time he made us cut all the neighbors' grass for free one summer 'cause we sassed two of our nosy neighbors?"

"Yeah." Madrid smiled. "Like it was anyone's business that we were kissing some girls on the front porch while Dad was out working late that night and Mom was at church playing bingo." Madrid laughed louder. "How about the time he took us fishing off those rocks and that kid next to us fell into the stream? Dad beat the kid's own father into the water."

"Yup, and saved that hard-headed kid's life, too, while nearly drowning his damn self." DeMar threw his head back against the sofa and laughed some more. Nathan stirred under the blanket momentarily. DeMar paused before continuing, "Dad didn't even know how to swim, huh?"

"Nope—just reacted. Always did, no matter what the circumstances," Madrid said. "What do you think he'd say about us now? Think he'd be proud of us?"

DeMar lifted his head off the sofa and grinned, tossing Madrid's questions around in his head. Would their father be pleased with the lifestyle he chose? Would he be disappointed that he still hadn't married at thirty-seven years old? Had kids? Purchased a home? It'd be hard to tell. So many years had passed, so many things had changed in the world. DeMar sighed. "I'm sure he'd be pleased. But to what degree . . ." De-Mar's voice trailed off.

"You're not sure," Madrid said, finishing De-Mar's sentence. "Personally, I think he'd be very proud of our choices and accomplishments."

"How you figure, Drid? I don't have any accomplishments worth celebrating. At least you're married with two children, a thriving career, and a home. I'm still single, living in a rented apartment, working in New York City as a so-called striving Wall Street wanna-be, and socking away my cash for them supposed 'rainy days' like dad instructed us to do. You know," DeMar said, sitting more erect, rubbing pieces of lint off his pant leg. "I should have majored in engineering like Dad advised me instead of majoring in women. Makes no sense," he mumbled.

"Ah, don't go whipping yourself upside the head for no reason. Allow me," Madrid teased, swinging playfully at his brother. "Seriously, De-Mar," he continued, "you're off to a running start with a growing company. And I'm sure you'll buy a house as soon as you feel the time is right. And as far as marriage is concerned—" Madrid paused and raised his brow "—let me just say that it ain't what it's cracked up to be sometimes. It's the hardest work I've ever done in my entire life. Period.''

"At least you got a partner willing to work with you. I know sometimes I give Mona a bad way to go. But overall, you've got yourself a good lady, Drid. So many people get into situations where only one person is pulling the weight of the two. That's ludicrous. At least you got Mona in your corner. Besides which, you have two lovely children who love you no matter what.''

Madrid really didn't want to hear about how good Ramona was, or how blessed he was to be married to her. Somewhere, deep down, he still harbored some ill feelings about how things had gone down between them a few days back. Somehow they would have to meet in the middle or call it quits—some way, somehow, something was going to have to change between them. Perhaps he could start by implementing some of the textbook's communications skills. Madrid sighed unintentionally.

"Speaking of Mona . . .'' DeMar said, taking time to read his brother's body language as he shifted the conversation.

"Her sister's husband had a heart attack,'' Madrid told him.

"Gordon? Is he all right?''

"They're not sure yet. I'll find out when Mona gets home tonight,'' Madrid said, standing. "You want a beer or something? I think I have two left.''

"Sure. But do you have any champagne or wine?'' DeMar asked.

"No. Why?''

" 'Cause maybe you need to buy a bottle, chill

it and have a celebratory homecoming when Mona gets here." DeMar grinned slyly.

"She could celebrate by her damn self," Madrid mumbled defensively. "What the hell would we be celebrating for anyway?"

"Your life together. Her safe arrival, your beautiful children, your blessed career. Hell, anything you can think of. Matter of fact, when was the last time you romanced your wife, little brother?"

Madrid looked away. *Every night,* he said to himself, thinking about the three o'clock lovemaking he initiated with Ramona while she lay motionless waiting for him to reach his climax. Could it be the lovemaking, or the lack thereof, that was the underlying problem?

A wave of insecurity flowed over him. *Naw.* He always satisfied his wife, right? Though she *had* been complaining that they never kissed like they used to, didn't cuddle, or have the same kind of foreplay or afterplay they did in the old days—and that he didn't compliment her on her looks anymore. She had even dropped some hint about him rushing through the lovemaking like he was on a schedule.

Well, she wasn't doing anything magnificent to spark flames in their bedroom, either. She didn't dress as sexily anymore, during the day or at night. Nor did she paint her toenails that pretty red, or shave her legs as often as she had when they were first together.

The extra weight she had gained after Nathan was born didn't bother him as much as she accused him it did. A thought flashed through his mind, precisely what the paper eluded to; not directly telling Ramona that her weight didn't

bother him was another lost opportunity to effectively communicate with her.

Hell, he liked the way her breasts became fuller
and rounder, and her hips and butt spread out
after the pregnancy. The only thing he wanted
from her was a little more time, more effort to
make herself pretty and sexy like before, smelling
good all the time, purring around him, stroking
his back, riding him on top . . . Madrid caught
DeMar's eager smile.

"See, I told you, man. You can't recall the last
time you pampered Mona, huh?" DeMar stood
up beside him. "Listen, this is my present to you
and Mona for putting up with my trifling ways.
Since I'm on vacation this week, the kids can
spend the night with me tonight and I'll take
them to school in the morning. This way you and
Mona can get that heat going again, you know
what I mean?" DeMar grinned wickedly again.
"Get some action going with my pretty ass sister-
in-law, that's all ya'll need to get things started
again."

Madrid looked at DeMar curiously. Now how
the hell would his single behind know? There was
more to a marriage than throwing some romance
in every now and then. But he was right in some
ways. A little romance might spark something. It
could even be the truce he'd been hoping for.

"I don't know, DeMar . . . with Nathan having
his attack last night and all. I probably should
keep him here with me."

"What do I look like? Billy the Bozo?" DeMar
said throwing his hands up in the air. "I'm responsible. I can take care of my nephew. Just give
me all the necessary information, medicine and

whatever else. You and Ramona need this one night together at least."

Madrid shut his eyes for a minute, contemplating the pros and cons of letting Nathan go home with DeMar.

DeMar frowned. "Christ, Drid it's only for a night."

Hesitantly, Madrid nodded his head "okay." DeMar was right, Madrid thought, he and Ramona did need to sort things out between them, and it would be a lot easier and less inhibiting if the kids weren't around. Especially if things threatened to get ugly with a loud argument of some sort. And DeMar was right about something else—despite all the problems with Mona lately, deep down she was prettier and softer than a dove. And if DeMar was noticing it, he certainly needed to lay some good loving on his wife, at a better time than three in the morning, just to show DeMar and any other man mesmerized by Mona's unique beauty that in no uncertain terms Ramona Shaw was indeed his wife.

The world had a funny way of transforming a woman if she chose to allow it to happen. In two and a half hours, Leslie had gone from looking like a junior Chakka Khan to one of the many blossoming teenage singers. Madrid's feelings were mixed—both happy and sad. Happy that they had conquered the battle with Leslie's hair for a few months, and sad that the new hairdo made her look more grown-up than the eleven-and-a-half years she boasted.

But Leslie loved her new look. Her square shoulders, lifted head and attitude showed it. She stood in the kitchen as if on center stage, absorbing all the attention. Nathan was fascinated by the many thick braids dangling down Leslie's back. DeMar and Connie reveled in her perkiness, and Madrid . . . well, he felt it necessary to remind her that makeup was still off limits.

The house seemed stiller than it had even when it was home only to Madrid and Ramona a few years back. Nagging noises and nuisances would be nonexistent for the rest of the night. DeMar had coaxed the kids to spend the night at his house, although cajoling them wasn't difficult after he promised to make a pit stop at Applegate Farms for some fresh ice cream on the way. And DeMar was so ecstatic to finally offer a helping hand instead of a needy one, that Madrid hadn't wanted to pop his bubble by refusing to play along.

Now it was just Madrid, the fourteen or so candles he'd strategically placed throughout the house, and the many scattered CDs lying on the floor. A trip to the local Pathmark was responsible for the bottle of Mums chilling in the freezer and the tulips in the tall vase standing on Ramona's dresser. If Ramona had left Detroit when she planned to, she would be pulling into their driveway in two hours or less. And a couple of hours was all he needed to set the atmosphere.

Madrid would light the candles in the bathroom and bedroom and run a hot bubble bath about ten minutes before he thought Ramona would arrive. In the meantime, candles would be lit on the mantel and family room coffee table as the Isley Brother's greatest hits, Teddy Pendergrass, Phil Perry, Jay Spencer, Regina Belle and Chante Moore echoed throughout the house. Ma-

drid smiled. Lord knew they could make some
sweet harmony together if all went well.

Jasmine incense would greet her when she
stepped into the exceptionally tidy house. The
two dozen long-stemmed red and white roses
would be dropped throughout the house, the first
one at the foot of the door, the second couple
on the steps leading to their bedroom, the last
few around the tub and across her side of the
bed.

Banking on the fact that Ramona might be
hungry once she finally did arrive, Madrid decided to have a snack waiting. He placed the fresh
salmon spread, wheat crackers, cheese, grapes,
strawberries and slices of melon on one of Ramona's fine crystal platters. In a smaller crystal
bowl, he placed chips of ice sprinkled with pieces
of orange rind and rose petals.

Madrid filled the tub halfway with warm water
and immersed his body—he couldn't remember
the last time he took a bath by himself, or with
Ramona, for that matter. Quick showers had
served as his relaxation method for way too long,
he thought as he took in a deep breath then exhaled it slowly.

Gladys Knights' "You're Number One" piped
through the speakers softly for now. It was Sunday
night and WBLS' Quiet Storm session was beginning. Madrid leaned his head back against the
cool marble and shut his eyes. The song swept
him away as he sang aloud, "Your happiness is
my only concern . . . You're number one . . ."
Now that was a true statement—Ramona had sure
been number one in his book for many years.

He rinsed the tub out with some cleanser, a
chore he despised, then plugged the drain with

the stopper. In thirty minutes or so, he would run Ramona a nice hot bubble bath. He laid a fresh towel on the counter with two roses on top, careful not to place them too close to the candles. Though he wanted to get a fire going with his wife, he didn't want to burn the house down.

Madrid stood in the door of the bedroom absorbing it all, making sure everything was perfect. Candles on each nightstand, roses, champagne glasses . . . Good, good, he thought, walking over to his closet. He rummaged through piles of clothes until he found the black silk pajama pants and smoking jacket Ramona had purchased for him a few Christmases ago. He shook the items a few times, deciding that it would be best to run a warm iron over them to knock out some of the wrinkles.

He tossed the pajama set on the bed and walked back into the bathroom. Before he'd proceed any further, he needed to take the time to smooth some lotion over his entire body. His cologne collection took up the entire left side of the counter; he chose Kenzo for Men, splashing the cool liquid fragrance on his chest and neck. Mona preferred the new scent over all his others lately.

Madrid felt excitement sneaking up on him and fought not to let it overwhelm him. Grabbing the pajamas off the bed, he headed downstairs to the laundry room, where the iron and ironing board were stored. He felt his spirits rise as he glanced at the clock. Just a little while longer, he grinned. He only hoped and prayed that the evening would not be in vain.

Fifteen

Lalah threaded her thin fingers through Gordon's limp ones. He needed some lotion, she surmised quickly—his skin was rough and clammy. The surgery had been determined successful, for the time being. Now it was up to Gordon to fight on his end—to recover and vow to eat right, exercise and live right. Live right. That would be something to see, Lalah joked inwardly. Gordon hadn't been living right, at least regarding their marriage, for some years now.

Perhaps the frightening face of death would whip him into shape, she hoped selfishly. It sure would most folks. But then Gordon Trevell was not most folks, not by a long shot. If Gordon had an epitaph, it would read: A prominent, wealthy, powerful, successful and young, by American standards, man, with every type of stock, bond, mutual fund, partnership, and all the cars, clothes, jewelry and women he could ask for. So why had he chosen her again? Lalah wondered as she studied Gordon's closed eyes. Beauty—that was it. Her everlasting, exuberant, intoxicating beauty. At least that's what he'd told her those many years ago when he proposed to her.

Tears streamed down her cheeks, burning as

she reveled in self-pity. Had she lost her touch, her beauty, her class? Is that what drove him into the arms of a woman half her age? *Damn him. Pardon me Lord,* she quickly begged, burying her chin in her chest. *I've been by his side through the good and bad. I've given him everything! Everything but a child. But he said he never wanted any children. He insisted on it—made it a part of our unspoken marital proclamation.*

The warm sensation of a teardrop dropping on Gordon's hand caused him to stir. His hand tightened suddenly, squeezing Lalah's frail fingers and she raised her head. When her eyes finally met his, she swore she saw the sparkling of building tears. A timid smile creased Gordon's face. An enormous effort, Lalah supposed. She mimicked the same displayed faintness, at the same time using her other hand to wipe away traces of tears and smeared mascara.

Gordon looked worn and feeble, with various sizes of tubes scattered every which way. The pale cream hospital gown blended against his ashy and colorless face. Sweat beaded on the top of his head before sliding down his forehead and the bridge of his broad nose. Lalah smiled, grabbed the end of the sheet and dabbed the perspiration off his face.

"See, if you had some hair, it might have caught some of this stuff," Lalah whispered jokingly, dabbing at his nose.

Gordon squinted, wanting to laugh, chuckle or just plain grin. *Lalah the comedian.* His chest hurt too damn bad to even attempt to reply or laugh. Didn't she know that? He blinked his eyes twice, freeing the tears that had built either during the surgery or now, as he faced his wife, his life-long companion, his sidekick.

"I'm sorry, Gordon," Lalah whimpered. "I never meant for you . . . for this . . ." She paused. Her emotions overflowed, foaming like a lidded pot of boiling rice. She lowered her head again, letting the few teardrops fall onto her lap. Gordon squeezed her hand again—feeling weak and light like a two-year-old child trying to arm wrestle a seventeen-year-old.

Nurses had been in and out of Gordon's room constantly over the past two hours, and when Lalah heard a noise outside Gordon's door, she assumed it was another nurse in a pink, blue and white smock. But when she looked up and faced the door, she noticed a heavy-set young woman peering through the glass. A sudden twinge of anger erupted, causing her eyebrows to furrow.

Her intuition awoke. The woman gawking through the small window was Gordon's playmate, Lalah was certain of it. Within a matter of seconds, Lalah had unconsciously sized up her competitor. From where she sat, the woman seemed homely, if not outright ugly. *She has some nerve coming here,* Lalah thought. And Gordon had some nerve putting her down for the looks of that woman. How had she found out about Gordon already?

Lalah sighed heavily with disgust, her demeanor changing rapidly, alerting Gordon. His eyes struggled to follow hers. And when they finally rested on the spot, where Lalah had been keenly focused, he squeezed her hand a third time. A plea for help—or understanding.

"Is that her?" Lalah spouted instantly, her gaze averted as she waited for his response. A sort of safety precaution, in case he lied—which she would have detected easily.

Gordon shut his eyes, but not before another teardrop escaped and warmed the side of his face. His mouth opened slowly, exposing his tongue, which was coated with a thick white film, an after-effect from the anesthesia. His voice was strained as he spoke. "There's no love on my part," he gasped. "She was a client . . . I love you, Lalah. Truly." The tears were warmer and steadier now as they fell.

Lalah couldn't face him, mainly because her eyes told a different story. A mixture of emotions—disgust, anger, pain, pity and hate—stewed within her empty eyes. Improvise—that's what she needed to do now. It wasn't the time or the place for them to get into a discussion about Gordon's mistress. Later, she vowed. Much later, when he was well enough to handle her pain, and feel the back-stabbing blade of betrayal by a loved one.

Pensively, she looked up at the door again. The woman had disappeared and Lalah was relieved. Finally, she glanced over at Gordon. "Would you like something to drink?"

Gordon stiffly shook his head no, steadily keeping an eye on Lalah. "I want you—us. I'm sorry . . ." he tiredly whispered. His ability to talk to her was limited. It hurt too much to talk, and even more to discuss his promiscuity with his wife.

Lalah stood up and walked over to the sink, where she filled the tiny Dixie cup with water. Absently she sipped the lukewarm tap water, focusing and finding nothing particularly interesting about the room. Pastel walls with matching accessories served as the decor. Pale blue walls with a boring lavender, yellow and blue watercolor painting set the tone of the room, and the lavender plastic cups, water pitcher, serving tray, soap dish, toothpaste holder and urine pail were meant to accentuate it.

A wave of nausea swept through Lalah. She tossed the Dixie cup into the trash, leaving a swallow of water in the bottom of it. Suddenly the room became unbearably hot to her; she patted her forehead with one of the powder blue tissues. Gordon was still studying her from across the room, she could feel it.

"I'm going to call Ramona and let her know the surgery was successful. She'd want to know," Lalah said, walking past Gordon's slightly inclined hospital bed. "I'll be back in a few minutes, okay?" Her eyes remained fixed on the floor while she spoke to him and even as she stepped out of his room. Everyone had some type of phobia about something or another, she reasoned. The only other thing she dreaded more than death itself was coming face to face with the woman accused of sleeping with her husband.

The nurses' station in the ICU was strangely empty and quiet. Lalah flagged down one of the nurses who was returning from administering medication to a patient. The petite Filipino nurse carried a tray in one hand and a clipboard under her other arm. Her face lit up when she saw Lalah walking toward her.

"Mrs. Trevel," the nurse said, placing the tray on the counter. "You should get some rest. Mr. Trevel will be fine. He's in good hands." She smiled.

"I know he is. And thank you," Lalah said. "I think I'm going to stay overnight just in case. Is there any way I could get a cot or something?"

The nurse looked at her queerly, then replied, "A cot? I don't think we have any here. I'll check anyway." She picked up another chart and headed down the hall.

"Thank you," Lalah told her. That small verbal exchange with the little nurse had exhausted her. A cigarette, Lalah thought, that's what she needed now. It had been four hours since her last smoke and she was long overdue. She slapped the bottom of the pack until one cigarette fell out. She placed it in her mouth, longing to find an area in the hospital where she could light up.

The nurse turned around to face Lalah again, giving her a disapproving look. "By the way, Mrs. Trevel. Another one of your relatives came by to see your husband, but I told her only one visitor at a time. She's waiting outside those doors."

Lalah stood staring at the back of the nurse's head. She was too stunned to move. Another relative? There were no other female relatives but Gordon's two sisters, who were en route from Dallas, and Lalah's mother, who was currently on a job assignment with her father in Saudi Arabia. Pure agitation motivated her to pummel through the heavy double doors into the lobby, where, even from a distance she recognized the woman she had seen peering through Gordon's window earlier.

Her heart rate was past description, though if it had to be explained, it was thumping somewhere past a fast-beating congo rhythm. As Lalah got closer to the woman, whose head was buried in a magazine, she slowed her pace, mindlessly gazing at the midsection of the woman's body. *My Lord*, Lalah gasped mouth drooping open. *This child is more than a little pregnant.* Just as Lalah

fought to draw her lips shut, the woman lifted
her head from her magazine and Lalah knew that
she had come face to face, woman to woman, with
Gordon's side action.

The woman stood, probably more out of reflex
than as a defense mechanism. Lalah walked directly over to her, struggling all the while to remain calm and tactful. If only she could fire up
the cigarette she had clutched in the palm of her
hand.

"I hear you're here to see my husband, Gordon
Trevell," Lalah said crassly. The words had
tripped out of her mouth before she had a
chance to think them over.

The woman reeked of fear. She wasn't here to
cause a scene, only to check on the status of the
father of her baby—Gordon. Her cousin, a nurse
who'd worked on the earlier shift, had phoned
her with the news about Gordon, and a warning
that she wished, as she stood before Gordon's
wife, that she had heeded—to stay away for
awhile. She had often imagined, even practiced
a scenario like this in her head on so many occasions. The only difference was that tonight the
other member of her mental cast was not imaginary, but here, right in front of her, in the flesh.

"I just want to know how he's doing. That's
all," she said innocently enough.

Lalah studied the young girl intently. How in
the sweet Lord's name could such a young
woman be so damn dumb and naive? Or just
plain callous and reckless? A bead of perspiration
rolled down the girl's forehead. A sure sign of
nervousness—an amateur sign, Lalah thought.
Didn't she know that she was supposed to keep

her composure no matter what? Never let 'em see you sweat.

"How did you hear?" Lalah asked her.

The woman shifted her eyes to the floor then back to Lalah. "I have a friend who works here."

"Is that right?" Lalah said sarcastically. Didn't she even have the good sense not to answer the question? *So, the joke's on me, huh?* Lalah thought. Everybody seemed to know about this little affair except her.

"I'm not here to cause any problems," the woman said defensively.

"Well, it's a little too late for that," Lalah snapped, looking down at her rounded belly. She placed the cigarette in the corner of her mouth, grabbing the lighter out of her purse. Just a few more feet and this puppy was going to be burning, Lalah thought, anxious for a smoke.

There was a tight moment of nothing but silence and air between Lalah and the mystery woman she didn't care to know formally or informally. The girl reached down and picked up her purse and sweater from the chair. Lalah stood waiting, for what she didn't know.

"I'm sorry. I just want to make sure he's all right," the woman said with wet eyes as she gathered her things in one hand.

"He's all right," Lalah told her. "But since you're already here, you might as well make your visit worthwhile. I'm sure you two have a lot to talk about. I'll be back in twenty minutes. Try not to be here when I return." Lalah lit the cigarette and took a long drag before turning to walk toward the elevator doors.

* * *

Madrid leaned back against the sofa with his eyes shut tight, absorbing his surroundings. The stereo was humming as Ronny Jordan's fingers strummed the guitar strings, captivating Madrid, whisking him away on a miniature journey, a voyage to a time in his life when everyday seemed to be happy. When stress and pressure were never a part of his vocabulary or the people around him. When he and Mona couldn't bear to be without each other, without kissing and touching and hugging and loving. Yes, the loving was so good to him, he had to keep it, claim it, marry it.

The black silk robe lay off his shoulders, open wide and waiting, while the candlelight glowed off the tightness of his chest. The guitar was his favorite of all instruments, yes indeed. Plucking a guitar was much like pleasing a woman. Had to apply just the right amount of soft pressure to make the shrills, the sounds, the sighs needed to orchestrate the final plateau. Ramona would be his guitar tonight. He'd pluck and stroke and . . .

He would start with slow kisses all over her body, making sure not to miss any of the crucial and jolting spots. He'd give her all the foreplay she'd been complaining of missing and soft compliments in her ear as their bodies intertwined together. Yes, tonight would be one of those nights she'd have no choice but to lock away in her memory and her journal. A night that would send her running to her psychology books to search for the meaning, the reason for the new fullness in their lovemaking. Madrid sighed in delight. He was ready and so was Scooter, the nickname his wife had given his manhood.

Two jingles into Madrid's fantastic voyage, he realized that it was the telephone and not xylophones ringing in the background. He rose off the sofa slowly, deliberately, as if practicing his strut in advance. Take your time, Drid, he cautioned to himself. Now was not the time to lose composure if the person on the other end was Ramona calling to say she had decided against coming home. He lifted the cordless off the cradle and cleared his throat. *Please don't be Ramona telling me she's still three hours away. The anticipation is about to kill me.*

"Hello," Madrid said in his sexiest, deepest voice.

There was a pause before the other person spoke. "Madrid? This is Lalah. Did I wake you?"

"Lalah." He spoke now in his normal tone. "No. No, I was just relaxing. That's all. How's Gordon?"

"That's why I'm calling. He's fine. Came through the surgery like a champ."

Madrid sighed, and it wasn't till then that he realized how worried he had been for his brother-in-law. "I'm glad to hear that. Ramona was beside herself when she called me earlier today. She'll be happy to hear the news, too."

"Is she home yet?"

"Not yet," Madrid responded. "But I'm expecting her any minute now."

Lalah detected the gleeful note in Madrid's voice. That was a good sign, she reckoned, considering. "How's Nathan feeling?"

"Like nothing ever happened. You know kids." Madrid laughed. "They bounce back from anything at an amazing rate."

Of course, that was the problem. Lalah didn't know the first thing about kids and their amazing abilities and gifts. Perhaps if she had given birth

at least once, she would be able to truly understand, to empathize with Mona and Madrid about
a family that included children. The line had
fallen silent, neither party knowing what to say.
Then they both attempted to speak simultaneously. Madrid deferred to Lalah.

"Go ahead, Lalah, I'm sorry," Madrid said.

"No, no, don't be. The kids still awake?"

"Actually, they're spending the night at my
brother's house."

"Really?" Lalah responded coquettishly. "Planning a warm welcome home, are we?" The
thought of Madrid and Ramona rolling around
in a house empty of kids tickled her spirit. She
couldn't resist the Cheshire cat grin, either. "So,
what you got planned, Madrid?"

Madrid paused at first, unsure of a sudden
change in emotions toward his sister-in-law. Because had it been any other previous conversation,
he would have flatly but politely replied, "None
of your damn business." But tonight felt different;
he didn't have the urge to grapple with his sister-
in-law or cast her in the dim, damning light he
had so customarily done in the past. No, this time
he would answer her question truthfully and
openly. Besides, Lalah was the type of woman who
could give him the last-minute input he needed
to top off the evening.

"Oh, nothing real special. Maybe just some
chilled champagne and strawberries, a few tulips,
some two dozen roses sprinkled throughout the
house, seductive musical selections, and a soothing, candlelit bubble bath. That's all." He
grinned proudly.

"*My* goodness, Madrid," Lalah sang playfully.
"Sounds like Ramona's in for a pleasant sur-

prise." Lalah thought about the shock Madrid was in for when he laid eyes on Ramona and snickered. "Sounds perfect. Absolutely what the two of you need."

"You think?" Madrid asked.

"I know," Lalah said confidently.

Now this was the Lalah Madrid was accustomed to. The spicy, fiery, meaningful but meddling one. Sweetness only surfaced in her once and a while, everybody knew that, he thought. "Good," he said. "I want us to have an opportunity to work things out in a less intimidating, more neutral environment." He laughed nervously.

"I'll say," Lalah told him. "You better go on and finish getting the house ready," she teased. "Just let her know Gordon's all right, will you?"

"Sure thing," Madrid said. Silence lingered once again. "Lalah," Madrid finally said. "Is there anything else I'm forgetting that could hamper the evening?"

Lalah paused, taking a moment to shut her eyes and visualize the evening that lay ahead for her sister. Quickly, she replayed bits and pieces of her conversations with Ramona in her head. What, if anything, had Madrid forgotten? Everything sounded just right—flowers, champagne, bubble bath, candles . . . Then it hit her. She opened her eyes and smiled corruptly. "Yes, Madrid there is," she said after a few seconds.

"What?" Madrid said anxiously.

"A sincere 'I love you' and an occasional house-keeper."

Sixteen

Ramona pulled Meka into the familiar narrow driveway and choked off the engine. Finally, she was home. Nothing seemed out of the ordinary. The exterior of the house remained pretty much the same, except, thank God, for the blades of grass that had been chopped recently. Madrid had found time to cut the grass during her absence? A damp chill shivered her body. She wasn't sure if the feeling was weather-related or that of nervousness coupled with uncertainty.

She grabbed her bags and stepped out of the car to face the back of her home. It was 9 P.M. The house was dark despite the light of the quarter moon, and except for what appeared to be a dim glimmer flickering through the family room window. The butterflies that had accompanied her during her departure a few days ago had returned to the pit of her stomach, as she stood wondering about the life she had temporarily escaped.

Turning the key in the lock, she let out a heavy but relieved sigh. Thank God her key still worked. Chante Moore's, "Old School Love" greeted her upon her entrance, as did soft, sensual beams of fragrant candlelight. This had to be the wrong house, Ramona determined, dropping one of her bags—the heaviest one—in the middle of the floor. The house was spotless, eerily still and peaceful. At least from where she was standing.

She stood in the hallway for a few seconds with her overnight bag draped over her shoulder, absorbing the atmosphere. A slow grin crept over her face. No sounds of feet pitter-pattering overhead, no whines or cries for food or lost clothing echoing through the house, and no DeMar Shaw slouching over the furniture. This scenario was far more appealing than any dream she could have conjured of her own volition. But as her eyes became more accustomed to the dimly lit room, she noticed something lying on the floor a few feet away from her.

Ramona strolled further into the house. "Hello," she yelled out bending down to lift the two long-stemmed roses lying on the floor. The white and red petals were open and full. Ramona buried her nose in the flowers and inhaled the sweet aroma. Before long the butterflies fluttering within her had flown elsewhere. A warming sensation that she recognized as a blush heated her cheeks and her reserved smile formulated into an uncontrollable, permanently plastered smile.

"Hello," she called again, a little more seductively as she approached the stairs. Two candles encased in wooden holders, meant to serve as her guiding light, she supposed, had been placed on two steps. She had to stop at the fourth and fifth steps to collect two more roses. Madrid had absolutely lost his mind, she smiled inwardly with pure delight. Cautiously she continued up the steps, carrying the roses and overnight bag on one side and holding onto the banister for guidance.

The upstairs hallway was considerably darker than downstairs. But as she approached her bedroom, the sudden brightness of silhouetted candlelight shimmering made her tremble. Absolutely the most romantic thing he had done for her in a long, long time, Ramona thought breathlessly. She slung her bag onto the floor in pure excitement and walked around the room, absorbing the romance. Her hands softly glided across the walnut highboy dresser, where three of the five oversized candles sat. Turning, she sashayed over to her dresser where she lifted a grape from the artfully decorated tray of fruit and cheese. The hip sounds of Rick James' and Tina Marie's "Fire and Desire" spewed from the speakers of a makeshift stereo Madrid had obviously concocted just for the bedroom.

She stood motionlessly for a few seconds, chewing on a few pieces of cheese and grapes before her eyes roamed over to the partially cracked bathroom door. There was a note affixed to it. Ramona's desire overtook her as she strolled toward the bathroom and yanked the note off the door. She read, "My body's calling for your body to meet me real soon, baby. But first, do take a moment to relax. Join me . . ."

Ramona smiled coyly, stepping out of her shoes, then her pants and her top until she was completely naked. Her burning desire to join with her husband sent a warm sensation through her. How she longed to have her legs intertwined with his, have his hands caressing her back, her breasts, her inner thighs. Slowly, she pushed open the bathroom door, walking into more candlelight. Her heart beat wildly in anticipation. Bubbles overflowed the tub. A glass, filled with what she assumed to be champagne, sat on the edge of the tub. But still Madrid was nowhere to be found. She shut the bathroom door to keep the warmth in and the coolness out.

Feeling a bit disappointed but still very much appreciative, Ramona sank down into the tub, which hosted a few floating candles. As she sank further down into the warm aromatic bubbles, she saw another note was taped to the tile. "Where are you, baby? Scooter wants to dance with Sukie. Got a picnic planned for just you and I. Appetizers will be served at . . . well, just as soon as you can make it."

Ramona grinned seductively, rolling the soggy paper into a ball and tossing it to the floor. Sukie? He hadn't made reference to her loving like that in some time now. She'd make him wait a little while longer, she decided, leaning her head back against the cold tile. That quickly, Ramona had lost track of what she and Madrid had been fighting about to begin with. She closed her eyes and took a deeper breath. Phyllis Hyman's "Friends" filtered through the bathroom door. Life was too short and unpredictable to get caught up in nonsense, she decided.

Ramona retraced her steps from when she had first entered the house. He could be anywhere. Good thing they hadn't gotten to the financial point where they could afford a much bigger house than this. *So, he wants to play, do a little teasing, huh?* She took another sip of champagne. *Well, Mr. Shaw, Ms. Sukie got something for Mr. Scooter.* She laughed aloud before splashing further down in the water.

* * *

Madrid lay sprawled across the living room sofa waiting patiently, anticipating his contact with Ramona. It had been easy to hide from her, to initiate this cat-and-mouse game, because he knew she'd never look for him here. The entirely white living room was off limits to everyone in the house, as well as most frequent visitors.

The "looking room," as most everyone referred to it, was considered a show-piece only, an expensively decorated room to sit in occasionally whenever there were first-time guests in their modest home. It was the only area of the house that had established bragging rights, after many heated battles over the cost to furnish it.

His eyes scanned the *Better Homes and Gardens*-style room more thoroughly. Even in the dimness, he recognized the oversized Ernie Barnes oil painting portraying a joyous party. The characters strutting about in the hanging picture seemed so life-like, especially the woman in the tight dress with her body contorted awkwardly as she paraded in a sexy dance—the type of dance he desired of Mona tonight.

Obsessed. That's what Madrid was by the romantic evening he had planned for Ramona. He could hardly contain his anxiety as Scooter threatened to peek through the slit of his silk pajama bottoms. Would Ramona continue with the game and seek to find him? Or would he go upstairs and wait for her on their bed like he had imagined earlier? Knowing Ramona, she'd choose to wait him out, like she had done earlier on in their relationship.

Still no movement from overhead, though Madrid longed to hear Ramona's footsteps across the floor. A deliberate, heavy breath pushed through his mouth. What was taking her so long? Surely thirty minutes should be ample time to relax in the bubbles.

The Stylistics', "Hurry Up This Way Again" piped softly out of the tiny speakers in the living-room. Madrid dreamed of a house surrounded by built-in acoustics. However, until he was able to realize that dream, placing stand-alone speakers in the family room, living room and dining area would have to suffice.

He swayed back and forth, singing the lyrics to the song softly at first, then louder as he heard Ramona's heavy, authoritative footsteps above. Sweet music to his ears, he thought, closing his eyes, then lightly nibbling his bottom lip. Finally, she was out of the tub.

Ramona touched her favorite fragrance behind her ears and knees, on her wrists and down the middle of her chest before smoothing the avocado body butter over her body. The steaming bath was just what she'd needed to ease away any lingering tension. The champagne—well, that's what contributed to her feeling exceptionally relaxed and erotic.

She gazed at her new friend for awhile, admiring the new haircut and the translucent lip color she had just reapplied.

"Thank the Lord," she whispered to the mirror. Good thing Lalah had forced her to take some stock in herself by way of a new look and some thrilling, frilly undergarments, compliments of Ms. Vicki. She'd have to tell Lalah what kind of magic this merry widow was going to create, as she slid the spaghetti straps over her shoulders. She hummed to the sounds of the Isley Brothers' remake of Mr. Mayfield's "So Proud Of You."

Too many years had passed since she'd felt so proud and so self-assured. Prior to enrolling in the graduate program, Ramona's life had been one steady, uneventful, *blah* merry-go-round. Except, of course, for her most recent episode with Ronnie and her brother-in-law, Gordon. She probably should've phoned Lalah as soon as she walked in, but Madrid's unexpected thoughtfulness had captivated her. Perhaps she could sneak in a call before she and Madrid got too involved with their evening.

Madrid was somewhere in this house, hiding and waiting for her to appear. That thought prompted yet another dimpled smile. Knowing Madrid, he'd be lying butt-naked on their bed when she stepped out of the bathroom. She laughed at that Freudian wish. She'd done about all she could do to contain her excitement—she needed to climb atop her man and take him places only she could.

Hearing the familiar, usually annoying squeak of their bedroom door, Ramona knew Madrid had come to claim her. She eyed herself in the mirror one more time and grinned. *Yeah, baby. Sukie's got something real good for Scooter.* No longer would she be preoccupied by the extra pounds she'd struggled with after Nathan's birth. In due time, she'd implement an exercise program to shed the extra inches, she vowed, slowly turning the knob to the bathroom door that led to the bedroom. But right now, she'd start by guiding Scooter through a grueling workout.

Ramona had been partially right. When she

stepped out of the bathroom, Madrid was sensually positioned on their bed. His head rested on his hand while he laid on his side, his feet crossed. The only difference was, he had on the sexy silk pajamas she'd bought him a few Christmases past. Like magnets drawn to metal, her eyes immediately wandered down his body. Well, she thought as she leisurely walked toward him, if Scooter was the judge, she had definitely made a favorable impression on Madrid. Scooter had already begun to jut up and out of the slit in the pajamas.

"*Hey*, baby," Madrid drawled with a diabolical grin. "What did you do with my wife?" he teased, springing up suddenly, tucking Scooter back in his bottoms. He sat up and leaned back against the headboard. *Lord have mercy*, his mind screamed. This was not Ramona Shaw standing before him. No, this woman posing in front of him with the sexy, stylish haircut, the black, slinky, "come and get me" outfit cupping her full breasts, and the three-inch black pumps, was not the Mona he knew. This babe was somebody else's wife.

"I left her in Detroit," Mona whispered in her sexiest tone, placing one hand on her hip.

"Really?" Madrid grinned wider now. "How come?"

"Because," she said, walking closer to the bed. "She needed to be laid to rest for a long, long while. Do you like?" she asked, spinning around in a full circle.

"Like?" He laughed, then slid off the bed. "Love would be the proper definition." He was steaming with lust. "By the way, Lalah called. Gordon is doing fine," Madrid said, standing before her.

"Thank God," she exhaled, looking up at him. "I was worried."

"So was I," Madrid told her, placing his hands around her waist. The lace and satin material was inviting and soothing to his hands. He ran his splayed fingers up and down her back. "You miss me?" he said playfully.

Ramona closed her eyes, wrapping her arms around his back and burying her head in his chest. The heavy floral scent of his cologne smothered her nose. "Did you miss me?" she replied, kissing his bare chest softly. A chill ran through him. She felt him shake slightly.

"Of course I missed you, baby. And so did the kids," he said, squeezing her buttocks.

"Where are my kids, anyway?" she asked.

"DeMar took them for the night. He wants to be remembered as having done his part to make the evening more enjoyable for us."

"Well, check out DeMar," Ramona said softly. Her brother-in-law had actually come through in a way that was beneficial to someone beside himself. For that, she was grateful to him.

Ramona pulled away from Madrid's chest and looked up into his eyes. He was still hurt, she detected. He attempted to mask his pain, but she could still tell. "Drid, I'm sorry about the way I handled things. It might not have been the best way." Her eyes were pleading with his; his gaze was steadily affixed to hers.

"I understand, baby. It was something you felt you had to do. It's just that . . ." He hesitated.

"What?" she encouraged.

"Nothing. We'll talk about things later." He smiled, momentarily shifting his gaze to another part of the room. "I'm glad you're home," he said, eyeing her again. "I just hope if there is a next time, for whatever reason, we both handle it better than this last time. It was very difficult not having you around. You really are the backbone of this family, Mona."

She smiled sheepishly. "What? No luck finding your blue socks while I was gone?"

"Yeah, that, too. But I also realized while you were gone that the grass ain't greener." He smiled.

She grinned broadly at that statement. "You ain't never lied," she whispered. "I realized something, too," she said softly, kissing his chest again.

"What's that?" Madrid whispered, gripping her buttocks more firmly.

"You're a good man, Madrid, and I appreciate all that you do for me, for *us.*"

He smiled proudly. This was something any real man would want his wife to feel. "Really?"

"Really," she purred seductively. "By spending some time in the Motor City with Lalah, I now know in *no* uncertain terms that all that glitters ain't good for the soul." She squeezed him tighter and laid her head on his chest again.

They stood in that position for quite some time, rocking softly to their own heartbeats and the background rhythms of Angela Bofill. She could have stood that way forever, Ramona thought, squeezing her arms tighter around Madrid. Here, in her husband's bosom, is where she felt totally secure, most safe. She lay her wet lips on his soft skin again.

Madrid shivered once more. Hell, he didn't mind shivering all night as long as he had his wife home and wrapped tightly in his arms.

"I love your haircut, baby," Madrid finally said as the song ended. "It accentuates your beautiful features." He pulled her back and stared into her face, admiring her sparkling almond-shaped eyes, full lips and succulent complexion. "I guess I'm going to have to beat the men off you now for sure, with your fine self. Not like I didn't have to before. But now I'm really gonna have to watch my back," he teased.

"Ah, honey you don't have anything to worry about." She winked.

"And this outfit," he said, looking at her body. "This is going in my dresser drawer," he joked. "Damn, baby, I love everything I see."

"You do? Well—" she paused as she broke away from his embrace "—I've got more to show you." She slid one of the spaghetti straps off her shoulder.

"Show me, baby." Madrid smiled, grabbing her hand and leading her to their bed. No more selfish lovemaking, he thought. He would make it a point to satisfy her first tonight, and every night after that if he could. Just like in the beginning of their relationship, when he was determined to please her before taking for himself. He'd make her sing sweetly for sure.

Madrid lay on his back with his robe partially untied. Ramona swung her leg over the right side of his body until she had straddled him completely. She untied his robe and slid his arms out of the sleeves until the robe was entirely free. He lifted up so she could pull the silk garment from under him before tossing it onto the floor. She sat down on top of him, feeling the hardness of Scooter pressing close to Sukie. He reached up and slid her other strap down and off her shoulder until her breasts were exposed. Madrid smiled. He had missed her.

She removed his pants and her top, leaving just the panties, and bent down to kiss him. He reached up and captured her face with both hands. Their lips met softly at first, until desire swept through them both. Their tongues became intertwined, dancing to a rehearsed rhythm. Madrid flipped Ramona over onto her back, still burying his tongue in her mouth.

"I've missed you, Mrs. Shaw," he purred. He had begun kissing her breasts.

"I've missed you too, Mr. Shaw."

"How much?" he said, kissing her navel.

"Oh, Drid," she whispered. "A lot, baby. A lot."

"I don't believe you," he teased. "Let's just see."

Ramona lifted his head away from her thighs and motioned for him to roll onto his back. He gladly obliged.

"Yeah, let's," she whispered into his ear as she straddled him, using Sukie to capture Scooter. Ramona gasped with desire.

Madrid moaned hard with pleasure. "Don't kill me, baby," he whispered. "We got all night. I'm here for you, baby." He thrust with the movement of her hips till they were in sync. "Here for you."

Epilogue

7:40 A.M., three weeks later . . .

Ramona stood in the kitchen in a purple and
green silk, floral-patterned robe, stirring a pot of
grits and scrambling a frying pan full of eggs. It
was a Thursday-morning routine today. Nathan,
off from daycare, lay upstairs still asleep. Leslie was
in her room dressing for school, and more than
likely trying to figure out which way to wear her
braids.

Madrid raced downstairs carrying his briefcase
in one hand and his shoes in the other. He walked
into the kitchen, easing up behind Ramona.
"Morning, baby," he said, kissing her on the back
of the neck and squeezing her breasts. "I still
can't—" His words were cut off abruptly as Ramona turned around to place a kiss on his lips.

She pulled a pair of black socks out of the
pocket of her robe. "Here," she said, turning back
to the stove. She removed the pot of grits from
the hot burner as Madrid grinned at the socks.
Just like my baby, he thought, reaching down to
put them on.

"Thanks, sweetheart."

"You're welcome," she said, spooning food

onto the plates. "Leslie," Ramona called out. "Come on. Time to eat."

Ramona sat Madrid's plate in front of him and he fanned away the steam before taking his first bite of the hot grits. "Ouch!" he yelped, reaching for the glass of orange juice sitting before him and taking a big gulp. "I suppose that's what I get for not saying grace first," Madrid said, sucking his burning tongue. He lowered his head and said a fast prayer, before picking up his fork again.

Leslie bounced downstairs with her knapsack in her hand. She had on a pair of green denim jeans and a matching gold top. Her braids had been collected into a ponytail and positioned on top of her head.

"Good morning," Leslie said aloud.

"Morning," Ramona responded.

"Good morning, pumpkin," Madrid replied.

"Ah, now I like that hairstyle, Leslie," Ramona told her, placing her plate on the table.

"Thanks, Mona." Leslie blushed. "Yum, grits. My favorite," Leslie sang.

"Good." Mona smiled. "Is your brother still sleeping?"

Leslie shrugged. "I guess so. He seemed asleep when I went into his room to get my brush. How come he gets to sleep in?"

" 'Cause he doesn't have school today," Madrid told her. "Now eat your breakfast so I can drop you off at school. Mona, I'm probably going to work a little late tonight. I have to go over some vital things with Alyson for her meeting in Puerto Rico next week," Madrid continued with a full mouth. "I should be home no later than eight, eight-thirty."

"That's fine. I don't have class tonight anyway."
She yawned.

"Tired?" Madrid said with a raised brow. "You
should learn to lay on your back sometimes—
maybe you'd rest better," he teased.

Ramona grinned. Leslie was clueless about
their little sexual innuendoes.

"I have drill team practice at 6:30 tonight,"
Leslie finally said. "Sandra's mother is supposed
to take us. Can you pick me up, Mona?"

"Sure. What time do you finish?"

"Eight o'clock," Leslie told Mona. She had
dropped some grits on her shirt. "Shoot," Leslie
sighed. "This is a new shirt." She wiped the stain
with her napkin.

"Well, watch what you're doing." Madrid
laughed, then turned toward Ramona. "What's
on your agenda today, baby?"

"I suppose Nathan and I will run some errands
before we go grocery shopping, and Doris is coming to clean the house. Then, when he's taking
his nap, I'll get some studying in." She dumped
the dirty pots in the sink. "I want to get a garden
going with some tomatoes and peppers, too. We'll
see. The grass is so plush and green, I may not
want to dig it up."

Madrid smiled and stood up. "I think a garden
would be nice. Give Leslie something to tend to
besides the remote control," he teased, winking
at Leslie. "But it's up to you, babe. You know I'll
pitch in where I can. You know, help you fertilize
whatever you need me to." He grinned seductively.

Ramona rolled her eyes playfully. Leslie shot a
glance at her father, then at Ramona, before taking her plate to the sink. She could feel it—this

was obviously a grown-up conversation. She'd have to change the subject or wait outside in the car. Since Ramona had returned from Detroit, she and her father had been all lovey-dovey. "I just have one question," Leslie cut in. "What we having for dinner?"

"Who knows." Mona winked at Madrid. "Perhaps some pigsfeet or chicken necks and goose eggs. I'm not sure." Ramona handed her a brown paper bag lunch.

"Yuk!" Leslie screamed. "I'll eat at Sandra's house in that case. See you later, Mona." Leslie kissed her on the cheek, grabbed her book bag and her lunch and walked out the back door.

"You got your keys, young lady?" Mona called.

"Yes," Leslie yelled back. She was outside waiting for her father.

"See you later, baby," Madrid said, kissing her on the lips. "Have a good day."

"You too, darling. Tell Alyson I said don't keep you out too late. We've got a date with me on my back." She winked.

"Yeah, for a change," Madrid chuckled, walking out the back door.

Ramona watched the Jeep roll down the driveway before shutting the door. She walked into the kitchen and instinctively began rinsing off the dishes. She stopped suddenly when she began to wipe the table down. Doris would be here today— no need to make a fuss over the kitchen. Instead, she picked up the cordless phone and dialed Lalah's house.

Gordon answered on the fourth ring. His groggy voice told Ramona that she had phoned her sister's house a little bit too early.

"Good morning, Gordon. Did I wake you?"

"No, no. I was just about to get on the tread-mill. How are you, Mona?"

"I'm fine. And yourself?"

"Much better, praise God. I've had to give up a lot to get on the wellness road again, but it's worth it," Gordon chuckled. "How are Madrid and the kids?"

"Everyone is doing fine," she told him.

"Good. Hold on. Here's your sister."

"Gordon," Ramona said swiftly. "Thanks again." She was thinking back to that awful night with Ronnie, and the night that Gordon had had his heart attack—the night she had chosen not to share with Madrid. At least not yet.

"You're always welcome, Mona. Don't ever for-get that," Gordon told her. His voice was warm and sincere, more than any time Ramona could recall. "Here's Lalah. Kiss the kids for me."

Lalah mumbled something to Gordon before taking the phone.

"Mona, how are you?" Lalah asked, with a slight morning throatiness.

"Fine. How 'bout you? How you handling things?"

"Oh, I'm handling things all right, I suppose." Lalah yawned. "That merry widow still working wonders for you?"

Ramona let out a sultry laugh. "Honey, I've been back to Ms. Vicki's since our initial visit. Got me a hot red lace catsuit now." She giggled.

"Good for you, sis, good for you. See, that's all you needed to add some spice to Madrid's life. How's that housekeeping situation working?"

"Excellent. She comes once a week and does wonders with the house. Having Doris has cut down my housework load tremendously. I have more time to study and help the kids with their homework. Not to mention play taxicab to all their little events," Ramona said.

"Yeah, and let's not forget more time to be Madrid's little sex toy." Lalah snickered.

"Speaking of sex toys, how are things with you?"

"What? You mean with Drew? Please, child. I cut him loose that night his tired ass fell asleep on me. He's history." Lalah rolled over on her side, tucking the phone between her ear and shoulder.

"What about that other situation? You know, with Gordon and that girl?"

"She's still pregnant—and Gordon is still here. He's all apologetic and sympathetic and pathetic. He's afraid I might leave him or something."

"Will you?" Ramona asked.

"Hell no. For what? I'll tell you like I told him—I'm too old to be starting over with some young, green-behind-the-ears, clueless brother. I'm going stay right here in this house and do my thing. We'll just be roommates living under the same roof, if you get my drift."

"Yeah, I guess," Ramona said, startled. She *didn't* get Lalah's drift or understand her sister's bizarre marriage. But then again, that was their life—their business—their grass.

"Anyway, Mona, let me buzz you back later on. I'm supposed to meet a new client at his house in an hour."

"Really? Who?"

"Gustis, somebody or another who plays for the Lions. Who knows, he might do me some good other than monetarily." Lalah chuckled aloud.

"Lalah, you're a trip. Keep your butt out of trouble, will you?" Ramona pleaded.

"Don't you worry, little sis. I got this. You just hold onto yours and I'll handle mine. Love you. 'Bye."

Ramona stood listening to the dial tone. Lalah hadn't changed one bit. Ramona smiled and hung the phone back in the cradle. At least Lalah was consistent and somewhat predictable. She walked to the mantel over the fireplace and stared at the family photo of Madrid, Nathan, Leslie and herself. Life, unlike Lalah, was so unpredictable. *Hold onto mine?* Ramona repeated Lalah's words in her head. *You better believe it, sister,* Ramona vowed. Because nobody or nothing, with the grace of God, would wedge another fence between her, her husband and their grass. Ever.

Other books by the author:

No Ordinary Love
Hearts Afire

BEGUILED (0046, $4.99)

by Eboni Snoe

After Raquel agrees to impersonate a missing heiress for just one night, a daring abduction makes her the captive of seductive Nate Bowman. Across the exotic Caribbean seas to the perilous wilds of Central America . . . and into the savage heart of desire, Nate and Raquel play a dangerous game. But soon the masquerade will be over. And will they then lose the one thing that matters most . . . their love?

WHISPERS OF LOVE (0055, $4.99)

by Shirley Hailstock

Robyn Richards had to fake her own death, change her identity, and forever forsake her husband, Grant, after testifying against a crime syndicate. But, five years later, the daughter born after her disappearance is in need of help only Grant can give. Can Robyn maintain her disguise from the ever present threat of the syndicate—and can she keep herself from falling in love all over again?

HAPPILY EVER AFTER (0064, $4.99)

by Rochelle Alers

In a week's time, Lauren Taylor fell madly in love with famed author Cal Samuels and impulsively agreed to be his wife. But when she abruptly left him, it was for reasons she dared not express. Five years later, Cal is back, and the flames of desire are as hot as ever, but, can they start over again and make it work this time?

Available wherever paperbacks are sold, or order direct from the Publisher. Send cover price plus 50¢ per copy for mailing and handling to Penguin USA, P.O. Box 999, c/o Dept. 17109, Bergenfield, NJ 07621. Residents of New York and Tennessee must include sales tax. DO NOT SEND CASH.